Daily News

掌握NEWS關鍵字

Keywords Catcher

Catch me if you can!

透析英文報導的要訣

James Chiao ◎ 著

Well begun is half done!
（好的開始就是成功的一半）

掌握新聞關鍵字
就是戰勝英文報導的50%

另外50%由本書特別規劃的四大主題、精心設計的4大項目幫您達成新聞英文百分百！

四大主題：

政治　財經　民生　綜合

四大主題，網羅各式新聞英文關鍵字+彙整，讓您在查詢關鍵字時"糾甘單"

4大項目：

代表意義超理解　背景知識大突破　使用方式一把罩　主題文章

完整解析關鍵字，讓您無論是在生活對話、學校報告還是公司簡報中使用News關鍵字都能更加得心應手，通通"逮就捕"

作者序

因為工作的關係，養成平常閱讀英文新聞的習慣，這次有機會藉著這本《掌握 News 關鍵字》和大家分享平常整理國際新聞常看到的字彙常識，希望能對從事各種不同領域工作的讀者有所助益。

這本書依照不同領域，分為四個種類，共七十個常見英語關鍵字，有些是最近臺灣常見的新聞議題，其他則是國際上發生的重要事件。希望讀者能夠透過簡易的背景説明，對特定議題有初步認知，再透過閱讀主題文章，了解事件的新聞走向。

針對書中提及的各種議題，我都儘量以客觀、中立的方式陳述各方不同的意見，但限於篇幅的關係，並無法顧及所有不同的意見立場，在部分議題上若和讀者您所認知的資訊有所出入，也請多多包涵，這本書畢竟不是新聞宣傳，而是一本希望能輕鬆分享的英文知識的作品。

再次感謝各位讀者的支持，不管是工作需要，還是純粹把這本書當成輕鬆的讀物來看，都希望本書能對您有所幫助。如果有不同的意見，也請不吝指教。

James Chiao

編者序

不管是讀、聽還是看英文新聞，相信是許多有志學習英文的人最常使用的學習方式。而新聞顧名思義就是「最新的報導、資訊；或是任何報章讀者或廣播聽眾感興趣的話題、最新的潮流」。也由於新聞是最新資訊，所以在英文新聞中常會出現一些新的詞彙，常會令意欲學習英文的人摸不著頭緒，也會因此久而久之便失去了學習英文的興趣。

本書除了收錄了一般常用的詞彙之外，也包含了許多最新的用語。將新聞關鍵字分門別類為四大篇，其中有政治、財經、民生及綜合用語，並依照字母排序。每個單元中還有新聞關鍵字的意義、背景知識以及使用方法的介紹，再加上中英對照文章的閱讀，讓您在學習及運用新聞關鍵字時更加輕鬆，也更能得心應手！

請跟我們一起來讀「掌握 NEWS 關鍵字」，一起透析英文報導的要訣吧！

倍斯特編輯部

目　次

PART 1
政治 Politics

PART 2

財經 Finance and Economics

PART 3
民生 People's Livelihood

PART 4
綜合 Miscellaneous

...anagement, securities investment, information processing, civil engineering, asset management, etc. Their monthly salary will be set at NT$31,000.

There will also be 209 new office clerks to be recruited this year, with their starting salary set at NT$24,000 per month. The largest number of new employees, at 459, will be mail carriers, with their starting pay also set at NT$24,000 per month, plus an extra driving or delivery allowance of NT$5,732.

Based on the average employment rate of 2% to 6%, the expected number of applicants to take the examination is around 8,000, the spokesman...

For furth...

Inter-party consultations t...

The China Post news staff

The Kuomintang-controlled Legislative Yuan completed the first reading of an amendment to its own procedural bylaw yesterday, promising to make all closed-door inter-party consultations public record. Known popularly as "black box" operations, the inter-party consultations held behind closed doors may last as long as four months.

"The horse trading...

Moreover, the records will be published in the Legislative Yuan bulletin, together with the conclusions reached, Ting said.

Should there be discrepancies between the published conclusions and the results of action on bills, full explanations will be able to be discovered in the record, the Kuomintang legislator said. "We want the secret horse trading exposed under bright sunshine," Ting stressed.

Lawmakers have to complete the second and third readings before the legislature adjourns for the summer. "There won't be difficulty," another Kuomintang legislator said. The...

Kuomintang c... majority in the... Yuan.

In addition, ... cedural bylaw... The inter-party... can go on for f... to that article, ... in one month.

Democratic ... islators ... Kuomintang-p... as "going a littl...

"All of us a... party consult... improved, but... be seriously d... ment were ...

PART 1

NSC dismisses Ma death in war scenario

The China Post news staff

Taiwan's top security body yesterday dismissed a report that the military's upcoming war chess would drill a scenario where President-elect Ma Ying-jeou was assassinated. The National Security Council (NSC) described the Next Magazine report as unfounded, irresponsible and with a political agenda.

Next claimed that the war chess, to be conducted later this month, would assume that Ma's assassination would plunge the nation into chaos and trigger a surprise invasion by China. The drill was meant to see how different government and security bodies could cope with such a situation, and how Taiwan would interact with the United States, the tabloid magazine cited unnamed presidential sources as saying.

It would be a test to see whether U.S. intervention should be sought or whether other solutions would be possible, and whether a state of emergency should be declared, the report said.

Ma's spokesman Lo Chih-chiang declined to comment on the report, saying the Presidential Office owed the public an explanation. President Chen Shui-bian had invited Ma to the war chess, which is part of the NSC's annual drill, but the president-elect declined the invitation.

The opposition camp called for the drill to be postponed until Ma is inaugurated, but the NSC insisted on conducting it as scheduled. The NSC said yesterday that the drill, to be conducted in three stages between April 21 and 27, is a test of government bodies' responses to military crises and of the nation's defense facilities.

But Kuomintang legislators have repeated the opposition camp's call for the drill be postponed, so as to let Ma oversee it. KMT Legislator Lin Yu-fang said it is "very ridiculous and impolite" for an outgoing president to conduct a drill on the mock assassination of his successor. "The Chen administration has designed such a drill apparently to vent its anger over its loss in the presidential election," claimed Lin.

KMT Legislator Chang Hsien-yao said such a drill has already raised concern in the United States and Taiwan's neighbors.

More... Parki...

TAIPEI, CNA

An internat... ject has... Parkinson's-r... that only dev... Those who c... twice more... Parkinson's d...

The mutati... is found in... codes for... repeat kinas... paper produc... partially fund... National Scie... lished in the s... of Neurology.

Parkinson's... as Parkinson... erative disor... nervous syste... the patient's... ment.

A group of... Singapore, Ja... States have a... Parkinson's-r... linked to LRR... relations bet... groups and... For example, ... LRRK2-G201... of Parkinson's... and Ashkenaz...

In 2004, th... a mutation, G... linked to Pa... especially Ha...

Fugitive ex-Hsinchu Council speaker returns

TAIPEI, CNA

Former Hsinchu County Council Speaker Huang Huan-chi returned to Taiwan and was taken into custody Tuesday after fleeing to China two years ago, following his sentencing to eight years in prison on corruption charges, judicial sources said yesterday.

Following unsuccessful kidney transplant surgery in China, Huang recently informed Hsinchu County police that he would be returning to the Taiwan. Shortly after Huang's plane landed in Taiwan, he was escorted away by police, who later turned him over to the Hsinchu District Prosecutors Office.

Huang served two terms as Hsinchu County Council speaker before running in the legislative elections in December 2001 as a candidate of the Taiwan Solidarity Union. He ended up losing the election. In that race, Huang was accused of vote-buying violations for allegedly using the county council's budget to purchase tea and moon cakes for voters. He was later released on bail.

Two years ago, after being convicted on corruption charges related to an incinerator scandal in the county, Huang decided to flee to China to avoid serving his prison sentence. He was then placed on the Hsinchu District Prosecutors Office's wanted list.

政治篇

Politics

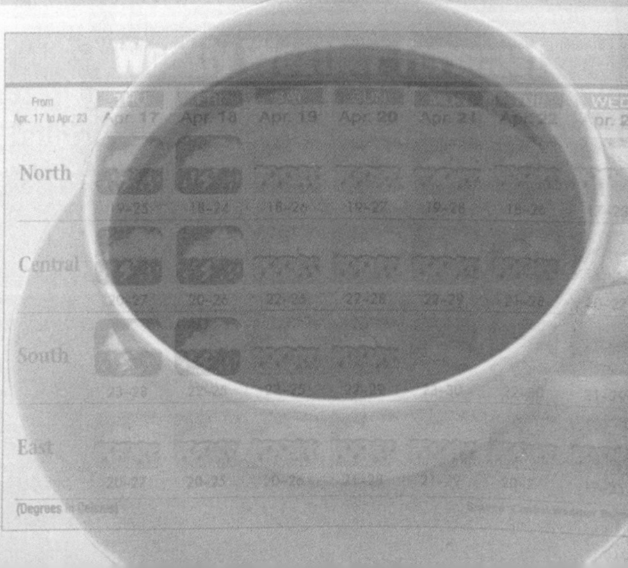

Unit 1

Air Defense Identification Zone
防空識別區

代表意義超理解

防空識別區是一個國家因國安需求所劃定的空域，以方便辨識、定位及掌控外來的飛行器。防空識別區通常跨越一國的領空，讓政府有更多的時間對外來飛機作出反應。

An Air Defense Identification Zone is an airspace in which the identification, location, and control of aircraft is required in the interest of national security. It extends beyond a nation's airspace to give more time to respond to foreign aircraft.

B 背景知識大突破 ackground

國際上並沒有對設置防空識別區的行為做出任何規範。2013 年 11 月，中國大陸設置東海防空識別區。這個舉動隨即引來包括日本、菲律賓、南韓、美國等周邊國家的關注。

The establishment of air defense identification zone is not regulated by any international body. In November 2013, the People's Republic of China established its East China Sea Air

---

* establishment　設立　　* regulate　規範

Defense Identification Zone. The announcement soon drew attention from most of the surrounding nations, including Japan, the Philippines, South Korea, and the United States.

M 使用方法一把罩 ethod

由於國際上並沒有對設置防空識別區的行為做出任何規範，因此各國政府可以單方面劃定防空識別區。大陸針對釣魚台海域劃定的防空識別區一般稱為 East China Sea Air Defense Identification Zone。與之相關的釣魚台列嶼，日本稱為尖閣諸島 (Senkaku Islands)，中國大陸稱為釣魚島 (Diaoyu Island)，我方則稱為釣魚台列嶼 (Diaoyutai Islands)。Air Defense Identification Zone，亦可縮寫成 ADIZ，例如：

Mainland China's Ministry of National Defense issued an announcement of the aircraft identification rules for the East China Sea ADIZ of the People's Republic of China in November 2013.

（中國國防部在 2013 年 11 月針對中華人民共和國的東海防空識別區中的航空器識別規則發表聲明。）

＊announcement　宣告、通知　　＊surrounding　周圍的、附近的

A 主題文章 Article

US official has warned China not to implement East China Sea Air Defense Identification Zone it has declared in November 2013, and certainly not replicate such an air defense identification zone in the South China Sea.

US stresses the deep concern that the United States feels over the rising regional tensions. The frequency and assertiveness of China's patrol are increasing, and China and Japan imposed competing regulations over disputed territory and nearby waters and airspace is raising tensions and increasing the risk of confrontation.

The official said the East China Sea Air Defense Identification Zone had caused confusion, threatened to interfere other nation's airspace. It also raised questions about China's intention, making surrounding nations nervous at a sensitive time. The United States had expressed its concerns about the air defense identification zone at a very high level, and US officials took much tougher stand than usual against Beijing's actions.

As rumors claim that China threaten to grow a second Air Defense Identification Zone in the South China Sea, the United States urged China to clarify or adjust its claims in the South China Sea, calling for a peaceful solution to end the incident. China, the Philippines, Vietnam, Taiwan, Malaysia and Brunei all have territorial claims across the waterway in the South China Sea, which provides 10% of the global fisheries catch and carries about five trillion in ship-borne trade.

China responded to US by saying as a sovereign state, China has all the rights to safeguard national security with any means, including establishing the ADIZ in response to the situation of air security. "No one is allowed to make irresponsible remarks" said

Chinese official in response to reports published by media saying that China plans to establish the second air defense identification zone and that the United States has warned against such a move.

美國官員警告大陸不要執行 2013 年 11 月發表的東海防空識別區，並強調大陸絕不應在南海複製相同的防空識別區。

美國強調，美國正密切關注區域中持續上升的緊張局勢；中國大陸在這個區域中巡邏的頻率和魄力都不斷增加，但中國大陸和日本對爭議地區的領土、海域和空域，都不斷增加雙方對抗的風險。

美國官員亦表示，東海防空識別區已對其他國家造成困擾，並威脅到其他國家的領空。他也認為，中國大陸表現出的意圖，已在這個敏感時機讓周邊國家感到緊張。美國已高分貝表達對防空識別區的疑慮，美國官員對中國大陸也採取比以往更強硬的立場。

至於外界傳言大陸將在南海劃立第二個防空識別區，美國則敦促大陸澄清其在南海的主張，並呼籲和平解決問題。中國大陸、菲律賓、越南、臺灣、馬來西亞和汶萊都對此區域提出主權，這片海域提供全球漁業 10% 的產量，並影響約五兆美元的貨品航運。

中國大陸方面則回應表示，做為一個主權獨立的國家，中國有權以包括劃立航空識別區等手段維護自身的國家安全。對於美國官員警告中國大陸不要設置南海航空識別區的報導，大陸官員回應媒體時説，沒有人能對此「説三道四」。

Unit 2

Annexation
併吞

代表意義超理解

在政治上，併吞指的是一個政治實體，例如一個國家或一個城市，將另一個政治實體的領土永久納入其中的行為。一般而言，是雙方中較強的一方，以擴張的方式，將較弱的一方合併而完成併吞的行為。

Politically speaking, annexation is the permanent incorporation of territory into an existing political unit such as a state or a city. It is also implied a certain measure of expansion of the stronger over the weaker in the merging of different entities.

B 背景知識大突破 ackground

在 2014 年，克里米亞半島以克里米亞共和國和塞凡堡聯邦市兩個實體被併入俄羅斯聯邦的一部分。這個兼併的過程是由剛從烏克蘭宣布獨立的克里米亞自治共和國舉辦的全民公投的結果。大部分的西方國家領導人認為這是一件非法的併吞行為，但俄羅斯強烈反對西方各國的說法。

＊permanent　永久的　　＊entity　實體
＊merge　合併

In 2014, Crimean Peninsula was incorporated into the Russian Federation as two federal subjects, the Republic of Crimea and the federal city of Sevastopol. The process was done by a referendum held by the Autonomous Republic of Crimea, which just declared its independence from Ukraine. Most of the western leaders considered it as an illegal annexation, but the Russians strongly opposed the western view.

M 使用方法一把罩 ethod

除了所謂的併吞 (annexation) 外，不同國家或不同政治實體間，還有多種方式可以達到領土或主權的變更。有別於併吞，統一這個詞 (unification / reunification) 一般用於較為正面的合併；割讓 (cession) 則是一個政治實體將領土給予或售予另一個政治實體。合併 (amalgamation) 則是雙方同意下的合而為一的行為，amalgamation 除了指政治實體的合併之外，也可以用以指相關單位或是公司企業的合併，例如：

The new company was formed by the amalgamation of three small businesses.
(這間新公司是有三家小型企業合併而成的。)

A 主題文章 rticle

Russia's annexation of Ukraine's Crimea region has deepened the worst East-West crisis since the end of the Cold War. Russia

---

* incorporate 把……合併；使併入
* referendum 公民投票
* declare 聲明

and the United States are still debating over the dispute, but the Russians seemed to take the hard stance, as a senior Russian diplomat remarked "U.S. policymakers need to calm down, maybe do some yoga and accept that Crimea is now part of Russia."

In the sovereignty dispute over the Crimean Peninsula, Google map appeared to have sided with Russian President Vladimir Putin–at least as far as the residents of Russia are concerned.

Google had updated its Google Maps of the said region that denotes the border between Ukraine and Crimea with bold, black line–many consider it indicating that Crimea is no longer a part of Ukraine, but a part of Russia.

The press spotted this recent change and suggested the Putin administration is behind it.

The said status is only visible when people visit map.google.ru, which is the map service for Russian users. For most of the users in other regions of the world, they will see a different version of the same map, with the border line between Ukraine and Crimea appears as bold but dotted, indicating its disputed status.

According to news articles, in respond to these changes, a spokesperson for Google Maps said, "Google Maps makes every effort to depict disputed regions and features objectively. Our Maps product reflects border disputes, where applicable. Where we have local versions, we follow local regulations for naming and borders."

According to newspaper report, politicians in the lower house of the Russian Federal Assembly had asked the Federal Mass media Inspection Service to evaluate foreign websites for labeling Crimea as disputed territory. At the same time, Russian search engine Yandex had already decided to show Crimea as part of Russia for Russian visitors, although it still showed it as Ukrainian territory to Ukrainians.

俄羅斯對烏克蘭克里米亞的併吞，造成冷戰結束以來東西之間最嚴重的危機。儘管美俄雙方仍對此事爭論不休，俄國方面似乎決定採取更為強硬的姿態。一位俄羅斯的高級外交官日前表示，「美國的決策者應該冷靜一下，去做些瑜珈活動，並接受克里米亞現在已經成為俄羅斯的一部分」。

而在雙方的主權爭議中，谷歌地圖似乎對俄羅斯總統普亭表示支持－至少在俄羅斯境內如此。

谷歌地圖日前已對該區域的地圖進行更新，將烏克蘭和克里米亞之間的邊界，改以粗黑線條進行標示。許多人認為，這代表克里米亞不再是烏克蘭的一部分，而屬於俄羅斯的一部分。

媒體發現這項變更，並推測幕後受到普亭政府的掌控。

目前只能在 map.google.ru 看到這個情況。這個網址是谷歌地圖對俄羅斯用戶提供的服務。對於世界其他地區的用戶，他們則會看到另一個版本的地圖，其中烏克蘭和克里米亞的界線，是以粗體虛線來表示其爭議地位。

新聞報導中提到，谷歌地圖的發言人對這些改變解釋說，「谷歌地圖力求客觀表現尚有爭議的地圖。我們在可能的情況下儘可能表現出有爭議的邊界。但若當地有不同版本的地圖，我們會按照當地的邊境和規則進行呈現」。

報紙報導則透露，俄羅斯聯邦議會下院中的政治人物曾要求媒體相關部門對將克里米亞列為爭議領土的外國網站進行觀察。同一時間，俄羅斯境內的搜尋引擎 Yandex 則已將克里米亞列為俄羅斯的一部分。但在烏克蘭境內的 Yandex 仍將克里米亞標示為烏克蘭領土。

Unit 3

Drone Attack
無人機攻擊

代表意義超理解

無人機攻擊，Drone 的原意為蜜蜂中的雄蜂，但近年來 Drone 則成為無人飛行載具（無人機）的別稱。無人飛行載具通常透過電腦或駕駛員進行遠距離操控。

Originally drones are male bees. The term Drone has become and commonly used as the name for unmanned aerial vehicle, which is an aircraft controlled remotely or by computer, without a pilot on board.

背景知識大突破 Background

自 2004 年開始，美國對巴基斯坦進行數百次的無人機攻擊。無人機造成的傷亡數字頗具爭議，但估計已擊斃 890 名平民，其中包括 197 名幼兒。部分人士認為，無人機對非武裝平民所造成的傷害可構成戰爭罪行。

The United States has launched hundreds of drone attacks in Pakistan since 2004. There is a debate regarding the number of civilian causalities, as an estimated 890 civilians had been killed,

---

* unmanned　無人的
* aerial　空中的
* causality　原因；因果關係

including up to 197 children. Some argue that drone attacks on unarmed civilians could amount to war crimes.

Method 使用方法一把罩

一般軍事用途的無人飛機，其正式名稱為 unmanned combat air vehicle(戰鬥用無人航空載具，UCAV)，簡寫 combat drone 或是 drone；而各種不同用途的無人飛機，則通稱為 unmanned air vehicle(無人航空載具，UAV)。早期無人飛機多用於警戒、偵查等任務，但新型的無人飛機已具備攻擊機的性能，引發爭議。例如：

UCAVs are small, elusive, and low-signature enough to exploit blind spots in enemy's air defense architecture.

（無人航空載具是小型且不易被發現的，辨識度夠低能利用空防體系當中的盲點。）

---

* civilian　平民、百姓
* combat　戰鬥

A 主題文章 Article

The United States had agreed to largely limit its drone attacks in Pakistan beginning in 2014. There have been no known drone attacks in Pakistan since 25 December 2013, and January 2014 is the first full month without any drone strikes at all in two years. Although politicians come to this agreement, they are still debates on whether US should send an army to clear out a region entirely controlled by militant groups in Pakistan.

The government of Pakistan has asked the United States to stop drone attacks, as they seek to negotiate with the Pakistani Taliban. According to the media, US has agreed to halt the attacks, and the use of drones in Pakistan has dropped dramatically.

US official proves that Pakistan's government had asked for a restraint of drone attacks as it pushes forward with peace talks with the Pakistani Taliban. US believes the stop of drone attacks would put more pressure on Pakistan, because by not using drones, it takes away any further excuse not to take action about the Taliban from the Pakistani government.

However, it is not the first time US has halted their drone strikes. There was a six-week hiatus in 2011, following the accident that 24 Pakistani troops were killed by the drones near the Afghan border. Pakistan denies it has any involvement in the drone program, regularly makes complains to the United States when drone attack occurs. But US official says that drone strikes would be impossible without some level of Pakistani consent. Senior officials in Pakistan regard drones as a necessary evil, but rarely say so in public.

A dramatic rise in drone attacks when Barack Obama took office, although they have fallen off again in the past 18 months.

Perhaps it is time for US to reconsider its drone attacks in Pakistan.

美國日前已同意自 2014 年起大規模縮減其在巴基斯坦的無人機攻擊。自 2013 年 12 月 25 日至今，巴基斯坦尚未遭到無人機襲擊。而 2014 年的 1 月則是兩年來巴基斯坦第一次度過一整個月未受到無人機的攻擊。美國政治人物雖然取得停止無人機攻擊的共識，但他們仍在爭論為是否應派遣軍隊對民兵組織占領的區域進行掃蕩。

巴基斯坦政府目前正尋求和當地的神學士組織進行談判，因此希望美國能停止無人機的攻擊。據媒體報導，美國已同意該要求，並大幅減少無人機的使用。

美國官員證實巴基斯坦政府因尋求與神學士組織談判而要求限制無人機攻擊。美國方面認為，停止使用無人機能對巴基斯坦造成更大的壓力，因為這樣一來，巴基斯坦就沒有藉口不對神學士組織採取行動。

這也不是美國第一次停止其無人機的襲擊。2011 年，有 24 名巴基斯坦士兵在阿富汗邊界被無人機擊殺，當時美國曾停止無人機的攻勢長達六星期。巴基斯坦否認該國和無人機有任何關聯，並在美國出動無人機時，固定提出抗議。但美國官員表示，若沒有巴基斯坦某種程度上的支持，無人機不可能在當地出動。部分巴基斯坦官員把無人機看做是一種必要之惡，但在公開場合他們不會這麼說。

自美國總統歐巴馬上台後，無人機的出動次數直線上升，但在過去一年半又逐漸下降。或許現在正是美國重新思考其無人機策略的時機。

Unit 4

Edward Snowden
愛德華 · 史諾登

代表意義超理解

愛德華 · 史諾登是前中央情報局職員及國家安全局技術員。他將國家安全局的最高機密文件披露給媒體，內容包括美國政府監聽、監視網路情資的資料。

Edward Snowden is a former Central Intelligence Agency employee, and former National Security Agency contractor who leaked top secret NSA documents to several media outlets, which reveal operational details of internet surveillance programs.

B 背景知識大突破 Background

史諾登逃往香港，並在香港將機密文件披露給媒體。美國政府隨即撤銷史諾登的美國護照，使得史諾登無法離開香港的機場，直到俄國政府給予他為期一年的政治庇護。史諾登目前仍被美國當局視為逃犯，他住在俄羅斯的一個祕密地點，並向俄國當局尋求永久性的政治庇護。

Snowden fled and released the documents to the media in Hong Kong. The United States officials had revoked Snowden's

---

* contractor　約聘員工
* leak　洩露
* surveillance　監督
* revoke　撤銷、廢除

passport, and he was not able to leave the airport until the Russian government granted him a one-year temporary asylum. Snowden is considered a fugitive by American authorities, and he lives in an undisclosed location in Russia where he continues to seek permanent asylum.

M 使用方法一把罩 ethod

史諾登將美國國家安全局關於稜鏡計劃監聽專案的秘密文件披露給英國衛報和美國華盛頓郵報。稜鏡計劃是國家安全局 2007 年起開始實施的機密電子監聽計畫，能對即時通信和既存資料進行深度的監聽，監聽對象包括美國以外的社群網路用戶，及任何與國外人士通信的美國公民。

稜鏡計劃在英文中稱為 PRISM（一般會以大寫表示），而監聽專案則是 surveillance program。稜鏡計劃監聽專案一般會寫做 PRISM surveillance program，PRISM surveillance，或是 Prism program。

＊grant 同意
＊asylum 政治庇護
＊fugitive 逃犯

A 主題文章 Article

Sweden's and Iceland's Pirate Party representatives have together nominated Edward Snowden for 2014 Nobel Peace Prize in February. Earlier in January, two Norwegian politicians had jointly nominated Snowden for the prize. They believe the public debate and policy changes in the Snowden incident had contributed to a more peaceful and stable world order.

The Nobel Peace Prize has been awarded annually since 1901 to those who have "done the most or the best work for fraternity between nations, for the abolition or reduction of standing armies and for the holding and promotion of peace congresses".

The nominators announce the nomination as they recognize Snowden's action had inspired thousands of people all over the world to speak truth to power and demand accountability and transparency in their own nations. Some of them also point that the United States government in international dealings have a long history of corruption, serious war crimes, and lack of respect for the sovereignty of other nations.

Ever since he released the documents, different people and group had nominated Snowden for Nobel Peace Prize. Being nominated means Snowden will be one of names that the Nobel committee will consider for the prestigious award. The committee will not confirm who has been nominated, but those who submit nominations sometimes declare their decision to the public.

Nominators include members of national parliaments, governments, and university professors. The prize committee members can also add their own candidates. From what we know, Snowden received as least four nomination for the prize.

瑞典和冰島的海盜黨（盜版黨）代表在二月份提名愛德華・史諾登競逐今年的諾貝爾和平獎。他們認為，在史諾登事件後各國在公眾討論和政策的改變，對世界的和平穩定是有相當貢獻。

自 1901 年起，諾貝爾和平獎都表彰「為促進民族國家團結友好、取消或裁減軍備以及為和平會議的組織和宣傳盡到最大努力或作出最大貢獻的人」，以資鼓勵。

本次的提名人認為，史諾登的行動激勵世界上成千上萬的人，在他們自己的國家中，勇敢面對強權，追求政治上的責任制和透明度。一部分的人甚至指控美國，認為美國犯下腐敗而嚴重的戰爭罪刑，且長久以來並不尊重其他國家的主權。

自從史諾登事件發生以來，已有數個不同的人或團體提名史諾登競逐諾貝爾和平獎。諾貝爾委員會將對此慎重考慮。該委員會並不會公布被提名人名單，但提名人有時會將他們的決定對外公開。

有權進行提名的人包括各國國會成員、各國政府和大學教授。評議委員會亦有權添加候選人。就目前所得知的消息，史諾登至少獲得四份提名。

Unit 5

Egypt Revolution
埃及革命

代表意義超理解

埃及革命發生於 2011 年 1 月 25 日，由群眾發起示威、遊行、罷工等各種運動，最後造成埃及總統辭職。

The Egyptian Revolution took place following a popular uprising that began on January 25, 2011. It was a diverse movement of demonstrations, marches, labor strikes, and riots. The President of Egypt eventually resigned from his position.

B 背景知識大突破 Background

在 2011 年革命期間，維安部隊和群眾發生衝突，至少造成 800 人死亡，100,000 人受傷。示威者要求結束埃及總統穆巴拉克的政權，而穆巴拉克最後辭職，將權力交給武裝部隊最高委員會。但 2013 年數百萬的埃及群眾再次遊行要求總統穆爾西辭職。穆爾西在 7 月 3 日被軍方驅逐，儘管軍方對強力鎮壓群眾，反軍方的示威活動仍在埃及上演。

During the revolution in 2011, there were clashes between protesters and security forces, resulting at least 800 people killed

---

* demonstration　示威遊行　　　* strike　罷工

and 100,000 injured. Protesters demanded to end Egyptian President Mubarak's regime, and Mubarak stepped down as president and turned power over to the Supreme Council of the Armed Forces. However, on June 30, 2013, millions of protesters across Egypt took the streets and demanded the immediate resignations of President Morsi. On July 3, Morsi was deposed by the military. Demonstrations against military rule are continuing despite brutality of security forces who fired to suppress demonstrations.

Method 使用方法一把罩

表達抗議的手段很多，常見的抗議手段包括示威 (demonstration)、遊行 (march)、和較為激烈的罷工 (strike) 等。但萬一群眾失去控制，則有風險演變為暴動 (riot)。快速而激烈的變革稱為革命 (revolution)，較為溫和的則稱為改革 (reform)。

＊ depose　罷免
＊ brutality　暴力行為
＊ suppress　鎮壓

A 主題文章 Article

In January 2014, rival demonstrations of supporters and opponents of the military-backed government took place in Cairo. More than forty people were killed in clashes since the beginning of 2014, and police broke up anti-government protests to arrest people. It has been three years since the Egypt Revolution, and it is hard to recall any of these events now. The revolution has now turned a full circle, back to where it was.

Since the last coup taken place in July 2013, Morsi's supporters have staged near-daily demonstrations to demand his return to position, with large events held on key anniversaries. Clashes erupted as security forces moved to disperse the demonstrations. Demonstrators would hurl stones at the police, and both demonstrators and bystanders were injured or killed when the police returned fire.

The military has backed the current government since the coup. Observers had labeled the present government as "fascist" or "totalitarian". Several key leaders of the 2011 revolution had been sentenced to jail. Police brutality is back, and government controlled media would label anyone who criticize the military as traitors. State media also claimed the demonstrators were supported by foreign powers.

Demonstrations against military rule are continuing despite brutality of security forces who fired to suppress demonstrations. No one knows when the unrest in Egypt would to an end.

2014 年 1 月，反對和擁護政府雙方的示威者持續在開羅遊行，雙方衝突已造成超過 40 人死亡；警察也開始逮捕反政府示威的群眾。埃及革命至今已超過三年，但現在已經很難回想起當年革命的場景。而這場革命繞了一圈，現在一切又從頭開始。

自 2013 年 7 月的政變以來，穆爾西的支持者幾乎每天都發動示威活動，要求政府讓穆爾西復位；示威者更在週五和各種紀念日發動大型活動。示威者和維安部隊每每發生衝突：示威者對警方投擲石塊，警方則開槍還擊，造成示威者和旁觀者傷亡。

政變後，軍方表態支持現任政府。部分觀察家已經將埃及政府列為法西斯政權或極權統治。2011 年革命時的主要領導人已被判處入獄。警察持續以暴力鎮壓民眾，政府控制的官方媒體動輒將批評軍方的人列為叛徒，並稱反抗行動的領導人都是國外勢力的代理人。

儘管維安部隊持續對示威者開火，各種反對軍事統治的活動仍在進行中。沒有人知道埃及的動亂何時會結束。

Unit 6

Government Shutdown
政府關閉

代表意義超理解

由於美國國會無法通過 2014 年度的預算法案，美國聯邦政府在 2013 年 10 月 1 日到 10 月 16 日間進入關閉狀態，關閉期間大部分的日常行政作業進入服務暫停狀態。

From October 1 through October 16, 2013, the United States federal government entered a shutdown and reduced most routine operations after Congress failed to enact the funds for the year 2014.

B 背景知識大突破 Background

國會在 10 月 17 日通過預算法案後，政府部門隨即恢復作業。在政府關閉期間，約有 80 萬聯邦政府員工被迫休假，另有 130 萬人處於無薪工作狀態。上一次的政府關閉事件發生在 1995-1996 年間，而這次的關閉事件是美國史上時間第三長的關閉事件。

Regular government operations resumed on October 17 after an interim bill was signed into law. During the shutdown, approximately 800,000 federal employees were furloughed, and

---

* enact　制訂法律；頒佈
* interim　臨時的
* furlough　休假

another 1,300,000 report to work without known payment dates. The previous federal government shutdown was in 1995-1996, and the shutdown in 2013 was the third-longest government shutdown in U.S. history.

Method 使用方法一把罩

由於美國歷史上曾多次因國會無法通過預算案而發生政府關閉狀態，因此一般提到政府關閉時，會在其後加上西元年分，做為區別。例如 government shutdown 2013。這種情況也可能發生在其他民主國家，為區別這種情況，也可以用 U.S. government shutdown 2013 這種方式強調這次事件。例如：

There have been eighteen U.S. government shutdowns in the political history. The longest one was the government shutdown 1995, and it lasted three weeks.

(在政治史上有 18 次的美國政府關閉。最長的一次是 1995 年的政府關閉，持續了 3 週的時間。)

A 主題文章 Article

The United States federal government entered a shutdown from October 1 through October 16, 2013. During the shutdown, approximately 800,000 federal employees were furloughed, and another 1,300,000 who were deemed essential report to work without known payment dates.

A lawsuit is now filed against the United States government seeking liquidated damages, with more than a thousand workers joining the suit in January 2014. According to the Fair Labor Standards Act, employers require to pay the workers at least minimum wage and overtime pay on their scheduled paydays. However, those who worked during the government shutdown weren't paid until the shutdown ended on October 16. The lawsuit says that the essential workers are entitled to liquidated damages, which the workers did not receive the minimum wages and overtime pay on time.

According to those who filed the lawsuit, even though the workers eventually collected the money, they are entitled to receive additional pay as damages, under the Fair Labor Standard Act. The amount of money each worker could receive depends on how many hours the person had worked during the shutdown, and their original salary.

In addition to those who already joined the lawsuit, lawyers also asked the court to send a notice about the lawsuit to the 1.3 million federal employees who worked during the shutdown. These federal employees could potentially join the lawsuit. There will be an oral hearing regarding this request, and the judge will rule on the issue.

There were no similar lawsuits filed in the past after each of the government shutdowns. The Congress seemed not too concerned

about how delayed paychecks would affect the lives of federal employees. The government has not yet issued a response regarding this lawsuit.

美國政府在 2013 年 10 月 1 日到 10 月 16 日間進入政府關閉狀態。在政府關閉期間，約有 80 萬聯邦政府員工被迫休假，另有 130 萬人必要人員處於無薪工作狀態。這些人工作時，並不知道自己何時能收到薪資。

目前許多人正對政府提出訴訟，要求政府對違約的行為進行賠償。在 2014 年 1 月就有超過一千名員工參加這場訴訟。根據美國的勞動基準法，雇主在預定的發薪日至少須將最低工資和加班費支付給員工。然而在政府關閉期間，政府並未完成上述條件。訴訟人認為，這些人都有權獲得違約賠償，因為他們在發薪日都沒有領到工資。

訴訟人強調，這些人雖然在關閉事件結束後領到薪資，但根據勞動基準法，他們有權獲得額外的薪酬彌補損失。每個人可得到的賠償將取決在政府關閉期間上班的時間，以及個人的的薪資所得。

除此之外，律師也要求法庭通知所有在訴訟期間工作過的 130 萬聯邦員工，通知他們參加訴訟。相關單位將舉行口頭聽證會，待法官決定是否進行通知。

在過去的政府關閉期間都沒有發生類似的問題，國會似乎也不怎麼重視遲發薪水對員工生活產生的影響。政府相關部門至今尚未對這場訴訟發表回應。

Unit 7

Immigration Reform
移民改革

代表意義超理解

政府對移民政策的討論與改革。移民政策泛指一個國家解決移民問題的原則和方針，包括出入國管理、取得國籍、公民的規範，及相關配套措施等。

Immigration reform means discussions and possible changes regarding current immigration policy. Immigration policy is the government's principle to solve immigration related issues, and it usually includes immigration control, nationality and citizenship regulation, and other related regulations.

B 背景知識大突破 Background

美國總統歐巴馬推動移民改革，並希望能在去年通過移民改革法案。參議院於 2013 年 6 月通過該改革法案，內容除強化美國邊境安全外，並為居留在美國的一千一百萬無證移民提供取得公民身分的管道。但共和黨主導的眾議院決定對該法案進行延宕，因此該法案未能在去年通過。

＊immigration　移民（指移入）

President Obama pushes for immigration reform, and he had hoped the Congress would pass the bill last year. The Senate passed the reform bill in June 2013, which would boost border security, as well as provide a pathway to citizenship for 11 million undocumented immigrants. However, the House of Representatives, led by the Republicans, decided to delay the bill, and it is not passed last year.

M 使用方法一把罩 Method

Immigration Reform 一般作名詞使用，多用於與政治相關的對話場合，例如：

What is your opinion on immigration reform?
（你對移民改革的看法如何？）

Do you support President Obama's immigration reform?
（你支持歐巴馬總統的移民改革嗎？）

這個辭彙也常在拉丁裔及亞裔族群中使用，例如：

I have lived in America for 10 years, but I had overstayed a tourist visa. I hope I can get my citizenship when the Congress passed the Immigration Reform Bill.
（我在美國住了十年，但我是用旅遊簽證滯留的。我希望國會通過移民改革法案後我能拿到公民身分。）

須注意的是，過去常出現在相關話題中的非法移民 (illegal immigrants) 一詞目前已較少使用，而改用詞性較為中性的無證移民 (undocumented immigrants)。

＊Congress　國會　　＊Senate　參議院

A 主題文章 Article

A man interrupted President Obama's speech on immigration reform in November 2013. This man is later identified as an undocumented Korean immigrant, who wants to president to halt deportation for all undocumented immigrant families.

According to this man's blog, he came to the United States from South Korea in his childhood, and he has lived in America for over 10 years. During his senior year in high school, he learned from his parents that they had overstayed a tourist visa.

The man claims that he was living in fear of deportation. He was not able to obtain a driver's license or receive financial aid from the government. When his parents were sick, they did not visit a doctor because they do not have health insurance. When their house was robbed, he refused to call the police because his family would be turned over to immigration office.

This said Korean American decided to interrupt President Obama's speech, despite that President Obama supports the immigration reform. He asks the president to use executive order to halt deportations for all the undocumented immigrant families. He argues that under Obama's administration, a total of 205,000 parents of U.S. citizens are deported in the last two years, and a total of nearly two million immigrants were deported in five years. In average, more than 1000 immigrants are deported every single day in America.

Many people disagree with the man's behavior. Some argue that the approach of screaming is disrespectful, and the man will not get people to listen to him by doing so. He cannot expect every problem to be solved by executive order–that is not how the government functions. That is why the Congress will vote on this reform bill–only the congress can pass an immigration reform.

Immigration reform is not a simple problem. Prior attempts by Congress have failed, and that's why President Obama has to push it himself.

2013 年 11 月，當歐巴馬總統針對移民政策改革發表演說時，一名聽眾打斷他的談話。稍晚後，此人被發現是一名韓裔的無證居民，他希望總統以行政命令停止相關的遣返作業。

根據這名男子的部落格所言，他幼年時跟隨父母從韓國來到美國，並在美國居住超過十年。他高三時從父母那裡得知全家人以旅遊簽證滯留在美。

該男子聲稱，他一直被遣返的恐懼中生活。他不能考駕照，也不能領取政府的獎學金；當他父母生病時，因為沒有醫療保險，他們不能去看醫生；當他們的房子被搶時，他們也不願報警，因為擔心會被移交給移民局。

儘管歐巴馬總統支持移民改革，此人仍決定打斷總統的演講，並要求總統以行政命令停止遣返所有無證居民。他強調，歐巴馬政府任內，過去兩年中，共有 205,000 名美國公民的父母遣返出境。過去五年中，共有近 200 萬無證移民被驅逐出境。美國政府平均每一天都將超過一千名的移民驅逐出境。

許多人不認同他的行為。他們認為，大聲打斷演說是很不禮貌的行為，也不會有人因此而聆聽他的主張。他不能指望行政命令能解決一切問題，政府並不是這樣運作的。這也是為什麼美國國會需要對這份法案進行表決，只有國會能通過移民政策改革。

移民改革不是一個簡單的問題。過去國會提出的改革都以慘敗收場，這也是為什麼歐巴馬總統要親自推動這項法案的原因。

Unit 8

Jihad
伊斯蘭教的聖戰

代表意義超理解

"Jihad" 是一個伊斯蘭教的名詞，也是穆斯林宗教上的義務。它字面上的意思是「奮鬥」，並延伸成為「和不信仰阿拉的人進行抗爭做奮鬥」的意思。這個字具有廣泛的含意，許多人將這個字視為伊斯蘭教中的聖戰。

Jihad is an Islamic term and a religious duty of Muslims. It means "struggle", and refers to struggle against those who do not believe in Allah. The word has wider implications, and many consider it as the Islamic term for "holy war".

背景知識大突破 Background

伊斯蘭的聖戰可分為兩種：大聖戰是指精神上的自我完善和完成義務，小聖戰則是指和伊斯蘭的敵人進行物體上的抗爭。物體上的抗爭又可分為暴力抗爭和非暴力抗爭。聖戰是伊斯蘭法條下唯一容許使用的戰爭型態，但聖戰的目的並非追求把非穆斯林轉化為穆斯林，而是指防衛伊斯蘭國家。

There are two commonly accepted meaning of jihad: the "greater

---

＊religious　宗教的　　　＊implication　含意

jihad" is the inner struggle by a believer to fulfill his duties, and the "lesser jihad" is the physical struggle against the enemies of Islam. The physical struggle can take a violent form or a non-violent form. Jihad is the only form of warfare permissible under Islamic law. The primary aim of jihad is not the conversion of non-Muslims to Islam by force, but rather the defense of the Islamic state.

M 使用方法一把罩 ethod

Jihad 這個字的原意並非聖戰，而是在信仰上對一個理念進行奮鬥。類似的概念也可用於基督教的 Crusade。Crusade 原本是指中古時代基督教發動的聖戰（十字軍），但在現代社會也可以使用再基督徒或基督教國家所推行的某種觀念或改革運動。不管是哪一種宗教，如果專指狹義上的宗教戰爭行為，可以考慮用 holy war（聖戰）取代 jihad 或 crusade 兩個字。

A 主題文章 rticle

An Israeli soldier was killed in a cross-border attacked caused by an online video. An Islamist militant group based in Sinai Peninsula, Egypt, has claimed responsibility for the attack.

The online video, "the Innocence of Muslims," which mocks the prophet Muhammad, had triggered protests across the Muslim

＊ inner　內心的；精神的

＊ warfare　戰爭、鬥爭

world.

Three gunmen were also killed in this Israeli-Egyptian border incident. Israeli officials say Al-Qaeda-inspired jihadist groups had grown to launch attacks in the desert region since the Egyptian revolution last year.

A group calling itself "Partisans of Jerusalem" had revealed itself on internet, calling the deadly cross-border attack a "disciplinary attack against those who insulted the beloved Prophet," referring to the video mentioned above.

"Partisans of Jerusalem" claims that three of its members had infiltrated into Israel earlier and remained hiding until they spotted and attacked an Israeli patrol squad.

The jihadist group also posted videos claiming responsibility for several previous attacks from Sinai Peninsula to Israel. The attacks include two rockets strikes last month, and an earlier strike on a pipeline carrying natural gas to Israel.

The group announced to launch another attack to avenge one of its members, who was killed by Israeli soldiers during a blast in Sinai weeks ago. According to the video, the said jihadist member had led an attacking last year, killing 8 Israelis on a road near the Red Sea.

The jihadist group also launched attacks on Egyptians bases earlier, killing 16 border guards. Egyptian forces tried to launch a crackdown on militants in Sinai using armored vehicles and helicopters.

Ever since the attack, there have been calls in Egypt to revise the 1979 peace treaty with Israel to allow more Egyptian troops in the border. The 1979 peace treaty has limited the size of Egyptian forces in Sinai. Israel has agreed to allow Egypt to send more troops to the region earlier, but Israeli Foreign Minister

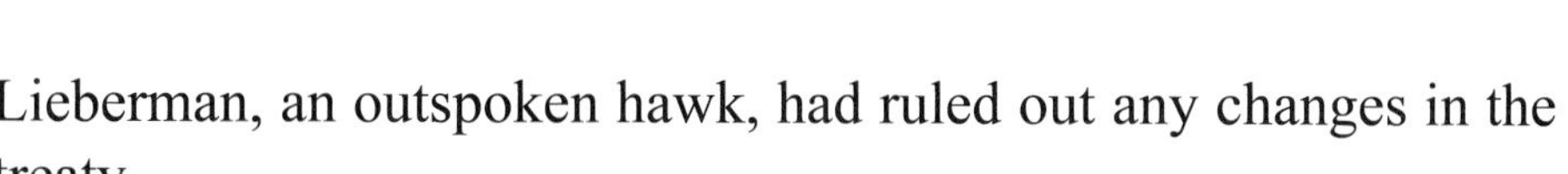

Lieberman, an outspoken hawk, had ruled out any changes in the treaty.

"There's no chance that Israel will agree to any kind of change" in the treaty, announced Lieberman on air.

一段網路上的影片引發跨國界的攻擊事件，一名以色列士兵因而身亡。一個位在埃及西奈半島的軍事組織聲稱他們在幕後規劃整起攻擊事件。

網路上一段嘲笑先知穆罕默德的影片「穆斯林的無知」在全球各地引發穆斯林的抗議。

這起位於以色列與埃及邊境發生的事件中，有三名持槍匪徒已遭到射殺。以色列官員表示，自從去年埃及革命以來，受蓋達組織啟發的聖戰團體已在沙漠區域發動數次攻擊。

一個自稱「耶路撒冷游擊隊」的組織在網路上現身，並將這起邊境攻擊事件稱為「對冒犯我們敬愛的的先知之人進行懲罰攻擊」。他們所指稱的就是上述影片。

「耶路撒冷游擊隊」聲稱，三名組織成員事前即潛入以色列，並在發現以色列巡邏隊後發動攻擊。

這個聖戰組織也在網路上發佈影片，證明他們涉及數次從西奈半島發動的攻擊。這包含兩次的火箭攻擊，以及對以色列天然氣管的襲擊。

該組織表示，他們還會持續發動攻擊，為在數週前攻擊以色列時喪生的成員報仇。網路上的影片顯示，該聖戰組織在去年就曾攻擊以色列，並在紅海一帶造成八名以色列人死亡。

聖戰組織先前也對埃及軍隊發動攻擊，擊斃 16 名邊境守衛。埃及軍隊曾試著以裝甲車和直升機瓦解該組織的軍事成員。

在攻擊事件發生後，埃及有意修改 1979 年與以色列簽定的和平協定。1979 年的和平協定限制埃及在西奈半島的駐軍規模。雖然以色列在稍早曾同意讓埃及進駐更多軍隊，但以色列的鷹派外交部長利柏曼，已經否決修改協定一事。

利柏曼在廣播中說，「以色列不會同意對協定做出任何修改」。

Unit 9

Militia Organization
民兵組織

代表意義超理解

民兵組織是由公民、平民等非職業軍人所組成的軍事力量，和其相對的則是由職業軍人所組成的軍隊。在許多國家，政府則承認預備役的軍人，這些非現役的軍人也被視為民兵，例如美國的國民兵。

A militia is a fighting force that is composed of non-professional soldiers such as citizens or commoners. It is the opposite of professional army or full-time military personnel. In many countries, the "part-time" professional forces are also recognized by the government, such as the National Guard of the United States.

背景知識大突破 Background

許多游擊戰都是由民兵組織發動的。這些民兵組織無法公然和正式的軍隊抗衡，因此他們派出小型的非軍事隊伍，以突襲後迅速撤離等方式和機動性較差的正規軍進行抗爭。有些民兵組織會強迫平民加入他們，藉此獲得人員上的補充。

＊compose　組成　　＊guerrilla　游擊戰

A lot of guerrilla warfare is launched by militia organizations. These militia organizations are not capable of fighting against a formal army; instead, they fight in small group of combatants of armed civilians or irregulars, use military tactics such as ambushes and hit-and-run to fight a larger and less-mobile traditional army. Some militia organizations also force civilians to join them in order to get more personnel supply.

M使用方法一把罩 Method

Militia 這個字專指各種非職業性質的軍事力量，包括國家承認的預備役軍人，和不為國家所認可的各種民兵組織。Military 這則是指正式的軍隊，或是廣義上一切和軍事有關的知識及事務，例如軍事戰術 (military tactics)、軍事戰略 (military strategy)、或是軍事支出 (military expenditures)。

A主題文章 Article

Two Islamist militias in Libya announced their disbandment under public pressure. The anti-militia anger has overwhelmed Libya since the attack on an American diplomatic mission on September 11.

The local government announced that one of the militia had surrendered their bases in the city. According to Reuters, a

---

＊combatant　參戰的人；戰士　　＊ambush　埋伏

＊tactic　手段、策略

second militia group also declared that they had agreed to disband.

Tens of thousands of protesters marched in Benghazi, the second largest city of Libya, demanding the dissolution of all militia groups formed during the revolt against Colonel Muammar el-Qaddafi, the formal strongman of the country. Angry protesters routed a rouge militia group whose members were linked to the attack on the American mission, in which the American ambassador, John Christopher Stevens, and three other Americans were killed.

During the revolt, the militia groups had been the security force in different cities; however, as the revolt ended, they had turned into destabilizing forces in many regions. Many of these militias were led by hard-line Islamists, including veterans of the war in Afghanistan. Other militias were led by Colonel Muammar el-Qaddafi's prisoners. These hard-line Islamist militias have openly spoken of creating Libya an Islamic state.

Politicians in Libya believe the government can work with the militias, if the militias are willing to cooperate. However, other militias not working with the government ought to be disbanded.

Some officials, though, suggested that any direct confrontation with the militias would be risking civilian lives. These officials claim that the problem could not be solved easily, and the government should seek negotiations with unfriendly militias.

Others proposed swift and vigorous efforts in order to end the militias' reign, especially those led by hard-line Islamists. They believe the militias provide nothing but chaos – assassinations, bombings, and kidnappings are common in the cities under militia influence.

兩團利比亞回教民兵組織在輿論壓力下被迫宣布解散。自從美國大使館在 911 受到攻擊後，利比亞全國充斥著反對民兵組織的憤怒氛圍。

當地政府表示，其中一個民兵組織已向政府投降，並將基地移交給政府。而根據路透社的報導，另一個民兵組織也向外界公告同意解散。

數萬名群眾在利比亞的第二大城市班加西示威遊行，要求對所有在格達費政府垮台後成立的民兵組織進行解散。被認為與襲擊美國大使館事件有關的民兵基地遭到憤怒的群眾包圍。美國駐利大使史蒂文斯與三名美籍人員在該事件中喪生。

當利比亞群眾起義反抗格達費時，民兵組織成為許多城市中維持秩序的力量。但在抗爭結束後，民兵反而成為治安的包袱。許多民兵組織的領導都是強硬的伊斯蘭分子，其中甚至包括許多參加過阿富汗戰爭的老兵；另一部分則由被格達費囚禁的犯人領導。這些強硬的穆斯林公然宣稱要將利比亞打造成伊斯蘭國家。

利比亞的政治人物認為，在民兵願意配合的前提下，政府應能與民兵組織合作。但若有民兵組織不願意配合，則政府應將其解散。

但亦有部分官員表示，倘政府與民兵衝突，遭殃的會是無辜百姓。這些官員認為事關重大，政府應嘗試與不友善的民兵組織展開對話。

有人認為政府應強勢、迅速的解決民兵問題，尤其是針對由強硬派回教徒所領導的組織。他們認為，包括各種刺殺、炸彈攻擊、及綁架事件在內，民兵組織的行為只會為社會帶來更多動亂。

Unit 10

National Security Commission of CCP

中央國家安全委員會

代表意義超理解

中央國家安全委員會是 2013 年 11 月在中國共產黨第十八次全國代表大會第三次中央委員全體會議（十八大三中全會）所通過設置的組織。

The National Security Commission of the Communist Party of China was established after the third plenary session of the 18th Chinese Communist Party Central Committee in November 2013.

背景知識大突破 Background

中央國家安全委員會的目的是將一切現有的國安機構進行整合，並受中共領導人直接指揮的單一機構。根據大陸官員的說法，該委員會的主要目標在於防患恐怖主義、分裂主義和宗教極端主義的危害。

It aims to bring all the security apparatus that China already has into a single committee under the direct command of the leader of the People's Republic of China. According to Chinese

＊plenary　全體出席的　　＊apparatus　機構

officials, the committee's primary target is to prevent terrorism, separatism, and religious extremism from endangering the nation.

M使用方法一把罩 ethod

大部分國家都有國安組織，名稱也大同小異。包括大陸、美、英、日等都有國安會 (National Security Council)，因此使用時通常會附上所屬的國家名稱以資區別。大陸和日本由於近來關係緊張，雙方政府新設立的國安會受到周邊各國的關注。

中國共產黨的正式英文名稱是 Communist Party of China，簡稱 CPC，有時也寫作 Chinese Communist Party，簡稱 CCP。

大部分國家都有國安組織，名稱也大同小異。包括大陸、美、英、日等都有國安會 (National Security Council)，因此文中若提到複數國家時應附上所屬國家名稱以資區別。

在台灣，國安局 (National Security Bureau, NSB) 和國安會 (National Security Council, NSC) 又不同，使用上要特別注意，例如：

The National Security Bureau (NSB) rejected a report that National Security Council Secretary-General suggested that the military should intervene in and handle major demonstrations.
(對於媒體報導國安會秘書長曾建議以軍隊干涉示威，國安會提出反駁。)

---

* terrorism　恐怖主義
* separatism　分離主義
* extremism　極端主義

主題文章 Article

The Chinese Communist Party's newly created National Security Commission will be led by the top three members of the supreme Politburo Standing Commission to monitor domestic and foreign security issues. President Xi Jinping will be the head of the commission, with Premier Li Keqiang and top legislator Zhang Dejiang as deputy chiefs.

Observers say that Xi, Li, and Zhang are the top three figures in the country. The structure tries to avoid conflicts with the current seven-seat Politburo Standing Commission system. Xi Jinping had told the party it was essential for the party to strengthen its control to maintain political stability, and the National Security Commission will help deal with threats at home and overseas.

The commission would be in charge of making overall plans and coordinating major issues concerning national security. It will not be considered a government department, and will report to the Politburo and its Standing commission.

The commission was established after the third plenary session of the 18th Chinese Communist Party Central Committee in November 2013, but few details were given. It is not yet known whether a parallel version of the commission will set up under the state, as is arrangement for the top military decision body. It is common to see the same people are in both state and party groups in China.

Experts also point out that the creation of the National Security Commission within the party would help strengthen the party's rule, and it did not require to go through the legislative processes for approval.

中國共產黨新成立的國家安全委員會以中央政治局常委會前三名成員為領導，將監控國內外的安全問題。中共國家主席習近平將成為該委員會的負責人，總理李克強和人大委員長張德江則是副手。

觀察者指出，習、李、張三人是全國前三位的領導人，這種佈局能避免委員會和現有的七人中央政治局常委系統發生衝突。習近平曾對共產黨內部表示有必要加強對黨的控制，以保持政治穩定；而國安委的設置，有利於處理海內外的威脅。

該委員會將統籌規劃、協調有關國家安全的重大問題。它並不是政府部門，而是向中央政治局和證治局常委提出報告。

國安委是由中國共產黨第十八大三中全會所通過設置的組織，但中共並未公開細節資料。目前外界仍不知道國安委是否會和中共的軍事決策機構一樣在黨和政府設置兩套並行的人馬；這種政黨和政府組織並行的措施在大陸非常常見。

專家指出，在黨內成立國家安全委員會將有助於強化習近平對黨的控制，這些措施並不需要通過立法程序批准。

Unit 11

Nelson Mandela
尼爾森 · 曼德拉

代表意義超理解

曼德拉是南非的政治家、於 1994-1999 年間擔任南非總統，致力於反種族隔離運動。他是南非第一位非裔總統，也是南非第一位在民主選舉中選出的總統。曼德拉於 2013 年 12 月去世。

Nelson Mandela was a South African politician who dedicated on anti-apartheid movement. He served as President of South Africa from 1994 to 1999, and he was also South Africa's first black president, and the first elected in a fully representative democratic election. Mandela died in December 2013.

B 背景知識大突破 Background

曼德拉因陰謀推翻政府的罪名在獄中服刑超過 27 年，出獄後於 1994-1999 年間獲選為南非總統。曼德拉任內致力於解除南非深根蒂固的種族歧視、貧困、不平等等問題，並全力促進族群間的和解。曼德拉於 2013 年 12 月 5 日去世，享年 95 歲。

Mandela served over 27 years in prison, being convicted of

＊apartheid　種族隔離制度　　＊convict　宣判有罪

conspiracy to overthrow the state. After he is released from prison, he served as President of South Africa from 1994 to 1999. During his office, he focused on dismantling the legacy of apartheid through tackling institutionalized racism, poverty, and inequality, and fostering racial reconciliation. Mandela died on 5 December 2013, at age of 95.

Method 使用方法一把罩

曼德拉一生中最為人所稱道的是他所領導的反種族隔離運動 (Anti-Apartheid Movement，簡寫 AAM)。種族隔離 (Apartheid) 是南非在 1948 年到 1994 年間所施行的制度，將人口分類為白人、有色人、印度人、黑人等四類，從地理上分離不同族群的人，強制他們住在類似保留區的區域中，同時防止非白人族群得到投票權或影響力。

* conspiracy　謀反
* dismantle　廢除
* reconciliation　和解

Nelson Mandela died on 5 December 2013 at the age of 95. The president of South Africa announced a national mourning period of ten days, with the main event held in Johannesburg on 10 December 2013, and a state funeral was held on December 15.

A nine-meter bronze sculpture of Mandela was unveiled after the event, which is billed as the largest statue of the South African leader. The giant statue stands with arms outstretched, symbolizing Mandela's devotion to inclusiveness. However, people also found a tiny, barely visible sculpted rabbit inside one of the bronze ears.

The bronze rabbit is about half the height of the ear canal. It was added by the two sculptors who built the statue because the officials of South Africa would not allow them to engrave their signatures on the statue's trousers. They also explains the rabbit represented the pressure of finishing the sculpture on time because the word for rabbit in the Dutch based language also means "haste."

The Department of arts and cultures says it did not know the sculptors had added the rabbit. South Africa officials request the miniature bunny removed from the statue as quickly as possible. The sculptors had apologized for any offence to those who felt the rabbit was disrespectful toward the legacy of Mandela.

There was also another incident during Mandela's memorial. A fake sign language interpreter was presented on stage whose gestures did not make sense. The fake interpreter was watched by millions as he stood beside speakers at the event. Thousands of people express their anger at the interpreter's gestures, and several deaf groups confirmed his signing did not reflect the comments made to honor Mandela. People were shocked by

the quality of sign language interpretation at the memorial–if it could be called interpretation at all.

尼爾森・曼德拉於 2013 年 12 月 5 日去世，享年 95 歲。南非總統宣布全國進行為期十天的哀悼，紀念活動則在 12 月 10 日在約翰尼斯堡舉行，並在 12 月 15 日舉行國葬。

南非當局塑造一個高約九公尺曼德拉銅像，並標榜這是南非領導人中規模最大的雕像。巨型雕像張開雙臂，象徵著曼德拉的對族群包容的貢獻。然而，人們卻在銅像的耳朵中，發現一隻小到幾乎看不見的兔子雕像。

這支青銅兔子大概有銅像耳道的一半高度，是這座銅像的兩個雕塑家，因為南非官員不讓他們在銅像的褲子上留下他們的簽名而自行加進去的。這兩名雕塑家解釋，兔子象徵著他們需要趕工完成雕像的壓力，因為兔子這個詞，在當地的語言中有也著「匆忙」的意思。

南非政府的藝術文化部門則表示，他們並不知道作者在銅像中刻了兔子。南非官員則要求儘快移除這支兔子。銅像的兩名雕塑家已經就所冒犯之處，表達歉意。

曼德拉的紀念式中還發生另一起事件。一名假的手語翻譯人員在台上進行手語翻譯，但他的手勢沒有任何意義。這名假的翻譯員在全球數百萬人的觀看下比手畫腳。上萬人表達他們對這名翻譯的憤怒，數個聾人團體也證實他的手勢和追悼曼德拉的演說內容毫無關係。群眾被這名翻譯的行為所驚訝－如果他的行為稱得上是「翻譯」的話。

Unit 12

North Korea Peace Letter
北韓和平公開信

代表意義超理解

2014 年 1 月 28 日，北韓在南韓與美國聯合軍事演習前發表公開信，希望雙方正式結束敵對狀態，並達成朝鮮半島非核化的目標。

North Korea had written an open letter to South Korea ahead of its joint military drills with the United States calling for end to hostilities between two nations and the denuclearization of Korean Peninsula on January 28, 2014.

B 背景知識大突破 Background

北韓發表公開信致南韓當局要求停止軍事敵對狀態，並要求在朝鮮半島達成非核化。信中並警告說，南北雙方的緊張局勢可能導致核戰爭。南韓當局的回應則表示，對於北韓的真實意圖仍抱有疑慮。

North Korea has called for an end to military hostilities with South Korea in an "open letter" sent to South Korean authorities. The letter also requests to achieve the denuclearization of Korean Peninsula. It also warned that the tensions between the North and the South could lead to an all-out nuclear war. South Korea

＊drill　訓練、操練

＊denuclearization　非核化、非核武器化

responded that there are still doubts over the true intentions.

M使用方法一把罩 ethod

北韓的正式名稱是朝鮮民主主義人民共和國 (Democratic People's Republic of Korea)，南韓的正式名稱則是大韓民國 (Republic of Korea)。朝鮮勞動黨 (Worker's Party of Korea) 是北韓唯一的執政黨，目前的領導人是金正恩 (Kim Jong-un)。南北韓關係稱為 South Korea-North Korea relations，例如：

South Korea-North Korea relations are the political, diplomatic, and military interactions between South Korea and North Korea, from the division of Korea in 1945 following the end of World War II。

(南北韓關係是南北韓在二戰後分裂至今，雙方在政治、外交、軍事等各方面的交流互動。)

＊interaction　互動　　＊division　分裂

A 主題文章 Article

Although North Korea has announced an open letter to call for an end to military hostilities with South Korea, recent event may show otherwise. In February 2014, North Korea threatened to cancel reunions of Korean War-divided families because the United States and South Korea are going to have military drills together. North Korea also accused that the United States are flying nuclear capable bombers near Korean Peninsula, raising tensions in the region.

North Korea and South Korea decided to resume the family reunions earlier. The reunion event had not been held since February 2010. Experts claimed that North Korea approved the reunion program because it needs to improve the relationship with South Korea to bring foreign investment and aid. Many believed that it is unlikely North Korea would cancel the reunion.

In its announcement, North Korea calls the drills between South Korea and the United States a preparation for war. It also considers the nuclear-capable bomber a great threat to its security. South Korea and the United States responded that the exercises are purely defensive.

The National Defense Commission of North Korea warned that the reunions may not happen if South Korea goes ahead with the drills. The North seemed to link the military drills and the nuclear-capable bomber together as a nuclear strike drill. The North says that a reunion negotiation is meaningless when there is a nuclear strike drill going on.

However, not everyone takes North Korea's threatening seriously. North Korea has a history of threatening to pause cooperation with the South to protest the drills between South

Korea and the United States. During the last year's drills, North Korea had the same responds; it had issued threats so often, that many believe the North is just doing its daily routine.

儘管北韓日前發佈一封公開信呼籲與南韓結束軍事敵對狀態，最近發生的事件卻顯示雙方關係並未和緩。2014 年 2 月，北韓對南韓和美國間的軍事演習提出抗議，並威脅取消兩韓間在韓戰中失散的親人團聚行動。北韓並指責美國讓有核作戰能力的轟炸機在朝鮮半島活動，增加區域間的緊張情勢。

南北韓原先決定恢復在 2010 年 2 月中斷的團聚活動。專家表示，北韓認可這次的團聚活動，因為北韓需要改善與南韓的關係，並藉此得到國外的投資和援助。許多人認為，北韓不可能取消這次的活動。

但在北韓的聲明中，北韓認為南韓和美國的軍事演習是在為戰爭作準備，並批評有核子攻擊能力的轟炸機是對區域安全的一大威脅。南韓和美國則回應表示，演習是純粹防禦性的。

北韓的國防委員會警告說，如果南韓照常舉辦演習，探親團聚將會被取消。北韓似乎把軍事演習和有核攻擊能力的轟炸機聯想在一起，認為這是一次核子打擊演習。北韓表示，當核子攻擊演習上演時，探親團聚的活動毫無意義。

並不是每個人都認真看待北韓的威脅。長久以來北韓就有對南韓和美國合作演習表達抗議的習慣。去年演習時，北韓也持續進行一樣的威脅。因此，很多人認為北韓的威脅不過是例行公事。

Unit 13

Obamacare
歐巴馬醫療改革

代表意義超理解

患者保護與平價醫療法案，又稱為歐巴馬醫療改革，是美國總統歐巴馬於 2013 年 3 月 23 日簽署的聯邦法。該法案的主旨是對一般大眾提供較好的醫療服務。

The Patient Protection and Affordable Care Act, also known as "Obamacare," is signed into law by President Obama on March 23, 2010. The purpose of Obamacare is to provide better medical service to the common population.

背景知識大突破 Background

歐巴馬醫改的主旨是對一般大眾提供較好的醫療服務。它的目標是向美國民眾提供高品質且平價的醫療保險，提升健保投保率，同時降低個人和政府的醫療成本。目前該法仍面臨部分州政府、保守團體及少數營利組織的反對。

The goal of Obamacare is to increase the quality and affordability of health insurance, lowering the uninsured rate, and reducing the

＊affordable　付得起的

costs of healthcare for individuals and the government. The law continues to face oppressions from certain state governments, conservative advocacy groups, and some business organizations.

Method 使用方法一把罩

Obamacare 是患者保護與平價醫療法案的簡寫，一般譯為歐巴馬醫改，英文簡寫亦稱為 PPACA (Patient Protection and Affordable Care Act) 或 ACA (Affordable Care Act)。很多時候也和醫療改革 (health care reform) 相互使用。

Obamacare 提供的健保，並不取代一般私人保險、聯邦醫療保險 (Medicare)、低收入醫療補助 (Medicaid) 等舊有的醫療保險制度。

* advocacy　擁護

* Medicaid　美國的公共醫療補助制度

主題文章 Article

The retailing company Target Corporation declared that it will stop providing health-care benefits to its part-time workers and directs them to purchase other insurance through the health law's exchange. Target is not the only company to do this – a good number of companies had dropped their health care benefits for part-time workers, as a result of Obamacare.

Like other companies that had dropped health benefits for part-time workers, Target claims that the change will actually help their part-time employees. It argues that by offering part-time workers insurance, it would actually disqualify most of them from being eligible for newly available insurance, which would reduce their overall health insurance spending.

But is Target's argument true? It will really depend on each individual part-time employee. For those who are already enrolled in the company's health insurance, they may be angry to see that their benefits are going to an end. However, for those who are not enrolled in the company's health insurance, they are likely to find themselves in a better situation, with access to more affordable health care, as promised by the president.

How many people would be affected by the new policy? According to Target, there are less than 10% of part-time employees enroll in the company's health insurance, which means 90% of them are not enrolled. This is what Target means the offer of insurance may prevent workers from the federal insurance, thus having negative impact. The 10% will lose access to an employer-sponsored insurance; while the other 90% will gain access to government-subsidized insurance.

Of course, Target comes up with this new policy for its own financial purpose: it will transfer much of its insurance spending

to the government. Obamacare is changing how employers offer coverage to their employees, but whether those changes are positive or negative depends on how much you earn and whether you are getting benefits right now. Like many other parts of the health-care policy, its complicated, and varies a lot from one individual to another.

美國銷售業 Target 百貨公司日前宣布，將停止該公司提供給兼職人員的醫療福利，讓他們能夠購買健保法案通過後的新的醫療保險。Target 不是唯一一家這樣做的公司－在歐巴馬健改後，已有數家企業放棄他們對兼職人員的健保福利。

和其他放棄對兼職人員的福利的企業一樣，Target 宣稱，此一改變實質上是在幫助他們的員工。Target 認為，他們取消兼職人員的保險，能讓員工符合購買新保險的資格，有利於減少他們的總體健保支出。

但這樣的說法是否屬實？這還是要看個人而定。對那些已經參加公司健保的人來說，他們可能會感到生氣，因為他們既有的利益將被取消。但對那些沒有參加公司健保的人來說，他們很可能面臨一個較好的局面，如同歐巴馬總統所承諾的，他們能參加更為平價的健保計畫。

但有多少人會受新政策影響？根據 Target 的資料顯示，目前只有 10% 的兼職員工有投保公司的健保，也就是說，有 90% 的兼職人員沒有參加公司健保。所以 Target 才說，新的措施能避免員工陷入無法購買新保險的窘境。雖然 10% 的員工會失去雇主提供的健康保險，但另外 90% 的人將能購買政府補助的健保。

當然，Target 是為了自己的財務打量而決定這項新政策：它把大部分的保險支出轉嫁給政府。歐巴馬健改改變了雇主與員工間的健保計畫，至於這些改變是正面的或是負面的，則取決於你的薪資，和你既有的福利。這就像醫改本身一樣，對每個人來說，變化很多，也很複雜。

Unit 14

Peacekeeping Operations
聯合國維和行動

代表意義超理解

依據官方定義，聯合國維和行動是經過聯合國授權的軍事行為，其目的在於協助在有衝突的國家間創造條件，以維持持續性的和平。

Peacekeeping operation, as officially defined by the United Nations, is an authorized military operation that helps countries to create conditions for sustainable peace.

B 背景知識大突破 Background

依聯合國規定，一般的維和行動以各種手段解決勢力間的紛爭，並以外交行為使敵對各方在談判中達成協議。其對象包括外交使節、國家、區域組織、或聯合國屬下的各種組織。有時候維和行動也可以經由非官方及非政府組織進行。

According to the United Nations, peacekeeping generally includes measures to address conflicts in progress and usually involves diplomatic action to bring hostile parties to a negotiated agreement. Peacemakers may also be envoys, governments, groups of states, regional organizations or the United Nations.

---

* hostile　敵對的　　　　* envoy　外交官、談判代表

Peacekeeping efforts may also be undertaken by unofficial and non-governmental groups.

Method 使用方法一把罩

Peacekeeping operation 是一個範圍較為廣闊的詞彙。聯合國及國際間解決爭端的各種方式，包括談判 (negotiation)、調查 (enquiry)、調停 (mediation)、和解 (conciliation)、斡旋 (good offices)、仲裁 (arbitration)、司法解決 (judicial settlement) 等；若聯合國安理會認定某個國家在對外關係上使用武力或戰爭手段，安理會亦有權決議採取強制和平手段 (peace enforcement action)。

＊judicial　司法的

＊enforcement　強制、執行

A 主題文章 Article

After a recent NATO conference, Kazakhstan Defense Ministry announced that Kazakhstan's peacemakers are operationally compliant and ready to participate in UN peacekeeping operations.

The event was attended by representatives from Great Britain, Germany, Turkey, Austria, Azerbaijan, Armenia, Bosnia and Herzegovina, Georgia, Jordan, Macedonia, Moldova, Mauritania, Norway, Serbia, Ukraine, Finland, Sweden, and Montenegro. Representatives from each country exchanged their experience in peacemaking missions, and discussed military cooperation in future peacemaking operation.

NATO experts started reviewing battalion from Kazakhstan in August 2013. It is well organized, and the soldiers are trained to patrol an area, repulse possible attacks and arrest suspicious people. The military men practiced in urban areas.

The Defense Ministry of Kazakhstan also announced that Kazakhstan peacemakers will not participate in mission causing mixed public reaction, According to the Defense Ministry, the United Nation is currently performing 15 peacemaking operations. Kazakhstan Defense Ministry had coordinated with the Foreign Ministry and submitted to Kazakhstan Government and then to seek the Presidential Administration's approval. Although the battalion is ready for peacekeeping operations, it is still too early to talk about any particular missions before the President makes the decision and the Parliament approves the suggestion.

Kazakhstan is a contiguous transcontinental country in Central Asia, and it is the ninth largest country in the world. It has 17 million of people, being the 62nd largest population in the world.

Kazakhstan is the largest economy of the post-Soviet region, which also includes Kyrgyzstan, Tajikistan, Turkmenistan and Uzbekistan. Foreign companies have invested billions of dollars in the nation's mineral and oil wealth since its independence from the Soviet Union in 1991.

在近期的北約組織會議上，哈薩克國防部表示，哈薩克的維和部隊已作好準備參加聯合國的維和行動。

出席本次會議的成員包括英國、德國、土耳其、奧地利、亞塞拜然、亞美尼亞、波斯尼亞、赫塞哥維那、喬治亞、約旦、馬其頓、摩爾多瓦、茅利塔尼亞、挪威、塞爾維亞、烏克蘭、芬蘭、瑞典和蒙特內哥羅等國的代表。各國代表在會議中交流維安任務的經驗，並討論在未來針對維安行動成立軍事合作。

北約的專家自 2013 年 8 月起開始對哈薩克的部隊進行視察。部隊的情況良好，士兵受到在城市中巡邏、反擊、以至於逮捕可疑人士等各方面的訓練。

哈薩克國防部同時表示，該國的維安部隊不會參與有爭議的維安行動。國防部聲稱，雖然目前聯合國共有 15 項進行中的維安任務，但在哈薩克外交部、行政當局、國會和總統的批准前，哈薩克並不會參與特定的維安行動。

哈薩克是一個領土跨越歐亞的中亞國家，同時也是世界上領土第九大的國家。哈薩克共有 1700 萬人口，在世界上排名第 62。哈薩克是蘇聯解體後中亞五國中的經濟大國，其他四國包括吉爾吉斯、塔吉克、土庫曼和烏茲別克。自 1991 年從蘇聯獨立出來之後，外國公司已經在哈薩克投資數十億美元，以開發該國豐富的礦產和石油資源。

Unit 15

Reforming Leading Group
深化改革領導小組

代表意義超理解

深化改革領導小組的正式名稱是（中共）中央全面深化改革領導小組。和國安委一樣，改革小組是中共十八大三中全會中決定設置的機構。

The reforming leading group is formally known as the Central Leading Group for Comprehensively Deepening Reforms. Like the National Security Commission, the decision was made in the third plenary session of the 18th Chinese Communist Party Central Commission.

背景知識大突破 Background

中共十八大三中全會決定設置全面深化改革領導小組，該小組由中共國家主席習近平親自擔任領導人。一般認為，改革小組將有權力跳過官僚體系直接推動政策法案，同時也幫助習近平鞏固對中央政府的掌控。

The third plenary session of the 18th Chinese Communist Party Central Commission had decided to create the Central Leading

＊comprehensively　全面地；包括地

Group for Comprehensively Deepening Reforms. The group is led by President Xi Jinping himself. It is believed to going to have the power to push policies past the bureaucracy system and help Xi Jinping to consolidate his power over the central government.

Method 使用方法一把罩

全面深化改革領導小組和中央國家安全委員會都是中共十八大三中全會後受國際關注的新組織，簡寫中央深改組；但與國家安全委員會不同，由於各國沒有類似組織，因此相對容易辨別。各國對該組織的稱呼，有時也簡化為 reforming leading group 或 leading group。

Article 主題文章

On January 2014, China's Central Leading Group for Comprehensively Deepening Reforms held its very first meeting in Beijing. The group is chaired by President Xi Jinping, with about another twenty members. Outsiders wondered about its operations ever since the third plenary session in November 2013, and following its first meeting, a rough picture has emerged.

---

* bureaucracy 官僚主義；官僚體系
* consolidate 把……合為一體、合併

President and Party Secretary Xi Jinping is in charge of the group shows the importance the leadership has placed on the group's role driving tough reforms, including integrating millions of farmers into cities, helping local government sweep their excessive reliance on debt, and allowing market-driven private enterprises a larger role in the economy.

The three deputy chiefs of the group are all members of China's decision-making body, the standing Committee of the Politburo. These deputy chiefs are Premier Li Kenqiang, Vice Premier Zhang Gaoli, and Liu Yunshan, who is the head of both propaganda department and the party school. Having four of China's top seven leaders inside the reform group is expected to help the group dealing with powerful vested interests that may put up obstacles to economic changes. There are tough battles ahead, and Xi said in the meeting that officials of the government should speed up their reform work and at the same time move forward with steady steps.

According to state media, the reform group is going to have six separate departments, giving it responsibilities and power that appear to extend far beyond the economy. These departments include divisions for party construction, discipline and supervision, democracy and justice, culture, and society. Observers believe the discipline and supervision department is likely to help fight the corruption, as well as the party construction department. Many wonder what kind of policy the democracy and justice department will push, but it probably won't include direct elections.

Another notable creation is the economy and ecology department. It reflects the leaders are aware of serious environmental problems after decades of rapid economic growth.

2014 年 1 月，中共領導人在北京召開全面深化改革小組領導小組第一次會議。該小組由習近平親自主持，約有 20 名成員。自十八大三中全會後，外界一直想知道該小組的運行狀況，這次會議則讓外界對改革小組有初步的認知。

由大陸國家主席、中共總書記習近平親自出任改革小組的領導人，已顯示該小組的重要性。改革小組的任務是帶領大陸進行艱困的改革，內容包括將數百萬的農民移向都市、協助地方政府克服它們對債務的依賴，以及讓市場導向的民營企業在總體經濟中發會更大的作用。

該小組的三名副領導人都來自中共的最高決策機構－政治局常務委員，包括國務院總理李克強、副總理張高麗，以及文宣部門和黨校主管劉雲山。由中共排名前七名領導人中的四人出任改革小組的領導人，將有助於排除經濟改革時既得利益集團對改革造成的障礙。習在會議上表示，政府官員應該加快改革腳步，同時穩步向前。

根據官方媒體報導，改革小組將設有六個獨立的專項小組，其職權遠超過經濟方面的改革。這些專項小組包括黨的建設制度改革、紀律檢查體制改革、民主法治領域改革、文化體制改革、社會體制改革等。觀察者認為，紀律檢查體制和黨的建設制度改革將有助於對抗貪腐。許多人對民主法治領域的改革感到好奇，但其內容應不包括人民直選。

另一個值得注意的焦點是經濟體制與生態文明體制改革。這反映出中共領導人已意識到十幾年來的急速經濟成長已造成嚴重的環境問題。

Unit 16

Same-sex Marriage
同性婚姻

代表意義超理解

同性婚姻是指在性別認同上相同的兩個人之間的婚姻關係。法律上對同性婚姻的認同也被稱為婚姻平等或平等婚姻權。世界上目前共有 17 個國家承認同性婚姻。

Same-sex marriage is marriage between two people of the same gender identity. Legal recognition of same-sex marriage is also referred to as marriage equality. Same-sex marriage is legally recognized in 17 countries.

B 背景知識大突破 Background

在美國，同性伴侶只能在 16 個州及華盛頓特區結婚。但 2013 年美國政府對溫莎的判決成為同性婚姻的里程碑：在該案中，美國最高法院認為，聯邦政府僅將婚姻限制在異性聯姻的做法是違憲的。

In the United States, same-sex couples can only marry in sixteen states and Washington D.C. 2013 United States v. Windsor became a landmark case because the United States Supreme Court held that restricting U.S. federal interpretation of marriage

---

* gender　性別
* landmark　里程碑
* restrict　限制、限定

to apply only to heterosexual unions is unconstitutional.

M 使用方法一把罩 ethod

Same-sex marriage 是指一個國家從法律上承認同性之間聯姻。除了有 17 個承認同性婚姻的國家外，另有 15 個國家雖然在法律上不稱作婚姻，但在實質的權利義務方面給予同性民事結合制度或生活伴侶制度。這種制度一般以伴侶 (partnership) 或同居 (cohabitation) 等詞語表示。例如：

Lawmakers in Luxembourg have approved changes in marriage legislation that will allow people of the same sex to wed and to adopt children。

(盧森堡的通過法案修正案，允許同性結婚及收養小孩)

Council approves benefits for same-sex partners of metro employees。

(議會通過大眾運輸系統雇員的員工福利可及於同性伴侶。)

＊ heterosexual　異性戀的；異性的

＊ unconstitutional　違反憲法的

A 主題文章 Article

The Scottish Parliament recently passed the Marriage and Civil Partnership Bill, a bill which allows same-sex marriage to take place. The vote number was 105 to 18. It received cross-party backing, despite both the Church of Scotland and the Scottish Catholic Church opposite the bill.

The Scottish government says the move was the right thing to do, and the first same sex wedding will be able to hold in the following autumn. However, groups who oppose same-sex marriage say it was s sad day for those who believes in traditional marriage, arguing that the Scottish Parliament had ignored public opinion and beliefs.

During the debate, members of the Scottish Parliament rejected amendments which would protect individuals and groups who oppose same-sex marriage. A member of the Scottish Parliament says that the bill is similar to the bill passed by the United Kingdom Parliament allowing same-sex marriage in England and Wales.

The bill that allows same-sex marriage to take place in England and Wales was passed in July 2013. The first same-sex wedding will be able to take place in March 2014. In Scotland, the Scottish Parliament decriminalized homosexual acts between two adults in 1900, and recognized same-sex partnership in 2005. Same-sex couples currently have the option to enter into a recognized partnership, but the Scottish National Party brought forward the Marriage and Civil Partnership Bill, saying it is an important step for equality.

Northern Ireland becomes the only part of the United Kingdom where same-sex marriage legislation has not been passed. The Northern Ireland Executive has stated that it does not intend

to introduce such a bill. However, same-sex partnership is recognized in Northern Ireland.

Scotland became the 17th country in the world to legalize same-sex marriage after the bill was passed.

蘇格蘭議會最近以 105 比 18 的票數通過婚姻與同性伴侶關係法案，該法案將允許同性別的人結婚。這項法案收到跨黨派的支持，但遭到蘇格蘭天主教會和蘇格蘭國教會的反對。

蘇格蘭政府表示，這是一項正確的決定，第一場同性婚禮可望在 2014 年秋天舉行。但對反對同性婚姻的團體來說，這卻是悲哀的一天。這些人支持傳統的婚姻，並認為蘇格蘭議會漠視反對者的意見和信仰。

在表決法案前的辯論中，蘇格蘭議會否決了保護反對同性婚姻團體的意見。一位蘇格蘭議員說，這次通過的法案，和英國議會允許英格蘭和威爾士同性結婚的法案相似。

允許英格蘭和威爾士同性婚姻的法案在 2013 年 7 月通過。第一場同性婚禮將能在 2014 年 3 月舉行。而在蘇格蘭，蘇格蘭議會在 1900 年時通過了兩個成年人之間的同性戀行為合法化的法案，並在 2005 年認可同性間的伴侶制度。同性間可以進入一個受到法律認可的伴侶關係。儘管如此，蘇格蘭民族黨仍提出這次的婚姻與同性伴侶關係法案，聲稱這是邁向完全平等的一大步。

北愛爾蘭則是聯合王國 (英國) 中唯一未立法通過同性婚姻法的地區。北愛爾蘭行政人員表示，目前沒有這樣的打算。但北愛爾蘭仍承認同性間的伴侶制度。

這次立法工作完成後，蘇格蘭成為世界上第 17 個將同性婚姻合法化的國家。

Unit 17

Scottish Independence Referendum 2014
2014 蘇格蘭獨立公投

代表意義超理解

蘇格蘭政府和英國政府同意於 2014 年 9 月針對蘇格蘭是否應成為獨立國家進行公投。據英國選舉委員會建議，公投題目將定為「蘇格蘭是否應成為一個獨立的國家？」

Following an agreement between the Scottish Government and the United Kingdom Government, a referendum on whether Scotland should be an independent state will take place in September 2014. The question to be asked in the referendum will be "Should Scotland be an independent country?" as recommended by the Electoral Commission.

B 背景知識大突破 Background

蘇格蘭王國自中世紀早期就存在，一直持續到 1707 年為止。蘇格蘭國王詹姆士六世在 1603 年繼承英格蘭和愛爾蘭的王位，英格蘭和蘇格蘭最後發展為大不列顛王國。在 1801 年時，大不列顛王國和愛爾蘭王國合併，成為現在的大不列顛和愛爾蘭聯合王國。

＊ agreement　協議、協定

The Kingdom Scotland emerged as an independent sovereign state in the early Middle Ages and continued to exist until 1707. King James VI of Scotland succeeded the throne of England and Ireland in 1603, and eventually the Kingdom of Scotland entered into a union with the Kingdom of England to create the Kingdom of Great Britain. The Kingdom of Great Britain entered into a union with the Kingdom of Ireland in 1801 to create the United Kingdom of Great Britain and Ireland.

Method 使用方法一把罩

英國的正式名稱是 the United Kingdom of Great Britain and Ireland（大不列顛和愛爾蘭聯合王國），一般簡稱為 the United Kingdom（聯合王國）或 Britain 不列顛。英國雖然因為英格蘭的關係，長期以來被稱為英國，但英國並不是正式的名稱。

＊ sovereign　獨立自主的
＊ throne　王位、寶座
＊ succeed　繼位、繼任、繼承

A 主題文章 Article

The British Broadcasting Corporation (BBC) is to suspend its membership of Confederation of British Industry (CBI), which is Britain's leading business lobby group, after deciding to join a number of organizations protesting over the CBI's move to officially campaign against Scottish independence.

BBC is a British public service broadcasting statutory corporation. It provides impartial public service broadcasting in the United Kingdom. It's the world's oldest national broadcasting organization, and one of the largest broadcasters in the world.

Both the BBC and the CBI issued statements saying the publicly-funded broadcaster would suspend its membership during the campaign period, which is from May 30 until the independence referendum on September 18.

BBC is one of a list of public agencies and universities to sever ties with the CBI after it registered with the Electoral Commission to support the campaign to stop Scotland from leaving the United Kingdom. In UK, organizations or individuals have to register if they want to spend more than ten thousand pounds on campaigning during the referendum.

It also highlights the fact that growing divisions in Scotland over the referendum. Recent polls showed that the race had tightened, with the pro-independence campaign remained behind.

Scotland has been part of the United Kingdom for over 300 years. General speaking however, businesses operating in Scotland had tried to avoid taking sides on whether Scotland should be independent from the United Kingdom, saying that they have no vote in the process, so they should not take sides.

The CBI had argued against independence, saying it would

cause uncertainty over taxation, financial regulation, currency, and European Union membership. However, most of Scotland's universities and several public agencies had left the organization after it registered to join the campaign.

英國工業聯合會是英國數一數二的商業遊說團體，這個組織在蘇格蘭獨立公投中登記反對蘇格蘭獨立。和其他數個團體一樣，英國廣播公司宣佈決定中止它在工業聯合會中的會員資格，以對工業聯合會的態度表達抗議。

英國廣播公司是英國法定的廣播服務機構，並提供給英國公正的廣播服務。它是世界上最古老的國家級廣播公司，同時也是世界上最大的廣播公司之一。

英國廣播公司和英國工業聯合會都發表聲明指出，在公投期間，也就是從 5 月 30 日到 9 月 18 日的公投日為止，英國廣播公司將中止其在工業聯合會的會員資格。

英國工業聯合會已向選舉委員會註冊，反對蘇格蘭從英國獨立。在英國，任何組織或個人都需要經過登記，才能在這場公投中支出一萬英鎊以上的資金表態助選。英國工業聯合會表態後，已有多個公共機構和大學表態和工業聯合會斷絕關係，英國廣播公司只是其中之一。

這也顯示在蘇格蘭獨立公投中雙方的分裂。最新的民調顯示，雙方的差距已在縮小，但支持獨立的一方仍處落後。

蘇格蘭和英格蘭合併已超過 300 年。一般來說，在蘇格蘭有業務的企業，都試著避免在這次公投中選邊站。這些企業表示，他們並沒有投票權，因此他們不會偏袒任何一方。

英國工業聯合會曾極力反對獨立，聲稱蘇格蘭的獨立將導致稅收、金管、貨幣、和歐盟會員資格等各方面的不確定性。但在工業協會登記反對獨立後，它的蘇格蘭公共企業會員和大學會員已紛紛離開這個組織。

Unit 18

South China Sea Dispute
南海主權紛爭

代表意義超理解

南海主權紛爭有來已久，在這個區域的各個國家都對海域中的島嶼和領海聲稱擁有主權彼此競爭。在南海中有主權爭議的國家包括汶萊、中國大陸、中華民國（臺灣）、印尼、馬來西亞、越南、及菲律賓。

There have been territorial disputes in the South China Sea, involving both islands and maritime claims among the sovereign states within the region. Those who has claims in the region includes Brunei, mainland China, Taiwan (Republic of China), Indonesia, Malaysia, Vietnam, and the Philippines.

B 背景知識大突破 Background

南海的糾紛十分複雜，因為每個不同國家都有不同的要求，並與其他國家相互競爭。例如越南、馬來西亞、汶萊和菲律賓之間有海上國界的糾紛。上述七個國家在南海也為南海上的島鏈進行爭奪，因為海底可能藏有可供開採的原油和天然氣。

The disputes in South China Sea are complex, as different

＊dispute　爭論、糾紛
＊maritime　海運的；海事的
＊complex　複雜的

countries have different claims and disputes with other countries. For example, Vietnam, Malaysia, Brunei, and the Philippines have disputes include the maritime boundary in the area. Each of the seven countries listed above have disputes among the island chains in the region. Each of them argues for the potential exploitation of crude oil and natural gas under the water.

Method 使用方法一把罩

Dispute 這個字可以用來表示各種國家間的紛爭，例如領土紛爭 territorial dispute、領海紛爭 maritime dispute、國界紛爭 border dispute 等。一般國家對海域的區分，則可分為領海 (territorial sea)、毗鄰區 (contiguous zone)、專屬經濟海域 (exclusive economic zone / EEZ)、大陸棚 (continental shelf)、公海 (high seas) 等。

＊boundary 界線；範圍
＊island chain 列島、島鏈
＊crude 原油

A 主題文章 Article

On 31 May 2014, Japanese Prime Minister Shinzo Abe said that Japan would help Southeast Asian countries secure the seas and pledged strong support for Vietnam and the Philippines in their maritime disputes with China. The speech comes at a time of rising tensions in the East and South China Sea, as China has sea disputes with Japan in the East China Sea, and with Vietnam and the Philippines in the South China Sea.

"Japan will offer its utmost support for the efforts of the countries of ASEAN as they work to ensure the security of the seas and the skies, and thoroughly maintain freedom of navigation and freedom of overflight." Abe made the above statement in Singapore, referring to the ten members of ASEAN.

According to Abe's speech, Japan is willing to provide aid, military training, and defensive equipment to help ASEAN countries protect the seas. Japan has already agreed to do so for the Philippines and is in talks to provide them to Vietnam. Abe increased Japan's defense budget for two years in a row after it had slid for more than a decade. He loosened restrictions on defense exports and is seeking to reinterpret the pacifist constitution to allow Japan to send its troops to defend allies.

Bilateral talks between China and Japan had stopped by the dispute over the islands known as Diaoyu in China and Senkaku in Japan, and Abe has not held a summit with China since he took office about 18 months ago.

Although the United States had repeated itself several times that its obligation to defend Japan extends to the disputed islands, President Barack Obama said in a speech on defense policy that the armed forces cannot be the primary component.

Anti-Chinese protests overwhelmed Vietnam in May after China

placed an oil rig in the disputed area in the South China Sea. The Philippines has started arbitration proceedings in the United Nations in its standoff with China over shoals off its coast.

2014 年 5 月 31 日日本首相安倍晉三表示，日本將幫助東南亞國家保護領海，並承諾在與中國的海上爭端上，將大力支持越南和菲律賓。安倍發表上述言論的時間點正值東海和南海緊張局勢持續升溫，因為中國分別在東海、南海和日本、菲律賓及越南有海域紛爭。

「日本將對東盟國家提供支援，全力支持他們以確保海上及空域的安全，徹底維護航行及飛行自由」。安倍晉三在新加坡對東協十國發表上述聲明。

根據安倍的說法，日本願意提供經濟援助，軍事訓練和防禦裝備，以幫助東協國家保護海洋權益。日本已同意對菲律賓進行援助，並和越南開啟相關談判。在安倍執政下，日本已連續兩年增加國防預算，在這之前日本已連續十年降低國防預算。日本也放鬆對國防軍火的出口限制，並尋求重新解釋和平憲法，讓日本能出兵保護盟友。

中日之間的會談已經因為中國方面的釣魚島或日本方面的尖閣列島之爭而停頓。安倍上任 18 個月以來，也從未和中國進行高峰會。

雖然美國已多次重申美日安保的義務範圍延伸及周邊有爭議的島嶼，但美國總統歐巴馬在針對國防政策的發言中也強調，軍事力量不能是美國的主要選項。

越南則在五月中爆發大規模反中抗議，原因是中國在南海的爭議海域架設油井。菲律賓則在聯合國申請仲裁，以處理中菲之前有爭議的沙洲。

Unit 19

Syrian Civil War
敘利亞內戰

代表意義超理解

敘利亞內戰是敘利亞政府和反對派之間的武裝衝突。2011 年時，政府和反對派之間的對立由動盪轉為衝突，2013 年真主黨加入這場紛爭，支持敘利亞政府。

The Syrian civil war is an armed conflict in Syria between the government and those who seek to oust it. Unrests broke into armed combat in 2011, and Hezbollah entered the war supporting the government in 2013.

背景知識大突破 Background

當真主黨開始支持政府軍後，卡達和沙烏地阿拉伯則為叛軍提供武器。敘利亞政府目前仍控制國內約 35% 的領土及 60% 的人口。由於在內戰中頻頻使用化學武器，而且政府軍及叛軍皆指控對方使用化學武器，因此敘利亞內戰引發國際間的密切關注。

When the Hezbollah entered the war supporting the government, Qatar and Saudi Arabia transferred weapons to the rebels. The Syrian government still controls about 35% of the country's

---

* oust　罷黜；驅逐
* rebel　反政府的人；反叛者

territory and 60% of the population. The war triggers massive international reactions because chemical weapons have been used in the war more than one occasion, and both sides claimed the other side launched it.

Method 使用方法一把罩

大規模殺傷性武器 (Weapon of Mass Destruction, WMD) 指的是核武器 (nuclear weapon)、放射性武器 (radiological weapon)、生物武器 (biological weapon)、或化學武器 (chemical) 等可利用來進行大規模屠殺的武器。有時候這些武器也被合併為縮寫，例如 CBRN 或 NBC 等，但這類詞彙指的都是各種大規模殺傷性武器。例如：

Saddam Hussein was well known for his use of chemical weapons in the 1980s during the Iran-Iraq War. In the 1980s he pursued an extensive biological weapons program and a nuclear weapon program, though no nuclear bomb was built。

(海珊在 1980 年的兩伊戰爭中使用化學武器而惡名昭彰。同一時期間他也開始發展生物武器和核子武器的計畫，但最後並未製出核彈)。

---

* trigger 引發、觸發
* massive 大的、巨大的

A 主題文章 Article

The Syrian civil war broke out in 2011, and the fight stills goes on today. The United Nation recently released a report, indicating that more than ten thousands children have been killed in the civil war, while many more become victims to various suffering, including rape, torture, and recruitment to become soldiers. The report also points out that thousands are forced to flee their homes during the past three years, and a large number of Syrian refugees flood into Jordan.

According to the report, both the rebels and Syrian government are guilty of abusing children. In the beginning of the civil war, most killings and maiming of children were attributed to government force; however, the rebel groups had increasingly engaged in such behavior in 2013. Government forces are primarily blamed for the arrest, ill treatment and torture of children, while the rebel groups are responsible for the recruitment of children in both combat and support actions. The rebels are also blamed for terror tactics, making civilian casualties, including children.

The report revealed that torture inflicted on children include beatings, electric shock, ripping of fingernails and toenails, sexual violence, cigarette burns, and exposure to the torture of relatives. It also warns that Syrian children had experience a high level of distress as a result of witnessing the killing and injuring of families and friends, or being separated from them.

The United nation estimates that more than 120,000 people have died in Syria since 2011, of those at least 10,000 were children. The report also notes that both sides of the civil war have seriously delayed the delivery of humanitarian assistance in areas affected by warfare. The United Nation secretary-general

Ban Ki-moon urged all parties to the conflict to take immediate actions to protect the rights of all children in Syria.

敘利亞自 2011 年爆發內戰以來，至今仍處於戰爭狀態中。聯合國最近發表一份文件指出，成千上萬的兒童死於內戰，更多的兒童則處於苦難中，他們面對的是強暴、拷打，並被徵募為士兵。報告還指出，過去三年來有數千人被迫遠離家園，大批的難民從敘利亞湧入約旦。

根據報導，敘利亞政府和反抗軍雙方都曾虐待兒童。在內戰爆發的那一年，殘殺兒童的多是政府軍，但自 2013 年以來，反抗軍也發生越來越多類似的行為。政府軍的罪行主要包括逮捕並嚴刑拷問兒童，而反抗軍則大量招募兒童負責各種戰鬥活動。反抗軍同時發動恐怖攻擊，造成大量的平民及兒童傷亡。

報告指出，對兒童進行的酷刑，包括毆打、電擊、拔除手指甲和腳趾甲、性暴力、菸頭燙傷，並在兒童面前對其親人進行折磨。報告也提出警告説，敘利亞兒童正經歷高度的磨難，因為他們必須與親友分離，甚至目睹親友遭到殘害。

聯合國統計，自 2011 年內戰爆發以來，共有超過 12 萬人死於戰爭，其中 1 萬人是兒童。報告也指出，雙方的戰事，已嚴重影響外界對戰區提供的人道援助。聯合國秘書長潘基文敦促各方採取行動，保護敘利亞的兒童。

Unit 20

Yasukuni Shrine
靖國神社

代表意義超理解

靖國神社是位於日本東京的神道教神社，是明治天皇為紀念在明治維新期間犧牲的人所建。現代靖國神社的意義則擴展到紀念過去所有戰爭中所陣亡的將士。

Yasukuni Shrine is a Shinto shrine located in Tokyo, Japan. It was founded by Emperor Meiji for the individuals who had died in service of the Japanese Empire during the Meiji Restoration. The purpose of Yasukuni Shrine had been expanded to commemorate all the dead from all wars fought throughout history.

B 背景知識大突破 Background

由於靖國神社內供奉有二戰期間的日本戰犯，因此常引起亞洲鄰近國家間的政治緊張。日本首相安倍晉三於 2013 年 12 月 26 日參拜靖國神社，此舉引發周邊國家抗議。根據媒體報導，美國官員希望安倍停止參拜靖國神社祭奠戰犯。

Yasukuni Shrine has often raised political tension in Asia due to

---

＊restoration　維新；復原　　　＊commemorate　紀念；慶祝

the enshrinement of war criminals from World War II. Japanese Prime Minister Shinzo Abe visited Yasukuni Shrine on December 26, 2013, which leads to surrounding nations to publish protests. Journalists reported that U.S. officials urge Abe not to visit the shrine and pay homage to war criminals anymore.

Method 使用方法一把罩

Shrine 這個單字的用途很廣，包括各種宗教的聖地、廟宇、神殿、祭祀地等皆可稱之為 shrine。在日本，佛教的各種寺、院一般稱為 temple，神道教 (Shinto) 的各種神社則稱為 shrine。Emperor 一字指的是西方歷史上的帝王，同時也是日本的天皇；有名的明治維新英文則稱為 Meiji Restoration。

Shrine 除了指神社之外，還可以指聖地、神殿等，其用法如下：

Many pilgrims knelt piously at the shrine of a local deity.
(許多朝聖者虔誠地跪拜在敬奉當地信仰的聖地中。)

＊ enshrinement 奉祀在廟中、置於神龕中

＊ war criminal 戰犯

＊ homage 崇敬、致敬

The president of the Republic of China (Taiwan) Ma Ying-jeou criticized Japanese Prime Minister Shinzo Abe's visit to the Yasukuni shrine, describing the move is to "rubbing salt into others' wounds," in an article posted on his Facebook page. In the article, Ma added that sixty-nine years have passed since the end of the World War II, yet the wounds left on those who suffered are indelible. The existence of "comfort women" keeps reminding Asian countries of the horrible crimes the Japanese invaders committed.

The Yasukuni shrine honors Japanese who died in wars, including convicted World War II war criminals. There are fourteen Class-A war criminals of World War II, and those criminals are the primary instigators and perpetrators of Japan's aggressive expansion and colonial rule during WWII. It has often raised political tension in Asia due to the enshrinement of these war criminals. Previously, President Ma said he is not only disappointed, but also puzzled by the Japanese leader's visit to the Yasukuni Shrine.

Ma is not the only one who criticized the Japanese leaders. Chinese officials and ambassadors to various nations also published commentaries criticizing Prime Minister Abe's visit to the Yasukuni Shrine. These commentaries are much more harsh than Ma's criticizes. One article said that the history of Japan in the past century was a brutal history of aggression and colonialism. The Japanese invasion caused huge casualties and property losses to the victim countries. Japan's war of aggression against China caused more than 35 million military and civilian casualties.

Chinese officials also condemned the Japanese prime minister's visit to the shrine insisted ignoring Japan's militant history. They

blamed right wing politicians as well as Prime Minister Abe for failing to reverse the reputations of the war criminals and even beautify the horrific crimes committed by them.

中華民國（臺灣）總統馬英九日前在臉書上批評日本首相安倍晉三參拜靖國神社的舉動是「在傷口上灑鹽」。馬英九在文中表示，二戰結束後至今已69年，但戰爭中受害者的傷痕無可磨滅；慰安婦的存在也不斷提醒日本侵略者在亞洲國家的罪行。

靖國神社中供奉著在戰爭中死亡的日本人，包括數名被定罪的二次世界大戰戰犯。其中共有二戰甲級戰犯14名，這些罪犯是日本在二戰期間侵略擴張和殖民統治煽動者與肇事者。也因為神社中供奉這些戰犯，靖國神社時常引起亞洲的政治緊張局勢。馬英九總統曾說，他對日本領導人參拜靖國神社的舉動感到失望與不解。

馬英九不是唯一一個批評日本的人。中國大陸官員和大使在各國發表評論，對安倍晉三參拜靖國神社的舉動提出批評。這些評論比馬的批評更為苛刻。一篇文章曾說，日本在上個世紀的歷史，就是侵略和殖民主義的殘酷歷史。日本的侵略行為造成被害國家巨大的人員傷亡和財產損失。日本侵略中國的戰爭造成3500多萬軍民傷亡。

中國大陸官員並譴責日本首相參拜靖國神社的舉動是無視日本的好戰歷史。他們指責右翼政客和安倍首相不但不正視戰犯的作為，反而致力於美化他們的可怕罪行。

anagement, securities investent, information processing, vil engineering, asset management, etc. Their monthly salary ill be set at NT$31,000.

There will also be 209 new ffice clerks to be recruited this ear, with their starting salary et at NT$24,000 per month. The argest number of new mployees, at 459, will be mail arriers, with their starting pay lso set at NT$24,000 per month, lus an extra driving or delivery llowance of NT$5,732.

Based on the average employment rate of 2% to 6%, the xpected number of applicants to ake the examination is around 8,000, the spokesm...

For furth...

Inter-party consultations t

The China Post news staff

The Kuomintang-controlled Legislative Yuan completed the first reading of an amendment to its own procedural bylaw yesterday, promising to make all closed-door inter-party consultations public record. Known popularly as "black box" operations, the inter-party consultations held behind closed doors may last as long as four months.

"The horse trading ...

Moreover, the records will be published in the Legislative Yuan bulletin, together with the conclusions reached, Ting said.

Should there be discrepancies between the published conclusions and the results of action on bills, full explanations will be able to be discovered in the record, the Kuomintang legislator said. "We want the secret horse trading exposed under bright sunshine," Ting stressed.

Lawmakers have to complete the second and third readings before the legislature adjourns for the summer. "There won't be difficulty," another Kuomintang legislator said. The

Kuomintang co... majority in the... Yuan.

In addition, ... cedural bylaw ... The inter-party ... can go on for f... to that article, s... in one month.

Democratic ... islators ... Kuomintang-pr... as "going a littl...

"All of us a... party consult... improved, but ... be seriously d... ment were ...

PART 2

NSC dismisses Ma death in war scenario

The China Post news staff

Taiwan's top security body yesterday dismissed a report that the military's upcoming war chess would drill a scenario where President-elect Ma Ying-jeou was assassinated. The National Security Council (NSC) described the Next Magazine report as unfounded, irresponsible and with a political agenda.

Next claimed that the war chess, to be conducted later this month, would assume that Ma's assassination would plunge the nation into chaos and trigger a surprise invasion by China. The drill was meant to see how different government and security bodies could cope with such a situation, and how Taiwan would interact with the United States, the tabloid magazine cited unnamed presidential sources as saying.

It would be a test to see whether U.S. intervention should be sought or whether other solutions would be possible, and whether a state of emergency should be declared, the report said.

Ma's spokesman Lo Chih-chiang declined to comment on the report, saying the Presidential Office owed the public an explanation. President Chen Shui-bian had invited Ma to the war chess, which is part of the NSC's annual drill, but the president-elect declined the invitation.

The opposition camp called for the drill to be postponed until Ma is inaugurated, but the NSC insisted on conducting it as scheduled. The NSC said yesterday that the drill, to be conducted in three stages between April 21 and 27, is a test of government bodies' responses to military crises and of the nation's defense facilities.

But Kuomintang legislators have repeated the opposition camp's call for the drill be postponed, so as to let Ma oversee it. KMT Legislator Lin Yu-fang said it is "very ridiculous and impolite" for an outgoing president to conduct a drill on the mock assassination of his successor. "The Chen administration has designed such a drill apparently to vent its anger over its loss in the presidential election," claimed Lin.

KMT Legislator Chang Hsien-yao said such a drill has already raised concern in the United States and Taiwan's neighbors.

More ... Parki...

TAIPEI, CNA

An internat... ject has ... Parkinson's-re... that only deve... Those who ca... twice more ... Parkinson's di...

The mutatic... is found in ... codes for ... repeat kinase... paper produc... partially funde... National Scier... lished in the s... of Neurology.

Parkinson's ... as Parkinson s... erative disor... nervous syste... the patient's ... ment.

A group of ... Singapore, Ja... States have al... Parkinson's-re... linked to LRRK... relations betw... groups and i... For example, t... LRRK2-G2019... of Parkinson's ... and Ashkenazi...

In 2004, the... a mutation, G2... linked to Par... especially Han...

Fugitive ex-Hsinchu Council speaker returns

TAIPEI, CNA

Former Hsinchu County Council Speaker Huang Huan-chi returned to Taiwan and was taken into custody Tuesday after fleeing to China two years ago, following his sentencing to eight years in prison on corruption charges, judicial sources said yesterday.

Following unsuccessful kidney transplant surgery in China, Huang recently informed Hsinchu County police that he would be returning to the Taiwan. Shortly after Huang's plane landed in Taiwan, he was escorted away by police, who later turned him over to the Hsinchu District Prosecutors Office.

Huang served two terms as Hsinchu County Council speaker before running in the legislative elections in December 2001 as a candidate of the Taiwan Solidarity Union. He ended up losing the election. In that race, Huang was accused of vote-buying violations for allegedly using the county council's budget to purchase tea and moon cakes for voters. He was later released on bail.

Two years ago, after being convicted on corruption charges related to an incinerator scandal in the county, Huang decided to flee to China to avoid serving his prison sentence. He was then placed on the Hsinchu District Prosecutors Office's wanted list.

財經篇

Finance and Economics

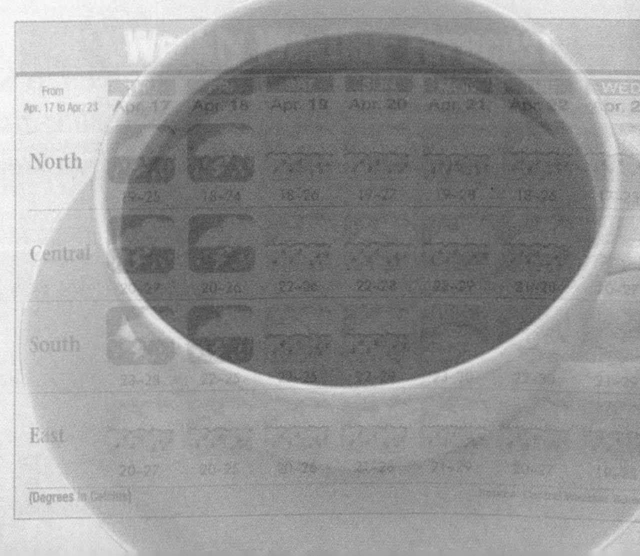

Unit 1

Abenomics
安倍經濟學

代表意義超理解

安倍經濟學是日本首相安倍晉三所推行的經濟政策的名稱。英文的安倍經濟學這個詞是安倍晉三的名字和經濟的混合詞，按照以往對特定人物的經濟政策所稱呼，例如雷根經濟學。

Abenomics is the name given to measures introduced by Japanese prime minister Shinzo Abe. The term "Abenomics" is a portmanteau of Abe and economics, following previous economics policies such as Reaganomics.

B 背景知識大突破 Background

安倍經濟學是日本首相安倍晉三的經濟政策總稱，他的目標是重振疲弱的日本經濟。安倍經濟學的具體作為包括大膽刺激金融、日本央行激進的貨幣寬鬆政策、以及鼓勵民間投資成長，並藉由這些方法達成增進國家競爭力的目標。這些政策也被稱為安倍的三隻箭。

Abenomics is the name given to Shinzo Abe's economic policies. His aim was to revive the sluggish economy with massive fiscal stimulus, aggressive monetary easing from the Bank of Japan,

---

* portmanteau　混成詞
* Reaganomics　雷根經濟學 (Reagan + economics)
* sluggish　不景氣的；緩慢的

and structural reforms to boost the nation's competitiveness. These measures are also known as Abe's "three arrows".

Method 使用方法一把罩

日本是君主立憲 (constitutional monarchy) 的國家，天皇 (the Emperor) 是虛位元首，國家的實際領導人是日本首相 (Prime Minister of Japan)。日本的國會稱為 National Diet，從國會成員中互選出首相後，由天皇任命之。日本國會又分為參議院 (House of Councilors) 和眾議院 (House of Representatives)，任期分別為六年和四年。總理大臣有權從國會成員中（亦有例外）任命政府各部會的大臣。

安倍晉三是日本有史以來最年輕的內閣總理大臣，迄今已兩度擔任內閣總理大臣。2006 年 9 月 20 日安倍晉三當選為第 21 任自由民主黨 (自民黨) 總裁，同月在國會中當選首相。其後，2012 年 12 月 16 日，在第 46 屆眾議院選舉中再度被指名出任內閣總理大臣。

＊boost 提高、增加　　＊measure 措施；程度

Japanese Prime Minister Shinzo Abe has been trying to revive Japan's economy with "Abenomics" for one year now. Japanese stocks and profits are soaring, and even shop prices are up, a key step after years of deflation. Abe has been successful in stoking inflation to convince consumers that deflation is over and to start shopping before prices get any higher. However, Abenomics is still at risk, as workers struggle to keep up with the inflation. How can the government expect the people to start shopping, if their wages remain the same while the price keeps going up?

So far, large enterprises and stock owners had benefited from Abenomics. For the prime minister's economic strategy to work, companies like Toyota must lead to higher pay. However, employees have yet to see the benefits. In 2013, pay for the average Japanese worker rose about 0.2%, but it had fallen 15% in the past 15 years. If the workers' wages cannot follow keep up with inflation, people are not likely to start shopping. The issue of wages is a test for whether Abenomics works or falls apart.

The situation will become worse, as Japan's sales tax is set to jump from 5% to 8% in April 2014. The increase of sales tax is believed to raise the cost of daily staples.

Recent poll also shows that despite global acclaim for Abe's economic project, 73% said that they do not feel they are benefiting from the policy. The poll also delivers another warning, as 66% said they do not expect to see a pay raise. Even worse, near 70% said that they are considering to curb their spending when sales tax increases in April.

過去一年來，日本首相安倍晉三一直試圖以「安倍經濟學」振興日本經濟。日本股票和企業利潤不斷成長，甚至商品的價格也在上升，打破日本過去長久以來通貨緊縮的困境。安倍晉三可以成功的告訴消費者，通貨緊縮已經結束，消費者應在物價持續上升前進行消費。但安倍經濟學目前仍面臨著危機，因為工人的薪資並未隨著物價上升而調漲，如果物價持續上升而薪資維持不變，政府又怎麼能期望民眾能增加消費支出？

到目前為止，大型企業和股票持有人都受益於安倍經濟學。但要完成安倍首相的經濟戰略，像豐田這一類的大企業必須給予員工更高的工資。但工人並未因安倍經濟學而受惠。在 2013 年，日本的平均工資上漲約 0.2%，但這個數字在過去 15 年下降了 15%。如果工資不隨著通貨膨脹上漲，民眾就不會增加消費。工資問題將是考驗安倍經濟學成敗的關鍵。

使情況更糟的是，日本的消費稅將在 2014 年 4 月從 5% 成長到 8%，消費稅的成長勢必引發另一波日用品的漲價。

最近的民調也顯示，儘管安倍經濟學在國際上受到好評，但有 73% 的人表示，他們不覺得政策對他們有好處。民調也帶來另一波警訊，因為有 66% 的人認為他們不會得到加薪。更糟的是，有近 70% 的人表示，因應四月銷售稅的增加，他們會考慮減少支出。

Unit 2

ANZTEC
臺紐經濟合作協定

代表意義超理解

像 ASTEP 一樣，臺紐經濟合作協定是紐西蘭和我方所簽訂的高規格綜合貿易協定。這份協定將會開放雙方的市場，讓貨品、服務業和投資更加自由便利。此外，臺紐經濟合作協定的內容也包括影視創投、原住民合作等，將現有的文創合作擴大為雙方交流。

Like the ASTEP, the Agreement between New Zealand and the Separate Customs Territory of Taiwan, Penghu, Kinmen, and Matsu on Economic Cooperation (ANZTEC) is a high quality, comprehensive trade agreement that will liberalize and facilitate trade in goods, services and investment between the two markets. It also includes innovative provisions on film and television, and indigenous cooperation that will expand existing creative, cultural and people to people links.

背景知識大突破 Background

臺灣與紐西蘭於 2013 年 7 月簽署臺紐經濟合作協定。臺灣是紐西蘭第十二大的貿易夥伴，據研究顯示，ANZTEC 將能擴大雙方在彼此的市場，同時增進消費者的權益。總體而言，ANZTEC 預期將對臺灣

＊ liberalize　使自由化、放寬限制

＊ facilitate　促進、增長

＊ innovative　創新的、革新的

的經濟成長和就業率帶來正面影響。ANZTEC 包含 25 個章節，覆蓋範圍很廣，從貨品貿易到原住民合作交流都是協議內容的一部分。

Taiwan and New Zealand announced the signing of ANZTEC in July 2013. Taiwan is New Zealand's 12th largest trading partner, and studies show that ANZTEC is expected to expand both Taiwan and New Zealand's market access and consumer welfare. Overall, ANZTEC is expected to have a positive effect on both Taiwan's national output and employment. ANZTEC contains 25 chapters, covering a wide range of topics from Trade in Goods to Indigenous Issues.

Method 使用方法一把罩

和 ASTEP 一樣，我國是以臺、澎、金、馬個別關稅領域 (the Separate Customs Territory of Taiwan, Penghu, Kinmen and Matsu) 的名義和紐西蘭簽訂協議。ANZTEC 是 the Agreement between New Zealand and Taiwan on Economic Cooperation 的縮寫，以臺灣作為臺澎金馬個別關稅領域的簡稱，但正式文件中仍使用 the Separate Customs Territory of Taiwan, Penghu, Kinmen and Matsu。

＊ welfare　福利、幸福

＊ indigenous　原住民；土生土長的

A 主題文章 Article

The Agreement between New Zealand and the Separate Customs Territory of Taiwan, Penghu, Kinmen, and Matsu (Taiwan) on Economic Cooperation (ANZTEC) came into effect in December 2013. ANZTEC would deliver the complete removal of tariffs on 99% of New Zealand's current exports to Taiwan in a four-year process, and removes 100% of tariffs within twelve years. It would immediately generate around forty millions of tariff savings on current trade between the two sides, and once it's fully implemented, tariff savings will reach an estimated 75 million each year.

70% of Taiwan's economic growth came from exports. The lack of formal diplomatic relations with many of its major trading partners made it difficult for Taiwan to sign trade agreements with its partners. According to the government of Taiwan, when ANZTEC took effect in November 2013, bilateral trade has increased by 73%, with New Zealand's exports to Taiwan grew 37%, and Taiwan's exports to New Zealand grew 120%.

According to the government, the recent signing of both ANZTEC and ASTEP also show that Taiwan is determined to approach trade liberalization. It is also interested in joining the proposed Trans-Pacific Partnership (TPP) and the Regional Comprehensive Economic Partnership (RCEP). To achieve its goal to complete its TPP and RCEP preparation, Taiwan will continue to push for trade liberalization and persuade the public to support its economic reform.

紐西蘭與臺澎金馬個別關稅領域間的合作協議 (ANZTEC) 於 2013 年 12 月起生效。 目前紐西蘭出口至臺灣的品項中，有 99% 的產品將在後續四年內陸續變為免稅，並自生效日的 12 年後完成 100% 的關稅全免。該協議的實施可立即對臺紐雙方帶來每年約 4 千萬元的關稅費用節省，待全部品項開放後，預計每年的費用節省可達 7 千 5 百萬美元。

目前臺灣有 70% 的成長仰賴於出口貿易。但受限於目前的外交現況，臺灣很難與我們主要的貿易夥伴們簽署貿易協定。據臺灣政府統計，當 ANZTEC 於 2013 年 11 月生效後，臺紐雙方貿易額增長了 73%，其中紐西蘭對臺灣出口增長 37%，而臺灣出口至紐西蘭則增長了 120%。

臺灣政府指出，近期簽署的 ANZTEC 及 ASTEP 兩項協議顯示臺灣將朝著貿易自由化的方向前進。同時府方也提出了對於加入 TPP 以及 RCEP 的興趣。為達成加入 TPP 與 RCEP 兩項目標，臺灣將持續地推動貿易自由化並說服民眾支持政府的經濟改革措施。

Unit 3

ASEAN
東南亞國家協會

代表意義超理解

東南亞國家協會（東協）是東南亞十國組成的政治經濟組織。東協的目的是透過平等互助的精神，加快成員國的經濟成長、促進社會進步和文化發展。東協也尊重聯合國憲章，透過成員國在區域中以法治精神維持區域的和平與穩定。

ASEAN is a political and economical organization of ten countries located in the Southeast Asia. It aims to accelerate the economic growth, social progress and cultural development in the region through joint endeavors in the spirit of equality and partnership. It also promotes regional peace and stability through abiding respect for justices and the rule of law in the relationship among countries in the region and adherence to the principles of the United Nations Charter.

B 背景知識大突破 Background

東協於 1967 年在泰國簽署東協宣言（曼谷宣言），正式成立東協，創始會員國包括印度尼西亞、馬來西亞、菲律賓、新加坡和泰國。隨著

＊endeavor　努力、力圖
＊abiding　持續的、持久的
＊adherence　信奉；堅持

汶萊於 1984 年加入、1995 年越南加入、1997 年寮國和緬甸加入，及柬埔寨於 1999 年加入，成為現在的東協十國。

The Association of Southeast Asian Nations (ASEAN) was established in 1967 in Thailand with the signing of the ASEAN Declaration (Bangkok Declaration). The original member included Indonesia, Malaysia, the Philippines, Singapore, and Thailand. Brunei joined ASEAN in 1984, Vietnam in 1995, Lao and Myanmar in 1997, and Cambodia in 1999, making up what is today the ten member states of ASEAN.

Method 使用方法一把罩

東協組織除積極拓展成員國之間的交流合作，也致力於和亞洲其他國家發展經貿關係。常見的 ASEAN+3 東協加三指的是東協十國加上中國大陸、日本、南韓等三國的自由貿易協定；ASEAN+6 東協加六指的是東協十國加上中國大陸、日本、南韓、印度、紐西蘭、澳洲的自由貿易協定。

* declaration 宣言；宣告

主題文章 Article

The Association of Southeast Asian Nations (ASEAN) consists of Brunei, Cambodia, Indonesia, Laos, Malaysia, Myanmar, the Philippines, Singapore, Thailand and Vietnam. ASEAN members had made a huge progress in economic integration by creating an ASEAN Economic Community (AEC) in 2015. Once the AEC is formed, it is said to bring both opportunities and challenges to its members.

The AEC marks the commitment of the ASEAN members to building and promoting a single market and production base, a highly competitive economic region tempered with equitable development. In addition, the ASEAN market is also fully integrated into the global economy. Once the AEC is formed, it would create greater opportunities for its members to export goods and services to the ASEAN market, yet the local business would face difficulties competing with all other members.

When the AEC is formed in 2015, its member countries could sell goods to all other ASEAN markets in ways that are similar to selling things at home markets, because all the trade procedures and certifying procedures would be largely simplified. It means more potential markets to all the member countries, as well as more potential competitions. However, most of the local enterprises within the ASEAN members know little about interests and challenges available for them in the coming integration. The lack of knowledge itself would be a great challenge for local business when the AEC is formed.

Moreover, since many of the ASEAN members are raw materials exporters, they would have to compete with one another in the same market in exporting raw materials and raw products. This includes raw products from farming, fishing, and mining, as well as basic electric and electronic components. Experts suggest that

domestic businesses should figure out a way to gain advantages in key products before 2015, as a business strategy to take full advantage once AEC is formed.

東南亞國家協會 (ASEAN) 是由汶萊、柬埔寨、印尼、寮國、馬來西亞、緬甸、菲律賓、新加坡、泰國、越南等國家組成。東協國家通過將在 2015 年成立東協經濟共同體 (APEC)，朝經濟整合邁進一大步。一旦東協經濟共同體完成，它將為成員國帶來各種機會與挑戰。

東協經濟共同體的成員國將會創造一個共同的市場和生產基地，並逐步成為一個極有競爭力公平貿易區。此外，東協市場也將完全融入全球經濟。一旦東協經濟共同體成立，它將為成員國創造更多的機會，使各國的貨品和服務業進入其他東協市場，但各國的本土產業也將面臨與其他所有成員國競爭的困境。

當 2015 年東協經濟共同體成立後，東協內部的貿易程序和認證程序都將大幅簡化，使它的成員國將能以國內銷售的方式，將產品賣到所有東協成員國的市場。這當然意味著更多的潛在市場，但所有成員國也將面臨同業的競爭。然後，大多數東協成員國內部的本土企業並不熟悉這些未來的機會及挑戰。資訊的缺乏將使東協經濟體內的企業面臨挑戰。

此外，由於許多東協成員國都是原物料出口商，這也意味著他們將必須和其他原物料出口商在相同的市場進行競爭。這些原物料包括農業、漁業、礦業等產品，並包括基本的電氣和電子零件。專家建議，東協的國內企業應該設法在 2015 年之前在關鍵產品取得競爭優勢，活用這種策略，才能充分從東協經濟共同體獲得利益。

Unit 4

ASTEP

臺星經濟夥伴協定

代表意義超理解

臺星經濟夥伴協定是新加坡和我方所簽訂的高規格綜合貿易協定。這份協定將會開放雙方的市場，讓貨品、服務業和投資更加自由便利。

The Agreement between Singapore and the Separate Customs Territory of Taiwan, Penghu, Kinmen and Matsu on Economic Partnership (ASTEP) is a high quality comprehensive agreement that will liberalize and facilitate trade in goods, trade in services and investments between both markets.

B 背景知識大突破 Background

臺星經濟夥伴協定於 2014 年 4 月生效，簽約雙方都是世界貿易組織的成員。雙方於 2013 年 11 月在新加坡簽訂協議，這份協議涵蓋貨品貿易、服務貿易、投資協議、爭端解決機制以及政府採購等各種領域。

The ASTEP will come into force in April 2014. Both Singapore

＊customs　關稅；海關　　＊come into force　開始生效

and the Separate Customs Territory of Taiwan, Penghu, Kinmen and Matsu (Chinese Taipei) are members of the World Trade Organization, and they had signed the ASTEP in November 2013 in Singapore. It covers areas such as trade in goods, trade in services, investment, dispute settlement, and government procurement.

Method 使用方法一把罩

我國是以臺、澎、金、馬個別關稅領域 (the Separate Customs Territory of Taiwan, Penghu, Kinmen and Matsu) 的名義加入世界貿易組織 (WTO)，一般國際場合中亦簡稱為中華臺北 (Chinese Taipei)。我們也用一樣的名義和許多國家簽訂相關的貿易協定。ASTEP 則是 the Agreement between Singapore and Taiwan on Economic Partnership的縮寫，將其中的臺澎金馬個別關稅領域簡稱為臺灣，以方便雙方作業，但在正式的文件中，我方仍是使用臺澎金馬個別關稅領域的名稱。

＊ procurement　採購、採買

A 主題文章 Article

Under the Agreement between Singapore and the Separate Customs Territory of Taiwan, Penghu, Kinmen, and Matsu (Taiwan) on Economic Partnership (ASTEP), Taiwan's alcohol exports to the city state of Singapore will receive duty-free treatment. When the trade pact between Taiwan and Singapore takes effect in April, the beer exports from Taiwan to Singapore are expected to grow from 50% to 100% in 2014.

Singapore has a large beer market, as the beverage accounts for over 90% of Singapore's total alcohol consumption. Taiwan beer exports to Singapore totaled around one million US dollar in 2013. Given the fact that Singapore has recently passed a law to increase alcohol taxes, liquor from Taiwan is likely to have an advantage in the Singaporean market. A 50% to 100% growth is expected in 2014 due to the zero-tariff treatment from ASTEP.

In addition to beers, Taiwanese food is also welcomed in Singapore. Exhibitors from Taiwan set up special pavilions to highlight alcoholic goods, food items, and deep-sea seafood from Taiwan. Anticipation over the said trade pact also drew other potential buyers looking to take advantage of reduced barriers.

Singapore is Taiwan's 11th-large export market in 2013, receiving about 96 million worth of products and accounting for 1.9% of Taiwan's total exports. The signing of the agreement in 2013 marked a breakthrough for Taiwan, as it is its first trade pact with a major trade partner in Southeast Asia.

據新加坡與臺澎金馬個別關稅領域簽署的經濟合作協議(ASTEP) 內容指出，臺灣的酒精類產品出口至新加坡將可獲得免稅優惠。當該協議於 4 月生效後，預計 2014 年從臺灣出口至新加坡的啤酒可成長 50% 至 100%。

啤酒在新加坡有非常廣大的市場，酒精類產品做為飲料在新加坡佔有 90% 以上的消費比例。2013 年臺灣啤酒出口至新加坡的總金額約為 1 百萬美元。而近期內才在新加坡通過的酒精類增稅法案，對於臺灣酒類產品在新加坡銷售可能會是一大優勢。在 ASTEP 免稅政策的優惠下，預計 2014 年出口成長可提升 50%-100%。

除了啤酒以外，臺灣飲食在新加坡也頗受歡迎。來自臺灣的展商們還特別針對來自臺灣的酒類、食品類、以及深海海鮮設立展館。這個貿易協議也吸引其他想藉此優惠牟利的業者

在 2013 年，新加坡是臺灣第 11 大的出口市場，年收入約為 9 千 6 百萬美元，占臺灣出口比例 1.9%。在 2013 年簽署的該項協議對臺灣來說代表一個突破，因為這是臺灣在東南亞主要的貿易夥伴中的第一個貿易協定。

Unit 5

Boao Forum
博鰲論壇

代表意義超理解

博鰲亞洲論壇是一個開放給世界各國政府、企業、及學界高階領袖的非營利性組織。各界領袖可以透過這個平台，分享他們對於亞洲的遠景，並促進亞洲的區域整合和合作。

The Boao Forum for Asia is a none profit organization with high level government, business, and academia leaders in Asia and around the world to share their vision in the region. It is committed to promote regional integration and bring Asian countries together.

背景知識大突破 Background

博鰲論壇以世界經濟論壇為模，致力於區域中的經濟整合。它的固定開會位置及總部設在中國大陸海南省的博鰲市，秘書處則設於北京。2014 年的博鰲論壇在 4 月間舉行，並於 4 月 10 日正式開幕。

The Boao Forum is modeled after the World Economic Forum, and it has a fixed site in Boao, Hainan, mainland China, with its secretariat based in Beijing. The forum focuses on economics,

＊integration　整合；結合　　＊secretariat　秘書處；書記處

regional integration, society, and the environment. The 2014 Boao Forum was held in April, with the official opening on April 10.

Method 使用方法一把罩

博鰲亞洲論壇的全稱是 the Boao Forum for Asia (BFA)，一般亦簡稱為 the Boao Forum，博鰲論壇。博鰲 Boao 則是海南島上的一個城鎮，是博鰲論壇固定的開會地點。

Forum 是一個極為常見的單字，從大型的世界論壇到網路上的社論論壇或討論串，都可以使用 forum 這個字。例如世界經濟論壇 World Economic Forum, WEF。例句如下：

The World Economic Forum is a Swiss nonprofit foundation committed to improve the states of the world by engaging business, political, academic, and other leaders of the society。

(世界經濟論壇是瑞士的非營利基金會，它的目的是藉由商界、政界、學術界及其他社會領袖的交流，還改善這個世界。)

除了論壇外，峰會 (Summit) 或對話 (Dialogue) 也是國際間常用的交流形式，例如 G8 Summit (八大工業國峰會) 和 the Shangri-La Dialogue (香格里拉對話)。

A主題文章 Article

The 2014 Boao Forum for Asia held its opening ceremony on April 10, in the province of Hainan. The economic forum attracted a wide array of regional leaders this year. Attendees include Premier Li Keiqang of mainland China, Prime Minister Tony Abbott of Australia, Prime Minister Jung Hong-won of South Korea, Prime Minister Serik Akhmetov of Kazakhstan, Prime Minister Thongsing Thammavong of Laos, and Prime Minister Nawaz Sharif of Pakistan. Former top government leaders from other countries including Japan, Malaysia, France, and the Philippines attended as well.

Representatives from both mainland China and Taiwan held a meeting on sidelines of the economic forum. The meeting was more than thirty minutes. After his meeting with Premier Li Keqiang, former Vice President Vincent Siew told reporters that he expressed hopes that Taiwan and mainland China would remove hurdles blocking further cooperation and adopt new views and approaches.

Siew said that he shared people's major concerns: the partnership between mainland China and Taiwan would become a rivalry, the barriers continue to complicate the entry of Taiwanese businesses to the mainland China market, and that Taiwan needs to take part in regional integration as quickly as possible. The former vice president also said that the changing global environment and developments on both sides of the Strait had created new challenges for exchanges between mainland China and Taiwan, and He suggested economic strategic dialogues and policy coordination between the two sides. The concerns over economic marginalization would be eased with Taiwan's participation in regional integration.

This is the ninth time Siew has attended the Boao Forum.

News also reported that Premier Li Keqiang urged the Taiwan public to seize opportunities for participation in regional integration through expansion of cross-strait cooperation. Li said that China is willing to open up to Taiwan before foreign countries in order to push for economic integration between the two sides.

2014 年博鰲亞洲論壇 4 月 10 日在海南舉行開幕式。今年的論壇吸引多國的領導人出席，出席者包括中國大陸國務院總理李克強、澳大利亞總理艾伯特、韓國總理鄭烘原、哈薩克總理艾哈邁托夫、寮國總理通辛、巴基斯坦總理謝里夫等。包括日本、馬來西亞、法國、菲律賓等國家的前政府高層官員也出席了這次會議。

兩岸雙方的代表在論壇外也進行會談，雙方進行約 30 分鐘的對話。前副總統蕭萬長和李克強對話結束後告訴記者，他希望兩岸雙方能以新的視野，排除障礙，進行進一步的合作。

蕭萬長說，他和眾多民眾一樣，擔心兩岸間競爭將使臺商在中國市場的處境複雜化，甚至成為雙方合作的障礙；臺灣應該要儘快參與區域整合。他也表示，全球環境變化為兩岸交流帶來新的挑戰，他建議雙方應該進行經濟戰略的對話和政策協調，才能讓臺灣加入區域整合，舒緩邊緣化的疑慮。

這是蕭萬長第九次出席博鰲論壇。

媒體同時報導，李克強呼籲臺灣民眾擴大兩岸合作，把握參與區域整合的機會。李克強說，中國大陸願意在對其他國家開放前，優先對臺灣開放，以推動雙方的經濟整合。

Unit 6

Cross-Strait Agreement on Trade in Goods

海峽兩岸貨品貿易協定

代表意義超理解

海峽兩岸貨品貿易協定將會降低臺灣與大陸間貨品的關稅。雙方原定於 2014 年前完成簽署貨貿協議，但由於服貿協議目前尚未在立法院通過，貨貿協議的談判也因而延宕。

The Cross-Strait Agreement on Trade in Goods will reduce tariffs between Taiwan and mainland China. It was originally planned to be signed before the end of 2014, but the negotiation is delayed as the service pact is ungratified in the Legislature Yuan.

B 背景知識大突破 Background

ECFA 的早收清單可視為貨貿協議的一部分，只是該部分隨著 ECFA 生效而提早進行。如果臺灣和大陸在未來完成貨貿協議，雙方將能進一步降低彼此間貨品的關稅。

The "early harvest" list of ECFA is part of the Cross-Strait Agreement on Trade in Goods that took effect with ECFA. If

＊tariff　關稅　　＊ungratified　不滿足的

Taiwan and mainland China sign the agreement on trade in goods in the future, it will further reduce tariffs on goods between the two sides.

M 使用方法一把罩
ethod

貨貿協議的正式名稱是 Cross-Strait Agreement on Trade in Goods. ECFA 的早收清單英文稱為 early harvest list。和服貿、貨貿相關的貿易用詞還包括 tariffs(關稅)、commercial barriers(商業障礙)等。由於目前貨貿協議尚未完成談判，新聞曝光也相對較低，未來外國媒體是否以使用其他簡稱稱呼貨貿協議仍待進一步觀察。但根據媒體消息指出：

"The possibility of concluding talks on the Cross-Strait Agreements on Trade in Goods this year is 'nearly non-existent' due to delays in talks," said the Deputy Economics Minister.

(據經濟部副部長表示，「因為談判延誤的關係，今年簽署兩岸貨貿協議的機會幾乎不存在。」)

* barrier 屏障、障礙

A 主題文章 Article

The cross-strait negotiation supervision legislation was approved by the Executive Yuan after the "Sunflower Movement." The new pact, which was one of the most important demands made by the protestors, is to ensure proper and fair cross-strait negotiations. The legislation is now awaiting the Legislative Yuan's review.

Chang Chia-juch, the Minister of Economic Affairs, said that he is pleased with the new legislation, which he believed is unlikely to delay future negotiations with mainland China. However, with the implementation of the Cross-Strait Trade in Services Agreement delayed, the impending cross-strait Trade in Goods Agreement may not be inked this year as the government had planned. Chang is not optimistic about the inking the agreement by mid-year as scheduled, and he is not even sure if it can be achieved by end of the year.

According to Chang, most countries are supportive of the government's efforts to continue trade negotiations with mainland China under the framework of the Cross-Straits Economic Cooperation Framework (ECFA), namely the United States. When asked about the Cross-Strait Agreement on Trade in Goods, Chang said that "we can't try to sign another agreement while the previous negotiated one is not yet put into effect."

When asked if it is possible for negotiations on the service trade pact to start over, Chang said in response that out of the 380 free trade agreements signed all around the world, only the U.S. and South Korea had initiated a renegotiation process before their FTA was put into effect. Other countries initiated renegotiations only after the FTAs were implemented a few years later.

Chang also explained that a renegotiation depends not only on Taiwan, but also on mainland China's willingness to cooperate.

He added that there is always a mechanism that allows for renegotiation after the pact is implemented, to amend and adjust any possible outcomes.

「太陽花」運動結束後，行政院通過示威者主要訴求之一的兩岸協商監督條例，以確保未來兩岸談判的公平性。該條例目前正在立法院等待立法委員的審查。

經濟部長張家祝表示，他很高興看到新的立法，並認為這不會延遲未來和中國大陸的談判。然而隨著兩岸服務貿易協議的延遲，兩岸貨品貿易協定很有可能無法按計畫在今年內完成簽署。張家祝對兩岸服貿在今年年中完成並不樂觀，並坦承他不知道服貿協議能否在今年內實現。

根據張家祝所言，大多數國家都支持政府在兩岸經濟合作框架(ECFA)下持續發展兩岸間的經貿合作，尤其是美國。當被問及兩岸貨品貿易協議時，張家祝表示，「在一個協議尚未完成前，我們不會嘗試簽署另一個協議」。

當被問及兩岸服貿協議能否重新談判時，張家祝則表示，世界上380個自由貿易協定中，只有美國和韓國間自由貿易協定得以在協定生效前重新談判。其他國家都是在自由貿易協定實施幾年後，才開始重新談判。

張家祝也解釋說，重新談判不僅是取決於臺灣，同時也關係到中國大陸的意願。他補充說，在協議實施後，有機制能重啟談判，對可能的結果進行修改或調整。

Unit 7

Cross-Strait Agreement on Trade in Services

兩岸服貿協議

代表意義超理解

兩岸服貿協議是臺灣與大陸間相互放寬服務業限制的貿易協定。雙方於 2013 年 6 月間簽訂協議，但目前臺灣的立法院尚未通過該協議。

The Cross-Strait Agreement on Trade in Services aimed to liberalize trade in services between Taiwan and mainland China. It was signed in June 2013; however, it is currently ungratified by Taiwan's Legislature Yuan, which is the law-making body of Taiwan.

B 背景知識大突破 Background

根據協議內容，「服務業」的範圍包括醫保、銀行、旅遊、電影、電信、印刷等行業，兩岸雙方將互相將這些產業開放，接受投資。兩岸服貿協議是 2010 年雙方簽訂 ECFA 後續的兩個協議之一，另一個後續協議則是兩岸貨貿協議。

Under the terms of the agreement, "services" include healthcare,

---

* aim　致力；旨在
* legislature　立法機關
* Yuan　院（音譯）

banking, tourism, film, telecommunications, and printings. These industries will be opened to investment under the agreement. It is one of two planned follow-up treaties to the ECFA signed in 2010. The other follow-up treaty would be the Cross-Strait Agreement on Trade in Goods.

Method 使用方法一把罩

兩岸服貿協議的官方英文名稱是 The Cross-Strait Agreement on Trade in Service，但國外媒體也會用 The Cross-Strait Service Trade Agreement (CSSTA) 稱呼服貿協議。另外一些報導為求方便，也會用 The Service Pact 或是 The Service Agreement 來稱呼服貿協議。和服貿相關的太陽花運動英文則稱為 Sun Flower Movement。

＊ treaty　條約、協議

A 主題文章 Article

In Taiwan, over 300,000 people joined a rally in front of the Presidential Office in April to expand a protest movement over a controversial service trade pact with mainland China. A massive sit-in was staged at the demonstration on Ketagalan Boulevard in front of the Presidential Office and nearby Zhongshan South Road.

The demonstrators were dressed in black with yellow ribbons while carrying sunflowers, a symbol of the protests, which have been dubbed the "Sunflower Movement". They chanted slogans such as "Withdraw Trade Deal" and "Protect Democracy", showing their discontent over what they consider a "black-box" deal, or the government's non-transparent handling of the trade-in-services agreement.

The organizers of the rally also pushed for a law-monitoring pact to prevent further "black-box" deals. They argued that the government should withdraw the service pact and refrain from negotiating or signing new agreements with mainland China until such a law is enacted.

The police authorities had counted 116,000 participants in this demonstration, including 15,000 in and around the Legislature Yuan office building, and 101,000 on Ketagalan Boulevard and nearby area. Meanwhile, the organizers of the demonstration claimed that at least 400,000 people had taken to the streets. Some also argued that the participants were over 500,000.

The National Police Agency said that Taipei city government had deployed 3,000 police officers to maintain order and control traffic in and around the rally site, with another 500 police assigned to keep order at the area.

The protesters are concerned that the service pact would give

mainland China too much economic influence over Taiwan. They are also concerned that mainland China's massive economic scale would hurt Taiwan's small and medium-sized enterprises. The government on the other hand, argued that the service pact would benefit Taiwan's economy, and help it joining other regional free trade blocs.

今年四月，臺灣有超過 30 萬人集結在總統府前對兩岸服貿協議展開抗爭運動。大規模群眾在總統府前及臨近的凱達格蘭大道和中山南路上靜坐示威。

示威者身著黑色衣服與黃色絲帶，並攜帶抗議的象徵品：太陽花。這場運動也被稱為「太陽花運動」。他們高喊「退回服貿」、「保護民主」等口號，訴求他們對「黑箱」協議的不滿，黑箱指的是政府在處理服貿協議中不透明的程序。

集會組織者同時推動兩岸協議監督條例，希望透過這個機制避免未來的黑箱程序。他們認為，政府應撤回服貿協議，並退回監督條例通過前兩岸所簽訂的所有協議。

警方表示，這場運動共有 116,000 人參加，包括凱達格蘭大道上的 101,000 名群眾，及 15,000 在立法院周邊的群眾。活動的組織人則表示，至少有 40 萬人走上街頭。同時也有人表示，參與者超過 50 萬人。

警政署表示，臺北市政府部署 3,000 名員警負責維持秩序、指揮交通，並指派 500 名的警力在特定區域維持秩序。

抗議者擔心服貿協議將使中國大陸在臺灣擁有過大的經濟影響力，他們也擔心中國大陸會以其龐大的經濟規模併吞臺灣的中小企業。但在另一方面，政府則認為，服貿協議將有利於臺灣經濟，並幫助臺灣加入區域中自由貿易集團。

Unit 8

ECFA
海峽兩岸經濟合作框架協定

代表意義超理解

海峽兩岸經濟合作框架協定是臺灣和大陸在 2010 年簽署的經濟互惠協議。ECFA 被視為 1949 年兩岸分治以來雙方最重要的協議。ECFA 一度被稱為 CECA — 兩岸綜合經濟合作協定。

The Cross-Straits Economic Cooperation Framework Agreement (ECFA), signed in 2010, is a preferential trade agreement between Taiwan and mainland China. It is regarded as the most significant agreement since the split in 1949. It was once called CECA, Comprehensive Economic Cooperation Agreement.

B 背景知識大突破 Background

臺灣和大陸簽定 ECFA 以降低彼此間的關稅和其他商業壁壘。其中關稅減讓的早收清單中，臺灣賣向大陸的產品共有 539 項，大陸賣往臺灣的產品共有 267 項。根據 ECFA 的架構，兩岸雙方應在未來完成服務貿易和貨品貿易的相關協議。

Taiwan and mainland China signed ECFA to reduce tariffs and

＊ framework　架構、框架　　＊ split　分裂；分割

commercial barriers. The early harvest list of tariff concessions covers 539 Taiwanese products and 267 mainland Chinese goods. Under ECFA, the two sides are to finish service trade and goods trade agreements in the near future.

M使用方法一把罩 Method

ECFA 在簽定前一度被稱為兩岸經濟協議，ECFA 訂立的是兩岸間經濟合作的框架，其下是經濟合作的各項細節措施；ECFA 簽訂後雙方依照條約內容，展開包括貨品貿易、服務貿易、投資保障、爭端解決機制等各方面的細節協商。

A主題文章 Article

Ma Ying-jeou, the President of Republic of China (Taiwan), said in April that the government is working to expand economic liberalization in Taiwan while strengthening cross-strait relations and communicating the benefits of free trade and regional integration to the public. Since the signing of the Cross-Straits Economic Cooperation Framework Agreement (ECFA) in 2010, significant progress has been made in concluding bilateral trade agreements with various economies, including Japan, Singapore, and New Zealand, he said.

According to the government, since the signing of ECFA with

＊concession　特許；特許權

mainland China, Taiwan had saved forty-two billion New Taiwanese dollars in customs duties, and it is only a result of the Early Harvest Program. Once Taiwan and mainland China finish the trade in goods agreement, exporters from Taiwan will be able to save even more, thus giving them the advantage in trade competition in China.

Since ECFA took effect in 2011, customs duties for goods covered by the Early Harvest Program had been gradually reduced to zero. According to the government, exports to mainland China in 2013 stood at US$81.8 billion, a year-on-year increase of 1.33%. However, exported goods covered by ECFA, namely those listed in the Early Harvest Program, increased by 10.62%. It signified the importance of ECFA and the Early Harvest Program, as the difference in growth between goods covered by ECFA and those not covered by ECFA is approximately a factor of eight.

After Ma took office in 2008, Taiwan and mainland China had signed 21 agreements in various areas, including transportation, food safety, investment, and crime-fighting. The government has sought to improve cross-strait ties under the constitution of the Republic of China. The administration had pushed for peaceful development on the bases of the so-called "1992 consensus" and the "one China with different interpretations" principle.

On the other hand, disputes had also risen between the ruling party and the opposition party over the question of trade in services. In April, massive protesters rallied, claiming that the service pact would damage Taiwan's economy and leave it vulnerable to political pressure from mainland China.

中華民國總統馬英九四月時表示，政府目前正積極擴大經濟自由化，並努力向大眾說明兩岸交流和區域整合的益處。海峽兩岸經濟合作框架協議 (ECFA) 自 2000 年簽署以來，臺灣在和其他經濟體締結雙邊協議的進步顯著，成果包括日本、新加坡、紐西蘭等。

根據政府資料顯示，自簽署 ECFA 以來，臺灣方面已省下 420 億臺幣的關稅，而這只是早收清單的成果。未來兩岸完成貨品貿易協定後，臺灣的出口商將可享受更多的優惠，使他們在中國大陸市場更有競爭力。

自從 2011 年 ECFA 生效以來，早收清單中的商品關稅已逐步減少為零。政府資料也顯示，去年對中國大陸的出口為 818 億美元，比去年同期成長 1.33%；但早收清單所涵蓋的項目成長 10.62%。也就是說，ECFA 涵蓋項目比沒有涵蓋的項目，相差將近 8 倍，這也顯示出 ECFA 和早收清單的重要性。

自從 2008 年馬英九上任後，兩岸已在各個領域簽定 21 項協議，內容包括交通運輸、食品安全、投資、打擊犯罪等各種項目。政府依據憲法以九二共識、一中各表的原則，來促進兩岸關係的和平發展。

但另一方面，兩岸間的服務貿易協定也引發執政黨和在野黨間的爭議。今年四月間臺灣爆發大規模的示威抗議，示威者認為服貿協議將損害臺灣的經濟，並使臺灣暴露於中國大陸的政治壓力之下。

Unit 9

FTA
自由貿易協定

代表意義超理解

自由貿易協定 (FTA) 是指兩個或多個國家間成立自由貿易區；在自由貿易區中，簽約國的貨品類商品和服務業商品將可自由進出貿易。

Free Trade Agreement, commonly known as FTA, is a treaty signed between two or more countries to establish a free trade area where commerce in goods and services can be conducted across their common borders.

B 背景知識大突破 Background

簽署自由貿易區的國家通常會相互同意取消大部分的關稅、進口配額等條件。與關稅同盟不同的是，自由貿易區的成員沒有共同的對外關稅，他們對其他國家有不同的配額、關稅、及貿易規章。

FTA member countries usually agree on eliminating tariffs and import quotas on most, if not all, goods and services traded between them. Unlike a customs union, members of a FTA do not have a common external tariff, which means they have

＊commerce　商務；貿易
＊eliminate　取消；排除
＊external　外部的、外國的

different quotas and custom, as well as other policies with other non-members.

Method 使用方法一把罩

FTA 有兩種意思，分別是自由貿易協定 (Free Trade Agreement) 和自由貿易區 (Free Trade Area)，其關係為：自由貿易協定是兩國或多國之間簽署的協議，而透過雙方或多方所簽署的協議，則使簽約方之間互相成為自由貿易區。有時一國國內也自主消除關稅和貿易配額，成立對經濟干涉較小的區域，稱為自由經濟區。例句如下：

A Free Trade Agreement would be advantageous to both countries.
（自由貿易協定對雙方國家都有好處。）

The ASEAN Free Trade Area project was launched in 1993.
（東協自由貿易區計劃是在 1993 年時開始的。）

＊ quota　配額；（正式限定的）定額

A 主題文章 Article

The Icelandic Parliament has passed a Free Trade Agreement (FTA) with China in February 2014. The parliament passed the agreement by 56-2, with three members abstained. Iceland and China began negotiating an FTA in 2006, but the talk was suspended in 2009 when Iceland tried to join the European Union. The talk was resumed in 2012, and after six rounds of negotiations, the FTA was signed between Iceland and China.

The said FTA covers trade facilitation, investment, competition, intellectual property rights and goods and services. It will enable the North Atlantic nation to join a booming market for years to come. Iceland Foreign Minister announced the news and indicated that the FTA will ensure the relationship between Iceland and China, and the two countries will have the chance to further strengthen in various areas, creating more business opportunities.

Iceland is the first European country to sign a FTA with China. According to the FTA, the two countries would put zero tariff on most of the traded items. Observers remark that China, with the ability to import more Icelandic fish with lower tariff, would seem to pale in comparison to the impotence of enhancing its influence in the region.

More importantly, although Iceland cannot offer much in the way of market growth, it could help China in its request for more influence in the Arctic, as global warming make the area increasingly accessible. Like South Korea, China is seeking to join the Arctic Council, an intergovernmental body that promotes cooperation in the region, as a permanent observer.

Trade between Iceland and China is small by global standards. China's exports to Iceland valued $341 million in 2013, while it

imported Iceland goods, mostly fish, totaled $61 million.

冰島議會在 2014 年 2 月以 56 比 2 的票數通過與中國大陸的自由貿易協定 (FTA)，另有三名議員棄權。冰島和中國大陸自 2006 年開始談判自由貿易協定，談判在 2009 年冰島試圖加入歐盟時中斷。雙方在 2012 年恢復談判，經過六輪談判後完成雙方自貿區的協定。

雙方簽署的自由貿易協定內容包括貿易便利化，投資，競爭，智慧財產權，商品及服務貿易等各種協定。這個北大西洋的島國將得以進入一個蓬勃發展的市場。冰島外交部長宣布此消息時表示，這份自由貿易協定將能確保冰島和中國大陸的關係，兩國將有機會進一步加強各個領域的合作，創造更多的商機。

冰島是歐洲第一個和中國大陸簽署自由貿易協定的國家。根據協定，兩國將消除雙方貨品絕大部分的關稅。觀察員表示，中國大陸有能力進口更多的冰島魚產，但更重要是，這將強化中國大陸在當地的影響力。

雖然冰島未來市場增加的機會不大，但它可以幫助中國大陸在極地增加影響力。隨著氣候暖化，北極航道的重要性與日俱增。和韓國一樣，中國大陸正尋求以永久觀察員的身分加入北極理事會，這是一個跨政府的地區合作組織。

以全球標準來看，冰島和中國大陸之間的貿易並不大。2013 年，大陸對冰島的出口價值約 3.41 億美元，而從冰島進口的總額約為六千一百萬美元。

Unit 10

G20
二十國集團

代表意義超理解

二十國財政部長和中央銀行首長會議簡稱二十國集團，是由二十個主要經濟體的財政首長和央行總長所組成的論壇，其目的是促進有關國際金融體系相關的合作與協商會談。

The Group of Twenty Finance Ministers and Central Bank Governors, commonly known as G20 or Group of Twenty, is a meeting of a group of finance ministers and central bank governors from twenty major economies. The purpose of the forum is to promote cooperation and consultation on matters pertaining to the international financial system.

B背景知識大突破 Background

20 國集團的成員包括 19 個主要國家和歐盟。19 個主要國家包括阿根廷、澳洲、巴西、加拿大、中國、法國、德國、印度、印尼、義大利、日本、韓國、墨西哥、俄羅斯、沙烏地阿拉伯、南非、土耳其、英國和美國。國際貨幣組織和世界銀行也都出席這個論壇。

The G20 includes 19 major countries and the European Union.

＊governor　銀行總長；（美國）州長；總督

＊consultation　諮詢；商議

＊pertain　有關、關於

The 19 major countries are Argentina, Australia, Brazil, Canada, China, France, Germany, India, Indonesia, Italy, Japan, South Korea, Mexico, Russia, Saudi Arabia, South Africa, Turkey, the United Kingdom, and the United States. The IMF and the World Bank also participate in the forum.

Method 使用方法一把罩

20 國集團從 2008 年開始召開領導人高峰會，其目的是讓有關國家就國際經濟、貨幣政策舉行對話，並藉此穩定國際金融及貨幣體系。隨著該集團的架構日漸成熟以及新興工業國家的重要性與日俱增，20 國集團已取代八大工業國集團成為全球經濟合作的主要論壇。

＊participate　參加、參與

A主題文章 Article

The G20 gave an ultimatum to the United States to pass reforms to the international Monetary Fund or risk being left out of new changes. Finance ministers from the G20 gathered in Washington for the spring meetings of World Bank and the IMF said that they were deeply disappointed by the US's failure to implement changes agreed in 2010, and gave the US until the end of the year to do so.

The reform will give emerging markets a more powerful voice at the IMF and shoring up the lender's resources appeared the most contentious issue for officials from the G20 leading economies and the representatives for all IMF members who met with them. It would double the Fund's resources and hand more IMF voting power to countries like the so-called BRICS - Brazil, Russia, India, China and South Africa.

"I take this opportunity to urge the United States to implement these reforms as a matter of urgency," Australian Treasurer Joe Hockey told reporters on the sidelines of the IMF-World Bank spring meetings.

The U.S. government under Obama administration supported the changes, but had been unwilling to meet the high political price demanded by the Republicans to get them through Congress. The G20 communiqué highlights how growing frustration with the US for holding up reform. "If the 2010 reforms are not ratified by year-end, we will call on the IMF to build on its existing work and develop options for next steps" says the communiqué.

Although the ultimatum is given, it is not clear whether the G20 would take the next stop, since the US has a blocking minority of votes at the fund. That's why the reforms were delayed in the first place.

The communiqué says the G20 is "committed to developing new actions" that "lift and rebalance global demand and achieve exchange rate flexibility." However, it does not single out any issue such as renewed currency intervention in China, or emerging current account surplus.

二十國集團對美國發出最後通牒要求美國對國際貨幣基金進行改革，否則二十國集團將另作打算。二十國集團的各國財政部長群聚華盛頓，對春季的世界銀行和國際貨幣基金會議作準備。公告表示，「我們對 2010 年國際貨幣基金改革方案遲遲未能實現深感失望，美國必須在今年內完成這些改革」。

這些改革將會讓新興市場國家在國際貨幣基金中擁有更大的話語權，並讓他們擁有更多的資源份額。對於巴西、俄羅斯、印度、中國大陸、南非等金磚國家來說，這項改革將讓他們的份額增加翻倍。

澳洲財政部長則在國際貨幣基金和世界銀行春季會議向記者表示，「我希望美國能儘快落實這些改革，這件事非常緊急」。

一般認為，歐巴馬政府支持這項改革，但卻不願在國會中滿足共和黨人在國會中提出的政治要求。二十國集團的公報則強調，美國對改革的延遲讓他們倍感挫折。「如果 2010 年的改革無法在 2014 年內獲得批准，我們將呼籲國際貨幣組織繼續完成既有工作，並制定下一步的行動方案。」公報上如此說。

雖然二十國集團已發出最後通牒，但目前外界仍不清楚二十國集團會下一步會採取什麼行動。這是因為美國在會議中擁有關鍵少數，這也是改革遭到延宕的首要原因。

公報上指出，二十國集團「致力於新的發展行動」，「追求世界匯率的平衡」，但並沒有提及任何現存的各種問題，例如中國大陸再次干預匯率、以及貨幣結餘等問題。

Unit 11

G8
八大工業國集團

代表意義超理解

八大工業國集團是由世界上八個主要工業國家所舉行的聯合論壇。論壇成員國可以藉由這個平台，分享他們對世界政治、經濟、及軍事方面的理念，並尋求更好的溝通及合作。

The Group of Eight (G8) is the name of a forum held by the governments of eight leading industrialized countries. The members would share their thoughts on politics, economy, and military to pursuit better understanding and cooperation.

B背景知識大突破 Background

八大工業國集團最早是由法國、德國、義大利、日本、英國、美國在 1976 所組成的六大工業國集團，隨著加拿大在隔年加入，成為七大工業國集團。俄羅斯在 1998 年加入該集團，成為一般所熟知的八大工業國集團。但在 2014 年的烏克蘭、克里米亞事件後，俄羅斯被其他成員國從論壇中剔除。

The forum was originated known as G6, which is hosted by France, Germany, Italy, Japan, the United Kingdom, and the

＊industrialize　工業化的
＊host　主辦、主持
＊pursuit　追求

United States, in 1975. Canada soon joined the forum in 1976, and it has become known as G7. Russia was added to it in 1998, and G8 became commonly known to the people. Nevertheless, Russia is removed from the forum in 2014, due to the recent incident in Ukraine and Crimea.

Method 使用方法一把罩

G8 這個名稱隨著他的成員變動而不斷改變，從最早的 G6 成為 G7，再從 G7 成為 G8。最近俄羅斯被踢出這個集團，因此短期內 G7 這個名詞將會較為常見。日後若俄國重回該組織，或由其他國家加入，則會重新回到 G8。

＊incident　事件、事變

Russia was kicked out of the Group of Eight (G8) of global powers at international summit. The US-led Group of Seven (G7) decided to suspend participation in G8. At the same time, they discussed measures to impose sanctions against Russia in energy, banking and national defense. US President Barack Obama and the other leaders of G8 have decided to exclude Russia from the G8.

Excluding Russia from the G8 may be intended as a warning from the US and its allies regarding the previous and current situation in Crimea and Ukraine, but Russia does not seem to care about the warning of G8.

President Obama had called an extraordinary meeting of the other seven members of the G8 to try to forge a united position on the worst crisis in relations with Russia since the end of the Cold War. So far, Washington had taken a tougher line than the EU, but Russia showed no sign to change its stance. Russian President Vladimir Putin says "If our partners do not want to come, so be it." Russia is not particularly concerned about the loss of membership of the "rich man's club."

Russia's reaction to it was also swift and scathing, as Foreign Minister Sergei Lavrov saying that the Kremlin does not "cling to this format" of the G8. Meanwhile, Moscow also imposed travel bans on 13 Canadian officials.

The fact is, G8 can no longer make unilateral decisions after the spread of the financial crisis and the rapid rise of new economies in the past few years. Russia plays an important role in many different multilateral mechanisms, including the UN, the G20, and APEC. Russia's active participation in international negotiation mechanisms also promotes positive development of

international situation and strategic cooperation.

As one of the major power in the world, Russia is inextricably linked to the west. It will continue to be an active participant in international affairs in the future.

俄羅斯在國際峰會中被踢出八大工業國集團。以美國為首的七大工業國集團決定停止八國集團運作；他們並討論從能源、金融、國防等各方面對俄羅斯實施制裁。美國總統歐巴馬和其他六國領導人已決定將俄羅斯排除在八大工業國之外。

將俄羅斯排除在 G8 之外的動作旨在對俄羅斯在烏克蘭和克里米亞事件中的行為作出警告。但俄羅斯對這些舉動並不十分在意。

歐巴馬總統要求八國集團的其他成員召開特別會議，以對這次冷戰以來和俄羅斯關係最僵的事件採取統一立場。華盛頓的立場比歐盟更為強硬，但俄羅斯並無任何妥協的徵兆。俄羅斯總統普亭說，「如果我們的合作夥伴不想來了，那就這樣吧」。俄羅斯似乎並不在乎被排除在「富人俱樂部」之外。

而俄羅斯官方的反應則是迅速而嚴厲。俄國外交部長拉夫羅夫說，克里姆林無須侷限於八國集團的框架，莫斯科方面並限制 13 名加拿大官員的出入境資格。

事實上，經過金融危機和新興經濟體的迅速崛起，世界格局不再是單邊關係。俄羅斯在聯合國、二十國集團、亞太經合組織中都發揮重要的作用，俄羅斯在各種國際機制中的參與也促進了國際間的交流與合作。

做為世界強權之一，俄國和西方國家有著密不可分的關係。其在未來仍會是國際關係中最重要的參與者之一。

Unit 12

GDP
國內生產總值

代表意義超理解

國內生產總值(GDP: Gross Domestic Product)是指一個國家或地區在一定時間內所生產的所有最終產品的市場價值總值。國內生產總值是用來觀察一個國家或地區經濟發展情況的重要指標。

Gross Domestic Product (GDP) of the market value of all final goods and products within a current country or area in a given period of time. GDP is an important tool often used to measure the economic development of the said country or area.

B 背景知識大突破 ackground

國內生產總值(GDP)和國民生產總值(GNP: Gross National Product)不同之處在於，國內生產總值是一個國家或地區內部生產的產品總值，而國民生產總值則是該國(地區)實際獲得的生產性總收入(包含海外生產)。

The difference between Gross Domestic Product (GDP) and Gross National Product (GNP) is that GDP is a country's gross

---

＊gross　y 總的　　＊domestic　國家的、國內的

product of internal production, while GNP is the country's actual production (including overseas production).

M使用方法一把罩 ethod

國內生產總值一般用來觀察一個國家或地區的經濟發展情況，通常是以年為單位進行觀察，但也常以季度 (quarter) 來作比較。常見的例子例如以 2012 年和 2013 年的經濟成長率作比較，或以 2012 年第一季 (2012 Q1) 和 2013 年的第一季 (2013 Q1) 作比較。

根據 2012 年的資料，GDP 前五名的國家分別是美國（15.6 兆，或萬億美元）、中國（8.2 兆，或萬億美元）、日本（5.9 兆，或萬億美元）、德國（3.4 兆，或萬億美元）、與法國（2.6 兆，或萬億美元）。中華民國（臺灣）則以 474 億美元，名列第 27。

A 主題文章 Article

Mainland China's GDP expanded by 7.4% in the first quarter of 2014, better than what many had expected. However, it is still a slowdown compared to its 7.7% growth in the final quarter of last year. Reduced momentum in investment and consumption are said to be behind the moderately weaker quarterly growth. The 7.4% growth is also slightly below the target of "around 7.5%" said by mainland China's leadership for the year of 2014.

Although most of the countries in the world may envy mainland China's current GDP growth level, experts say the world's most populous country needs high output levels to absorb legions of migrant workers and new graduates hunting for jobs. If the mainland Chinese leaders fail to maintain the growth, the unemployment rate would affect social stability. Mainland China has set a growth target of 7.5%, and experts believe the government has a floor of 7%. The Chinese government says 7.5% growth would generate 10 million jobs and that growth below 7% would cause high unemployment rate.

Meanwhile, industrial production was up 8.8% in March, below expectations for a 9% rise. Year-to-date fixed asset investment was up 17.6%, lower than the expectations for an 18% rise. Year-to-date retail sales were up 12%, higher than expectations for an 11.9% rise. For March alone, retail sales were up 12.2%.

Overall, mainland China's economic growth in the first quarter was within range, the employment rate remained stable, and inflation was also under control. However, this moderate growth means more unexpected elements to the world economy, as mainland China is a major global growth engine. These unexpected elements include whether the Chinese government would adjust its policies to bring up the slightly faster-than-expected growth. In early April, the government announced a

series of "mini-stimulus" measures to offset recent slippage in trade and industrial production. These included the rebuilding of shantytowns and increase of spending on railroad infrastructure.

中國大陸 2014 年第一季的國內生產總值成長率為 7.4%，較眾人所預期的為佳，但和去年第四季 7.7% 的成長率比起來仍有所下滑。一般認為，投資和消費減少是這次經濟成長率微幅下滑的主因。而 7.4% 的成長率也稍低於中國大陸領導人「7.5% 左右」的年成長率目標。

雖然世界上大部分的國家可能都對中國大陸現有的經濟成長率投以羨慕的目光，但專家表示，這個世界上人口最多的國家必須維持高經濟成長水平，才能提供農民工和應屆畢業生足夠的就業機會。如果中國領導人不能維持經濟成長，高失業率就會影響中國大陸的社會穩定。專家認為，中國大陸雖然制定了 7.5% 的經濟成長目標，但政府的底限應該在 7%。中國大陸政府方面則表示，7.5% 的成長率約能提供十萬個就業機會，若成長率低於 7% 則會帶來高失業率。

中國大陸三月份的工業生產成長 8.8%，比預期的 9% 稍低。年初至今的固定資產投資成長 17.6%，也稍低於預期的 18%。年初至今的零售量增長 12%，則略高於預期的 11.9%。三月份單月份的零售成長量則是 12.2%。

整體而言，中國大陸第一季的整體經濟大致保持穩定就業、通貨膨脹也在控制範圍內。然而，這對世界經濟而言並不是個穩定因素，因為大陸是世界經濟的成長引擎。而中國政府促進經濟成長的政策則成為不確定因素。在四月初時，大陸政府宣布了一系列的刺激經濟措施，以彌補微幅下滑的貿易和工業生產量。這些措施包括棚戶區改造和鐵路基礎設施投入的增加。

Unit 13

Globalization
全球化

代表意義超理解

全球化是一種經由自由貿易、資本流動、以及外來廉價勞動力而達到經濟發展，並走向全球性經濟整合的過程。

Globalization is a development process of an increasingly integrated global economy marked by free trade, free flow of capital, and the tapping of cheaper foreign labor markets.

B 背景知識大突破 Background

國際貨幣組織對全球化的定義包括四個基本面向：國際貿易、資本流動、人口遷移、知識傳播。各種不同的環境挑戰也常與全球化連結在一起。

The International Monetary Fund identified four basic aspects of globalization: trade and transactions, capital and investment movements, migration and movement of people, and the dissemination of knowledge. Different kinds of environmental challenges are also linked with globalization.

* capital　資本、資金
* monetary　貨幣的、金錢的
* aspect　方面；形式
* dissemination　傳播、散播

Method 使用方法一把罩

全球化，一般是指國與國之間在政治、經濟上的相互合作、依存，但亦可用來解釋在交通、通訊極為發達的現代，世界逐漸走向「地球村」的實際情況。近年來全球化的討論極為風行，但究竟是好是壞仍是見仁見智。globalize 則是全球化的動詞型態。

例如是民進黨主席蔡英文所提到的「民進黨要走向世界，再跟著世界走向中國，馬英九則是擁抱中國，離世界愈來愈遠」，而新聞報導中提及馬英九總統的回應：

In response to the comments of the chairwoman of Taiwan's opposition Democratic Progressive Party (DPP) – Tsai Ing-wen, Ma said that the DPP's notion of globalization was "globalization without mainland China," thus highlighting the differences between the two parties and their understanding of globalization.

（回應民進黨主席蔡英文的評論，馬英九總統説民進黨的全球化是「沒有中國大陸的全球化」，而這也明顯的顯示出兩個政黨之間對於全球化佈局的路徑差異。）

A 主題文章 Article

In the past couple decades; globalization had mostly benefited the world economies. The general stance is that the benefits of globalization outweigh the economic and social costs by providing GDP growth in several underdeveloped regions. Relatively speaking, developing countries also become wealthier based on per capita GDP growth rates. Benefits to economic development, international trade, and standards of living are obvious as the outcome of globalization.

However, experts argued that it is the world's most advanced economies which had mostly benefited from globalization, leading to a widening global gap between the rich and the poor. Studies showed that Finland, Denmark, Japan, Germany and Switzerland had become the largest beneficiaries of globalization. Germany had gained an extra two trillion euros in GDP, an average of 1,240 euros per person, per year since 1990.

While globalization generated an average fifteen hundreds euros annual per capita income gain in Finland, in developing countries such as China, Mexico, and India, per capita income rose by less than a hundred euros. From these numbers, it is clear that globalization tends to widen the gap between the rich and the poor in the international community.

Nevertheless, despite its low per capita income growth, mainland China is among the winners of globalization. Since the introduction of economic reforms in 1978, mainland China has become of the of world's fastest growing countries. As of 2013, it became the world's second-largest economy, and it is also the world's largest exporter and importer of goods. Mainland China is also a member of numerous formal and informal multilateral organizations, including the WTO, APEC, and the Shanghai Cooperation Organization.

Yet again, now mainland China sees the downside of globalization. Years of rapid economic growth had brought various of social problems, and mainland China is launching a series of reforms trying to solve these problems.

在過去數十年中，世界經濟是全球化潮流中的受益者。全球化在未開發地區帶來經濟成長的好處，整體而言，仍超過其背後所帶來的經濟和社會成本。從人均國內生產總值的成長率來說，發展中國家的確也變得更加富裕。國際貿易的增長、社會福利的增加、生活水準的改善，都是全球化所帶來的好處。

但專家也表示，在全球化中獲利最多的國家，也都是世界上最先進的經濟體，導致國家間的貧富差距不斷擴大。研究顯示，芬蘭、丹麥、日本、德國和瑞士都是全球化中最大的受益者；自1990 年以來，德國從全球化中多賺進二兆歐元，每年人均收入增加 1,240 歐元。

全球化為芬蘭帶來每年人均收入增加 1,500 歐元的成長，但在中國、墨西哥、印度等發展中國家，每年人均收入則增加不到 100 歐元。從這些數字來看，全球化顯然正在擴大國際社會上的貧富差距。

但儘管人均收入成長緩慢，中國大陸仍是全球化最大的贏家之一。自從 1978 年進行開放改革以來，中國大陸是全世界經濟成長最快的國家。2013 年中國大陸已成為世界第二大經濟體，同時是世界上最大的商品進出口國。它同時也是包括世界貿易組織、亞太經合會、上海合作組織等眾多正式及非正式多邊組織的成員。

但中國大陸在全球化的過程中也受到負面影響。常年的經濟高度成長帶來各種的社會問題，中國大陸目前正試著進行一連串的改革來解決這些問題。

Unit 14

RCEP
區域經濟全面夥伴關係

代表意義超理解

區域經濟全面夥伴關係，又稱為 RCEP，是東協十國和其他六個和東協有自由貿易協定的國家間的全面自由貿易協定。東協十國包括印尼、馬來西亞、菲律賓、新加坡、泰國、帛琉、緬甸、柬埔寨、寮國、越南；而其他六國則是中國大陸、日本、南韓、澳洲、紐西蘭和印度。

Regional Comprehensive Economic Partnership, also known as RCEP, is a free trade zone agreement (FTA) between the 10 ASEAN members (Indonesia, Malaysia, the Philippine, Singapore, Thailand, Brunei, Burma, Cambodia, Laos, and Vietnam) and its FTA Partners (China, Japan, South Korea, Australia, New Zealand, and India).

B 背景知識大突破 Background

RCEP 談判預定在 2015 年完成，將涵蓋超過 30 億人口和約世界貿易總額的 40%。RCEP 的內容將涵蓋貨品貿易、服務貿易、投資、技術合作、知識產權、爭端解決等問題。臺灣已於日前宣布有意願加入 RCEP，以避免在區域中遭到邊緣化。

＊regional　區域的

The negotiation of RCEP is to be concluded in 2015, and the FTA will include more than three billion people, with about 40% of the world trade. RCEP will cover trade in goods, trade in services, investment, economic and technical cooperation, intellectual property, competition, dispute settlement and other issues. Taiwan has announced its interest in joining it to prevent being isolated in the region.

M使用方法一把罩 ethod

東協的正式名稱是 Association of Southeast Asian Nations，簡寫為 ASEAN，中文稱為東南亞國家協會，有時候亦翻譯為東南亞國家聯盟(東盟)、東南亞合作組織(東合)。東協加三(ASEAN+3；中日韓)和東協加六(ASEAN+6；中日韓澳紐印)都是常見的關鍵字。東協和六國的 FTA 都將有各自的效益，而整個 ASEAN+6 則會進一步帶來更多的複合效應。據新聞中指出：

Simulations conducted by the ASEAN Secretariat suggest that an ACFTA will increase ASEAN's exports to China by 48% and China's exports to ASEAN by 55.1%. The FTA increases ASEAN's GDP by 0.9% while China's GDP expands by 0.3%.

（根據東協秘書處的模擬資料顯示，光是中國和東協雙方的自由貿易協定(ACFTA)，東協對中國的出口就將增加 48%，中國對東協的出口將增加 55%，同時為東協增加 0.9% 的 GDP，並為中國增加 0.3% 的 GDP。)

* negotiation　協商、談判
* conclude　結束、完成
* isolate　隔離、孤立

A 主題文章 Article

Taiwan's representatives in countries that are negotiating the proposed Trans-Pacific Partnership (TPP) and the Regional Comprehensive Economic Partnership (RCEP) are scheduled to return in February. These representatives will take four-day courses to be better prepared to seek support from their assigned countries in order to let Taiwan join the said regional trade blocs.

According to the Ministry of Foreign Affairs, Taiwan's representatives in countries that are related to TPP and RCEP are all expected to return for the training. These countries include the United States, Japan, Singapore, South Korea, India, Malaysia, the Philippines, Indonesia, Thailand, Brunei, Vietnam, New Zealand, Australia, Peru, Chile, Canada and Mexico.

In recent years, regional economic integration has accelerated globally, with TPP, RCEP, and the free trade agreement (FTA) talks among China, Japan, and South Korea. Negotiations for these agreements are expected to conclude before the end of 2015. Taiwan feels the pressure as its main competitor, South Korea, is about to complete its FTA chain in the region.

Taiwan is eager to join the two trade blocs in order to prevent itself from becoming marginalized in the region's economic integration. The TPP negotiating countries account for about 36% of Taiwan's trade, and the RCEP countries 57%. President Ma Ying-jeou made the remark that Taiwan must join TPP and RCEP as soon as possible; Taiwan will not be absent (in the region's economic integration) and cannot be marginalized. The government had set goals of completing its TPP preparations by July 2014.

In the past decade, Taiwan had signed the Economic Cooperation Framework Agreement (ECFA) with mainland China, and

economic cooperation agreements or investment pacts with New Zealand, Singapore and Japan. It had also resumed talks with the United States under the Trade and Investment Framework Agreement (TIFA). To achieve its goal to complete its TPP preparation, Taiwan will continue to push for trade liberalization and persuade the public to support its economic reform.

臺灣在擬參建太平洋夥伴關係 (TPP) 和區域全面經濟夥伴關係 (RCEP) 國家的駐外代表定於在二月返國。這些代表將參加為期四天的集訓，以為爭取上述區域貿易集團成員國家的支持。

外交部表示，臺灣目前在擬參建 TPP 和 RCEP 國家的代表都會回國參加集訓。這些國家包括美國、日本、新加坡、韓國、印度、馬來西亞、菲律賓、印尼、泰國、汶萊、越南、新西蘭、澳大利亞、秘魯、智利、加拿大和墨西哥。

近年來，區域經濟整合的風潮在全球不斷加快，包括 TPP、RCEP、以及中日韓之間 FTA 的談判都相繼進行中。這些談判預定將在 2015 年完成。臺灣對此感到極大的壓力，因為它的主要競爭對手韓國已將完成區域間的 FTA 鏈。

臺灣迫切地希望能加入 TPP 和 RCEP 兩個集團，以避免自身在區域經濟整合中邊緣化。臺灣與參與 TPP 談判國家的貿易總額約佔自身的 36%，與 RCEP 國家則佔 57%。馬英九總統日前指出，臺灣不能 (在區域經濟整合) 中缺席，必須儘快加入 TPP 和 RCEP，才不會被邊緣化。政府目前已建立起在 2014 年 7 月前完成 TPP 準備工作的目標。

在過去十年中，臺灣已與中國大陸簽署經濟合作架構協議（ECFA），並與紐西蘭，新加坡及日本完成經濟合作協定或投資協定。臺灣也恢復了與美國的貿易與投資框架協定 (TIFA)。為了實現上述目標，臺灣將繼續推動貿易自由化，同時努力說服民眾支持經濟改革，完成加入 TPP 的準備。

Unit 15

Shadow Banking
影子銀行

代表意義超理解

影子銀行系統指的是非銀行的金融設施，這些設施提供類似於傳統銀行的服務，並和傳統銀行一樣向各種機構和市場提供服務。但這些影子銀行較不受執政當局和傳統法規的限制，因此帶來潛在的危機。

The Shadow Banking System refers to non-bank financial facilities that provide services similar to traditional banks. It comprises a diverse set of institutions and markets that collectively carry out traditional banking functions, but only loosely linked to traditional regulations from official authorities. That's why shadow banks may cause potential problems.

背景知識大突破 Background

2009 年大陸金融系統暴露出的高風險貸款已引起各界的恐慌。大陸在 2014 年推動一連串的改革試圖解決影子銀行的問題。研究顯示，除非大陸能以市場改革解決信貸泡沫化的危機，不然這個問題將影響到全球的經濟成長。

＊comprise　包含、包括
＊diverse　多樣化的、形形色色的
＊collectively　共同地

The explosion of risky, undisclosed loans in mainland China's financial system since 2009 is certainly a cause for alarm. The Chinese authorities is launching a series of reforms in 2014, trying to solve the shadow banking problems. According to studies, unless mainland China can bring its credit bubble under control with market reforms, it could pose a significant threat to global growth.

Method 使用方法一把罩

影子銀行 (Shadow Banking) 又被稱為影子金融體系或影子銀行系統 (Shadow Banking system)，有時候也被稱為平行銀行系統 (The Parallel Banking System)。這些非銀行的機構從事放款，也接受抵押，通過槓桿操作持有大量證券、債券。影子銀行為金融體系帶來巨大的脆弱性，並成為全球金融危機的重要推手。

＊ explosion 爆發、激增

＊ undisclosed 秘密的、隱蔽的

A 主題文章 Article

In mainland China, trust companies are non-bank lenders that raise funds by selling high-yielding investments and funding loans to risky borrowers such as property developers and local governments. In order to prevent systemic risks posed by the country's shadow banking, mainland China had issued stricter guidelines governing trust companies.

The government had encouraged the rise of non-bank lending as means to diversify mainland China's bank-dominated financial system, while issuing targeted rules to curb the risky practices. The latest regulations appear consistent with regulator's overall approach to shadow banking, which has become an important yet dangerous founding source for weak borrowers in mainland China.

The said new regulations from the Chinese administration aimed to reduce liquidity risks by forbidding trusts from operating so called "fund pools" that enable them to fund cash payouts on maturing products. "Fund pools" refer to pools of cash and credit assets from various different wealth management products that banks and their trust companies maintain. The regulation also required trust companies to develop clear mechanisms for shareholders to provide support to the trust companies during periods of liquidity stress.

The government wanted trusts to strictly match each wealth management products with a specific set of underlying assets, rather than pooling cash and assets from different products together into common pools. It had also increasingly focused on such structures over the last year, targeting the liquidity risk posed by the practice of using proceeds from the sale of new wealth management products.

In addition to the focus on fund pools, the new guidelines also require trusts to reduce lending when their capital levels fall due to losses. The regulator also pledged to tighten the approval process for trusts to expand into new business lines. The purpose of these new regulations is to prevent the systemic risks behind shadow banking, and to prevent a potential financial crisis which may be similar to the one happened in 2008.

在中國大陸，信貸公司是非銀行的借貸組織，它們透過高利投資和借款給房地產開發商或地方政府等方式募集資金。為了防止影子銀行可能帶來的系統性風險，中國大陸已對信貸公司發布監管方針。

大陸當局曾一度鼓勵這種非銀行的貸款，以在銀行主導的金融體系外多元發展。而且同時發布具有針對性的規章，以遏制風險提升。最新發布的法規多半針對大陸的影子銀行，後者已成為一種重要但危險的借貸管道。

大陸當局這些新的規定旨在禁止信託操作能對成熟產品融資的「資金池」，以降低流動性風險。「資金池」包括各種不同的理財產品，由銀行和銀行的信託公司來維持現金和信貸資產。該法規還要求信貸公司制定明確的機制，要求股東在流動性壓力期間提供支援。

政府希望信貸公司嚴格管理每一項理財產品及特定的資產，並避免從不同的產品匯集現金和資產。政府也越來越注意過去一年中逐漸累積的結構，及這種作法所帶來的系統性風險。

除了針對資金池外，新規則還要求信託公司在因損失而造成資本額水平下降時需減少放貸。監管機構並將嚴格管理信貸發展新業務時的批准流程；這些新規定的目的，就是要避免影子銀行及其後續的系統性風險，並防止類似 2008 年金融風暴的危機發生。

Unit 16

The Doha Round
杜哈回合談判

代表意義超理解

杜哈回合談判是世界貿易組織成員間最新一輪的貿易談判，其目的是藉由降低貿易壁壘和修改貿易規則，以追求國際貿易體系的重大改革。

The Doha Round is the latest round of trade negotiations among the WTO membership. Its aim is to achieve major reform of the international trading system through the introduction of lower trade barriers and revised trade rules.

背景知識大突破 Background

杜哈回合談判最新的工作項目包括二十種不同領域的貿易項目。杜哈回合談判的也被稱作杜哈發展計畫，因為它的核心目標是要促進發展中國家的貿易現況。杜哈回合談判從 2001 年正式開始，談判項目包括農業、服務業、智慧財產權等各式議題。

The work program of the Doha Round covers about 20 areas of trade. The Round is also known semi-officially as the Doha Development Agenda as a fundamental objective is improve

---

＊aim　瞄準、對準
＊revise　修訂、修改
＊semi-officially　半官方地

the trading prospects of developing countries. The Round was officially launched in 2001, its topic included agriculture, services, and intellectual property topics.

Method 使用方法一把罩

在 WTO 的架構下，成員國會發起回合談判，以針對特定貿易議題進行大規模的多邊討論。例如 WTO 前身的 GATT，就 1986 年到 1994 年的烏拉圭回合談判達成共識，並創立 WTO。杜哈回合談判於 2001 年正式開始，該年於卡達首都杜哈展開新一輪多邊貿易談判。原定於 2005 年的 1 月 1 日完成談判，但一直到 2005 年年底都未能達到協議，於 2006 年 7 月 22 日在 WTO 總理事會的批准下中止。

* agriculture 農業
* property 財產、資產

A主題文章 Article

The Doha Round has long been delayed by its members for the differences over how to reduce tariffs on both agricultural and manufactured goods. World Trade Organization (WTO) members had finally agreed to come up with a work program by the end of the year to finish the Doha Round earlier this year.

During his first trip to Washington , WTO Director General Roberto Azevedo urged the US to reprise its leadership role in the multilateral trading system. He hopes the US may bring the long-delayed Doha Round of world trade talks to a conclusion.

Azevedo delivered a speech after meeting with US president Barack Obama and US Trade Representative. He praised the role of the United States to make it easier to transport goods around the world. "It's clear to me that the WTO needs America, I also think America needs to WTO," said the Director General.

Azevedo described his meeting with Obama a very important sign of US support for the WTO system at the time when the US is focused on two high-quality regional integration – the Transatlantic Trade and Investment partnership (TTIP) with the European Union, and the proposed Trans-Pacific Partnership (TPP) agreement with eleven other Pacific countries.

The Director General argued that although regional trade deals provided positive benefits most of the time, certain issues like trade remedies and agricultural subsidies can only be discussed in multilateral context. If the Doha work plan is to be concluded as quickly as possible, WTO members would receive huge gains, at the same time freeing up the global trade agenda to the next era.

Although WTO members continued to insist that any Doha Round agreement need to include outcomes on agriculture,

which is the main reason the Doha Round is blocked and delayed, Azevedo argued that negotiators need to figure out new approaches to finish the round. He encouraged the Obama administration to reflect "American values" and take its role in the WTO system.

長期以來杜哈回合談判成員受困於農業和工業產品關稅上的歧異而未能有任何進展。日前世界貿易組織成員終於同意提出一份計畫，並在今年底前完成杜哈回合談判。

世貿組織秘書長阿茲維多拜訪華盛頓時敦促美國在多邊貿易體系中扮演領導者的角色。他希望美國可以協助延宕多年的杜哈回合談判作出結論。

阿茲維多和美國總統歐巴馬及美國貿易代表會晤後發表談話。他稱讚美國在世界貿易中所扮演的角色。「很明顯的，我認為世貿組織需要美國，美國也需要世貿組織」，他說。

阿茲維多認為，美國目前正在推動兩個高階區域整合協議－和歐盟國家的跨大西洋貿易及投資夥伴關係 (TTIP) 以及和太平洋國家的跨太平洋夥伴關係協議 (TPP)；他和歐巴馬此時會面，象徵美國對世貿組織的支持。

他認為，雖然大部分時間區域貿易協定都帶來正面效益，但貿易救濟和農業補貼等問題必須經由多方談判才能決定。如果杜哈談判的工作計畫能順利完成，世貿組織的成員國將獲得巨大的收益，也將帶領全球貿易進入一個新的紀元。

儘管世貿組織成員堅持杜哈回合談判須包含農業議題造成談判受阻，但阿茲維多認為，各國需找出新的方法來完成談判。他鼓勵歐巴馬政府發揮美國價值觀，並在世貿體系中發揮作用。

Unit 17

TIFA
臺美貿易暨投資架構協定

代表意義超理解

臺美貿易暨投資架構協定(Trade and Investment Framework Agreement) 是臺美間高層級的經貿磋商機制。TIFA同時也是雙方解決貿易爭端、促進雙方貿易與投資合作的重要平台。

The Trade and Investment Framework Agreement (TIFA) is one of the most important channel for high-level economic and trade consultations between Taiwan and the U.S. It also serves as a platform for trade dispute resolution, trade promotion, and investment cooperation.

B 背景知識大突破 Background

臺美貿易暨投資架構協定創立於 1994 年，雙方後續在 2006 年的會議達成多項共識，內容包括農業、知識產權、政府採購投資等。臺美雙方會談於 2007 年中斷，直到 2013 年才恢復對話。

The Taiwan-U.S. Trade and Investment Framework Agreement was established in 1994, and the two held a productive meeting in 2006, covering issues related to agriculture, intellectual

---

＊channel　管道、通道
＊platform　平台
＊productive　富有成效的
＊issue　問題、爭議

property rights, and government procurement and investment. It was suspended from 2007 to 2012, and resumed in 2013.

M 使用方法一把罩 Method

在臺灣，一般使用 TIFA 時，多半指臺美間的貿易暨投資架構協定。但實際上，TIFA 也可以用來泛指所有國與國之間所簽訂的貿易與投資架構協定。若要特別指出是某方間的貿易與投資架構協定，則可在 TIFA 前加入簽約雙方的名稱，例如 Taiwan-U.S. TIFA。

A 主題文章 Article

The United States and the Republic of China (Taiwan) had concluded their latest round of Trade and Investment Framework Agreement (TIFA) talks in April. The two sides held in-depth discussions on agricultural trade issues, and according to the Office of the United States Trade Representative, both sides had made meaningful progress on several two-way trade issues.

According to a statement from the United States Trade Representative, the United States and Taiwan experts agreed to continue fully utilizing the investment and the Technical Barriers to Trade Working Groups launched at last year's TIFA Council meeting and build on recent positive steps taken by Taiwan. These "positives" include clarifying investment criteria, revising

＊ suspend　使中止

standards and multipack labeling requirements, and lifting data localization requirements in the financial sector.

According to the United States Trade Representative, representatives from Taiwan also outlined plans to devote necessary resources to strengthen intellectual property rights enforcement during the meeting.

However, Taiwan announced its stance again on U.S. pork, saying it will not lift the ban on U.S. pork imports containing the additive Ractopamine. The vice Economics Minister of Taiwan, Cho Shih-chao, said that the United States hopes Taiwan will present what it calls "scientific evidence" that Ractopamine is harmful to human body. However, he said that the government will keep the ban in place.

The TIFA was signed in 1994 as a framework for U.S.-Taiwan dialogue on trade issues in the absence of official diplomatic ties, but was suspended from 2007 to 2012 mainly because of controversies over imports of U.S. beef containing Ractopamine. The talks resumed in 2013 after Taiwan lifted the ban on certain US beef products. This 8th and final round of TIFA talks was held in Washington D.C.

In this round of talks, Taiwan's highest agenda is to bid to join the US-led Trans-Pacific Partnership (TPP). The TPP is a high-level free trade agreement involving Australia, Brunei, Chile, Canada, Japan, Malaysia, Mexico, New Zealand, Peru, Singapore, the United States, and Vietnam.

我國政府與美國雙方於四月份完成臺美貿易暨投資架構協定最新一輪的談判，雙方就農產品貿易問題進行深入討論。據美國貿易代表辦公室表示，雙方已就數個貿易問題上取得有意義的進展。

美國貿易代表辦公室的聲明表示，臺美雙方同意繼續發揮去年 TIFA 會議中發起的投資工作小組與技術性貿易障礙工作小組的功效，並朝臺灣近期努力的目標邁進。這些目標包括更明確的投資標準、修訂標示的標準，及減輕金融部門資訊數據化的限制。

美國貿易代表表示，臺灣方面也計畫投入必要的資源，以加強對知識財產權的保障。

臺灣在美豬進口方面則再次表達其立場，堅持不會進口含有萊克多巴胺的美國豬肉。經濟部次長卓士昭強調，雖然美國方面希望臺灣提出萊克多巴胺是對人體有害的具體證據，但政府會繼續禁止美豬進口。

臺美貿易暨投資架構協定源於 1994 年，由於雙方並沒有正式外交關係，因此以這樣的方式來建立對話框架。但該談判於 2007 年至 2012 年間一度中斷，其主因即為對含有萊克多巴胺的美國牛肉有所爭議。雙方於 2013 年臺灣解除美牛禁令後恢復對話，這次的會議是雙方第八次也是最後一次的會談，會談本身在華盛頓舉行。

在此次會談中，臺灣的最重要目標是申請加入由美國主導的跨太平洋夥伴協定 (TPP)。TPP 是一個含括澳大利亞、汶萊、智利、加拿大、日本、馬來西亞、墨西哥、紐西蘭、秘魯、新加坡、美國和越南的高階自由貿易協定。

Unit 18

TPP
跨太平洋夥伴協定

代表意義超理解

跨太平洋夥伴協定，簡寫 TPP，是目前正由美國、加拿大、日本、澳洲、帛琉、智利、馬來西亞、墨西哥、紐西蘭、秘魯、新加坡及越南等多國間協商的多國自由貿易協定。

The Trans-Pacific Partnership, also known as TPP, is a free trade agreement under negotiation by the United States, Canada, Japan, Australia, Brunei, Chile, Malaysia, Mexico, New Zealand, Peru, Singapore, and Vietnam.

B 背景知識大突破 Background

TPP 的目標是提高成員國間的貿易及投資量，並鼓勵創新和經濟發展。TPP 談成後成員國將佔世界經濟生產總值的 40%，同上囊括約世界總出口量的 1/3。臺灣和南韓都已公開表達參加 TPP 的意願，另外菲律賓、寮國、哥倫比亞、哥斯大黎加、印尼、柬埔寨、孟加拉和印度都是可能參與 TPP 的國家。

The goal of TPP is to enhance trade and investment among its members, and to encourage innovation, economic growth and

* trans-pacific　跨太平洋；越太平洋線
* enhance　提高、增加
* innovation　改革、創新

development. It will cover about 40% of world GDP and nearly one third of world exports. Both Taiwan and South Korea had announced interest in joining it, and countries including the Philippines, Laos, Colombia, Costa Rica, Indonesia, Cambodia, Bangladesh and India had also been mentioned as possible candidates.

Method 使用方法一把罩

TPP 的前身是 2005 年的跨太平洋戰略經濟夥伴協定 (Trans-Pacific Strategic Economic Partnership Agreement，簡稱 TPSEP 或 P4)，當時的成員只有帛琉、智利、紐西蘭、新加坡等四國；也因為這個名稱，在早期 TPP 也稱為 TPPA。當時的新聞曾表示：

The Obama Administration has begun talks with the Asian and Latin American nations to enter into the Trans-Pacific Strategic and Economic Partnership Agreement (TPPA).

(歐巴馬政府開始與亞洲和拉丁美洲國家為加入 TPPA 進行對話。)

---

* candidate 候選人、可能參加者

A 主題文章 Article

The White House is pushing Congress to give it the trade promotion authority, or "fast track" authority, which would make it easier for Obama to negotiate trade agreements with other countries. If Congress grants the president the trade promotion authority, it would give the administration more leverage with trading partners in its negotiations.

The White House is pushing for fast track authority because Obama seeks to complete trade agreements with European Union, known as the Transatlantic Trade and Investment Partnership, or TTIP, and a group of Pacific countries as part of the Trans-Pacific Partnership, or TPP.

The authority is putting time limits on congressional consideration, and it is trying its best to prevent the trade promotion authority from being amended by congress. Getting the trade promotion authority passed would be a major victory for the administration.

However, Americans in general do not favor the idea to give the President the fast track authority. Americans used to like the idea of free-trade agreements, but they are cooling to the idea now. Many Americans believe now that multinational agreements which bring down trade barriers will only favor large multinational corporations over the interests of small businesses. In additional, many Americans also believe free-trade agreements will take away their job opportunities.

There are public surveys released recently, by both Democratic and Republican pollster. The result shows that in the past ten years, there is a growing concern about an opposition to free-trade agreement in the country overall. The White House is likely to face a headwind as they try to push for the fast track. So far,

over 550 labor, environmental, and community groups have signed a letter in opposition to the fast track bill.

TPP would be history's largest single multinational free trade agreement that could significantly transform the US economy. But with mid-term elections in the United States in November 2014, talks about TPP are likely to be on hold until the end of the year.

白宮目前正在推動「貿易促進授權法」，以加速與其他國家進行貿易協定談判的速度。如果國會決定授予總統這種貿易促進權，將使美國和其貿易夥伴的談判更具效率。

白宮正積極推動這項「貿易促進授權法」，因為歐巴馬正試圖與歐盟及太平洋國家進行奧義協定談判，以完成跨大西洋貿易投資夥伴關係 (TTIP) 和跨太平洋夥伴協定 (TPP)。

行政部門希望國會儘量縮短審議時間，並盡力防止貿易促進授權法受到國會修訂。如果在國會順利通過貿易促進授權法，將會是歐巴馬的一大勝利。

然而，美國大眾並不傾向將這個權限授權給總統。過去自由貿易協定的想法較受到美國人的歡迎，但現在他們卻逐漸轉為冷淡。許多美國人認為，消除貿易壁壘只對大型企業有利，會影響小企業的生機，並奪走美國人的就業機會。

最近發布的民調結果中，無論是民主黨和共和黨的民調，都顯示民眾對自由貿易協定感到疑慮。白宮在這項法案的推動上可能會遭遇逆勢。目前已有超過 550 個勞工、環境和社區團體，聯署反對貿易促進授權法的推行。

TPP 簽訂後將成為歷史上最大的單一跨國自由貿易協定，可以顯著改變美國經濟。但隨著美國在 2014 年 11 月的期中選舉在即，有關 TPP 的討論在今年年底前都可能遭到擱置。

Unit 19

TTIP
跨大西洋貿易投資夥伴關係

代表意義超理解

跨大西洋貿易投資夥伴關係 (TTIP) 又被稱為跨大西洋自由貿易區 (TAFTA)，是美國和歐盟之間的自由貿易協定。

The Transatlantic Trade and Investment Partnership (TTIP) is also known as the Transatlantic Free Trade Area (TAFTA) is a free trade agreement between the United States and the European Union.

背景知識大突破 Background

TTIP 是美國和歐盟之間的自由貿易協定。美國和歐盟自 2013 年起開始談判，預定在 2014 年底完成協議。美國和歐盟加總後共占全球生產總值的 60%，貨品貿易的 33%，及服務貿易的 42%。加拿大、墨西哥、冰島、挪威、和瑞士都是未來可能的成員國。

The Transatlantic Trade and Investment partnership is a free-trade agreement between the European Union and the United States. The talk began in 2013, and it may be finalized by the end of 2014. The two together represent 60% of global GDP,

---

* transatlantic　橫跨大西洋的
* finalize　結束、完成

33% of world trade in goods and 42% of world trade in services. Canada, Mexico, Iceland, Norway, and Swiss are all its potential members.

Method 使用方法一把罩

歐盟的英文是 European Union，縮寫為 EU。歐盟的機構包括歐盟委員會 (European Commission)、歐盟理事會 (Council of the European Union)、歐洲理事會 (European Council)、歐洲議會 (European Parliament)、歐洲央行 (European Central Bank) 等。歐盟共有 28 個成員國，其中 18 個國家已經採納歐元為 (euro) 流通貨幣。

美國和歐盟之間高規格的「跨大西洋貿易及投資夥伴協定 (TTIP)」自 2013 年啟動談判，目前仍沒有突破性的進展。中國外交部則在日前表示，中國和歐盟應該展開中歐 FTA 可行性的研究。中國是歐盟的的第二大貿易夥伴，英國在去年就曾表態支持中歐 FTA，而法國等國家則擔心來自中國的廉價貨品競爭。無論 TTIP 和中歐 FTA 進展如何，歐盟都將是中美雙方經濟競爭的一大戰場。

A 主題文章 Article

European expert claims that the transatlantic Trade and Investment Partnership (TTIP) proposed between the United States and the European Union is likely to change the global trade rules and regulations.

The idea is, the combined economy scale of TTIP is so large that it will have an overwhelming standard-setting power for other countries. The two together represent 60% of global GDP, 33% of world trade in goods and 42% of world trade in services, and these number may still increase as Canada, Mexico, Iceland, Norway, and Swiss are all its potential members. Once TTIP is signed, even major competitor like China would almost certainly comply with whatever trade rules and regulations the West offered to the world.

TTIP aims to remove trade barriers in a wide range of economic sectors to make it easier to buy and sell goods and services between US and EU. The agreement is expected to increase the size of US economy by 128 billion US dollars (about 0.4% of its GDP) and the EU by 162 billion US dollars (about 0.5 of its GDP) permanently.

Many believe the negotiation between US and EU would be relatively simple, as economic barriers between the two are relatively low. However, as negotiations progress, civil society groups on both sides of the Atlantic are increasingly feeling uneasy, concerning on environmental protection, health and safety standards and consumer rights.

Many worried that by removing barriers to trade such as food regulations and chemical regulation, the EU will be accepting US standards which in many cases are lower than its own. Meanwhile, TTIP could open the gate for multinationals to sue

EU member states if new environmental or health legislation is introduced. Once TTIP is signed, Europe is likely to lose its position as a global frontrunner on public policies, including nature protection and food quality.

歐洲專家表示，美國和歐盟之間的跨大西洋貿易和投資夥伴 (TTIP) 可能會改變全球貿易的規則和條件。

他的主張是，TTIP 龐大的綜合經濟規模，將對世界造成壓倒性的標準制定權。洽談 TTIP 的雙方規模加總起來，將佔全球生產總值的 60%，世界貨品貿易的 33%，和世界服務貿易的 42%；而這些數字還可能持續增加，因為加拿大、墨西哥、冰島、挪威和瑞士的都是 TTIP 的潛在會員。一旦雙方簽訂 TTIP，就算是中國這樣的強力競爭對手，也必須在貿易中遵從歐美雙方提供的規範和法則。

TTIP 的宗旨在於消除各種形式的貿易壁壘，使歐美雙方能更容易的進行貨品和服務貿易。TTIP 預計將永久性的為美國增加 1280 億美元的產值 (約佔美國國內生產總值的 0.4%)，並為歐盟增加 1620 億美元的產值 (約為歐盟生產總值的 0.5%)。

許多人認為，歐美之間的談判相對單純，因為兩者間的經濟壁壘相對較低。然而，隨著談判的進展，大西洋兩岸的民間團體對 TTIP 帶來的環保、健康、安全標準和消費者權益越來越感到不安。

他們擔心，若消除貿易障礙，歐盟將在食品法規、化學限制等標準上和美國同化，這在很多情況下，都代表著歐盟必須降低自己的標準。同時跨國公司也將可以新的環保衛生標準對歐盟成員國家提出訴訟。一旦 TTIP 簽訂後，歐洲很可能會失去其在公共政策，包括自然保護和食品質量等在全球的領先地位。

Unit 20

WTO
世界貿易組織

代表意義超理解

世界貿易組織是一個提倡自由貿易的團體。這是一個各國政府針對貿易協定進行談判的論壇。世貿組織也是執行貿易協定、解決貿易爭議的平台。成員國可以在 WTO 內解決相互之間的貿易問題，並對世界貿易進行監督及自由化。

The World Trade Organization is an organization for trade opening. It is a forum for governments to negotiate trade agreements. It is a place for them to settle trade disputes. It operates a system of trade rules. The WTO is a place where members try to sort out the trade problems they face with each other. It intends to supervise and liberalize international trade.

背景知識大突破 Background

世貿組織的前身是 1948 年開始的關稅暨貿易總協定。世貿組織管理成員國間的貿易行為，並為各種貿易協議提供框架。世貿組織共有 159 個成員國，組織內的重大決定則由所有成員國採共識決議。出席世貿組織的通常是一國的經貿首長或特派大使。

＊ supervise　監督、管理　　＊ liberalize　使自由化

The WTO's predecessor, the General Agreement on Tariffs and Trade (GATT), was commenced in 1948. The organization deals with regulation of trade between participating members, and provides a framework for negotiating and formalizing trade agreements. It has 159 member states, and all major decisions are made by the membership as a whole, either by ministers or by their ambassadors.

M使用方法一把罩 Method

WTO的前身是GATT，當時的GATT只是一個多邊國際協定，在國際法中並不具有獨立法人人格，WTO則明訂為是獨立的國際組織。GATT 1994本身是一個獨立的貿易協定，而WTO的貿易協定除包括GATT 1994外，還包括服務貿易總協定、知識產權協定、爭端解決規則與程序等不同協定。例如：

According to WTO's official website, the WTO's procedure for resolving trade quarrels under the Dispute Settlement Understanding is vital for enforcing the rules for ensuring that trade flows smoothly. There is a web page in WTO's website for each of the disputes brought to the WTO.

（根據WTO的官方說明顯示，WTO用來解決貿易糾紛的爭端解決機制是確保貿易流暢的重要機制；在WTO的官方網頁保留有成員國對WTO提出的每一件貿易爭端。）

＊commence　開始、著手　　＊ambassador　大使、使節

Russia had threatened to take the US to the World Trade Organization (WTO) over sanctions imposed in respond to the US's move in the recent Ukraine crisis. The Russian official at the WTO council in Geneva talked about the possibility of filing lawsuits against the United States over the sanctions against Russian banks. The economy minister of Russia, Alexei Ulyukaev, said that the Russians hope to use the mechanism of the WTO to keep their partners in check regarding this issue.

Both the United States and the European Union had imposed travel bans and financial sanctions against Russia since the annexation of Crimea earlier in March. The United States took a relatively more serious stance against Russia, as Washington included one Russian bank and a number of tycoons who hold stakes in several large companies in the sanction list.

According to the WTO website, Russia expressed its concern about the executive order with financial sanctions signed by the US President Barack Obama would potentially violate the WTO agreements. Russia urged other members of the WTO "not to be drawn to political motivations when it comes to trade." If Moscow goes ahead with the said decision to fill the lawsuits, it would be the first formal challenge to trade sanctions in the World Trade Organization. Such act is believed to add to growing friction between Russia and other WTO members.

The United States government said that it anticipates more Ukraine-related sanctions on Russia, but suggested no action was likely before a diplomatic meeting in Geneva.

針對美國在烏克蘭危機中對俄羅斯所進行的制裁，俄羅斯揚言將在世界貿易組織中對美國提出貿易訴訟。俄羅斯官員最近在日內瓦的世界貿易組織理事會談及對美國制裁俄國銀行的行為提出貿易訴訟的可能性。俄羅斯經濟部長烏柳卡耶夫表示，俄國希望透過世界貿易組織的機制來牽制貿易夥伴。

由於俄羅斯在三月時兼併克里米亞，美國和歐盟都對俄羅斯進行金融制裁。美國對俄羅斯的立場較為強硬，華盛頓方面將一家俄國銀行和數名俄國富豪列入制裁名單。

根據世界貿易組織網頁的資訊，俄羅斯認為美國總統歐巴馬所發布的制裁命令可能違反世貿組織的相關規定。俄羅斯也敦促世貿組織的其他成員「在商言商，不要被其他政治動機所影響」。如果俄羅斯真的完成訴訟的程序，這將是世界貿易組織第一次挑戰制裁命令。一般認為，俄羅斯的行為將加大其和其他世貿組織成員間的摩擦。

美國政府則預期將對俄羅斯進行更多制裁行動，但也建議在日內瓦舉行外交會談前，不要有所行動。

PART 3

anagement, securities investent, information processing,
vil engineering, asset manage-
ent, etc. Their monthly salary
ill be set at NT$31,000.

There will also be 209 new
fice clerks to be recruited this
ear, with their starting salary
et at NT$24,000 per month. The
rgest number of new
mployees, at 459, will be mail
arriers, with their starting pay
lso set at NT$24,000 per month,
lus an extra driving or delivery
llowance of NT$5,732.

Based on the average employ-
nent rate of 2% to 6%, the
xpected number of applicants to
ake the examination is around
8,000, the spokesman ...

For furth...

Inter-party consultations t...

The China Post news staff

The Kuomintang-controlled Legislative Yuan completed the first reading of an amendment to its own procedural bylaw yesterday, promising to make all closed-door inter-party consultations public record. Known popularly as "black box" operations, the inter-party consultations held behind closed doors may last as long as four months.

"The horse trading ...

Moreover, the records will be published in the Legislative Yuan bulletin, together with the conclusions reached, Ting said.

Should there be discrepancies between the published conclusions and the results of action on bills, full explanations will be able to be discovered in the record, the Kuomintang legislator said. "We want the secret horse trading exposed under bright sunshine," Ting stressed.

Lawmakers have to complete the second and third readings before the legislature adjourns for the summer. "There won't be difficulty," another Kuomintang legislator said. The ...

Kuomintang con...
majority in the ...
Yuan.

In addition, A...
cedural bylaw ...
The inter-party ...
can go on for fo...
to that article, sh...
in one month.

Democratic P...
islators ...
Kuomintang-pro...
as "going a little ...

"All of us ar...
party consulta...
improved, but a...
be seriously do...
ment were ...

NSC dismisses Ma death in war scenario

The China Post news staff

Taiwan's top security body yesterday dismissed a report that the military's upcoming war chess would drill a scenario where President-elect Ma Ying-jeou was assassinated. The National Security Council (NSC) described the Next Magazine report as unfounded, irresponsible and with a political agenda.

Next claimed that the war chess, to be conducted later this month, would assume that Ma's assassination would plunge the nation into chaos and trigger a surprise invasion by China. The drill was meant to see how different government and security bodies could cope with such a situation, and how Taiwan would interact with the United States, the tabloid magazine cited unnamed presidential sources as saying.

It would be a test to see whether U.S. intervention should be sought or whether other solutions would be possible, and whether a state of emergency should be declared, the report said.

Ma's spokesman Lo Chih-chiang declined to comment on the report, saying the Presidential Office owed the public an explanation. President Chen Shui-bian had invited Ma to the war chess, which is part of the NSC's annual drill, but the president-elect declined the invitation.

The opposition camp called for the drill to be postponed until Ma is inaugurated, but the NSC insisted on conducting it as scheduled. The NSC said yesterday that the drill, to be conducted in three stages between April 21 and 27, is a test of government bodies' responses to military crises and of the nation's defense facilities.

But Kuomintang legislators have repeated the opposition camp's call for the drill be postponed, so as to let Ma oversee it. KMT Legislator Lin Yu-fang said it is "very ridiculous and impolite" for an outgoing president to conduct a drill on the mock assassination of his successor. "The Chen administration has designed such a drill apparently to vent its anger over its loss in the presidential election," claimed Lin.

KMT Legislator Chang Hsien-yao said such a drill has already raised concern in the United States and Taiwan's neighbors.

More ...
Parkin...

TAIPEI, CNA

An internati...
ject has ...
Parkinson's-rel...
that only devel...
Those who car...
twice more ...
Parkinson's dis...

The mutatio...
is found in g...
codes for p...
repeat kinase ...
paper produce...
partially funde...
National Scien...
lished in the sc...
of Neurology.

Parkinson's ...
as Parkinson s...
erative disord...
nervous system...
the patient's ...
ment.

A group of e...
Singapore, Jap...
States have alr...
Parkinson's-rela...
linked to LRRK2...
relations betw...
groups and ir...
For example, th...
LRRK2-G2019S...
of Parkinson's ...
and Ashkenazi ...

In 2004, the ...
a mutation, G2...
linked to Park...
especially Han ...

Fugitive ex-Hsinchu Council speaker returns

TAIPEI, CNA

Former Hsinchu County Council Speaker Huang Huan-chi returned to Taiwan and was taken into custody Tuesday after fleeing to China two years ago, following his sentencing to eight years in prison on corruption charges, judicial sources said yesterday.

Following unsuccessful kidney transplant surgery in China, Huang recently informed Hsinchu County police that he would be returning to the Taiwan. Shortly after Huang's plane landed in Taiwan, he was escorted away by police, who later turned him over to the Hsinchu District Prosecutors Office.

Huang served two terms as Hsinchu County Council speaker before running in the legislative elections in December 2001 as a candidate of the Taiwan Solidarity Union. He ended up losing the election. In that race, Huang was accused of vote-buying violations for allegedly using the county council's budget to purchase tea and moon cakes for voters. He was later released on bail.

Two years ago, after being convicted on corruption charges related to an incinerator scandal in the county, Huang decided to flee to China to avoid serving his prison sentence. He was then placed on the Hsinchu District Prosecutors Office's wanted list.

民生篇

People's Livelihood

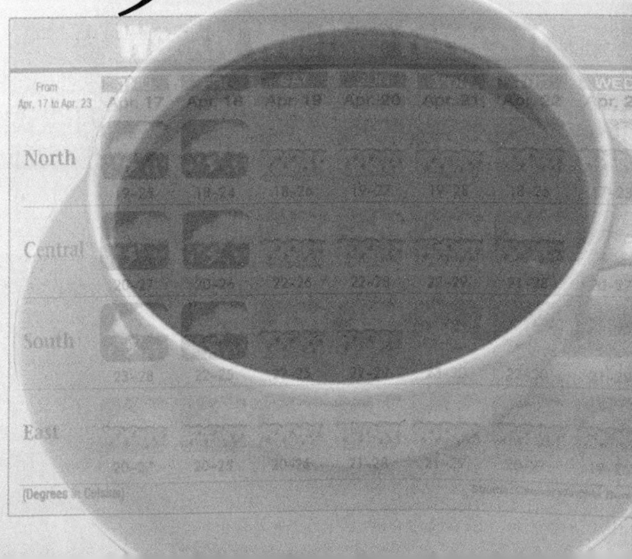

Unit 1

Argument on Freedom of Speech
言論自由爭議

代表意義超理解

在 21 世紀中，和宗教相關的不敬言論已成為聯合國中討論言論自由的問題。許多聯合國的成員國認為，言論自由不應延伸成對其他宗教侮辱行為的保護。

In the early 21st century, blasphemy related issues had become a freedom of speech problem for members of the United Nations. These states argue that the freedom of speech should not be extended to protect insults to other religions.

B 背景知識大突破 Background

聯合國大會通過多項決議，呼籲全世界對宗教毀謗行為採取行動。伊斯蘭領袖認為，各種反伊斯蘭教的言論，應該被視為仇恨言論而在世界各地受到禁止。

The General Assembly of the United Nations passed several resolutions which called upon the world to take action against the defamation of religions. Islamic leaders also consider anti-Islamic materials as hate speeches that should be banned around

---

* blasphemy　褻瀆神明的言論或行為
* argue　堅決主張；表明
* insult　侮辱
* defamation　誹謗、中傷

the world.

M 使用方法一把罩 Method

言論自由雖然已漸成為普世價值，但仍有其界線。一般來說，言論自由的界線有包括「傷害原則」（harm principle）和「犯罪原則」（offense principle），例如歧視性的仇恨性言論（hate speech）即有可能遭到法律制裁。

世界人權宣言 (Universal Declaration of Human Rights, UDHR) 第 19 條明定保障言論自由的權利：

Everyone has the right to freedom of opinion and expression; this right includes freedom to hold opinions without interference and to seek, receive and impart information and ideas through any media and regardless of frontiers.

（所有人有權享有主張和表達意見的自由；此權利包括保持主張不受干涉的自由，以及透過各種媒體，不受國界影響以尋求、接受、及傳遞資訊和思想的自由。）

A 主題文章 Article

In the annual United Nation General Assembly meeting, which is intended to celebrate the world's common values, Muslims and the West had been divided by perspectives on freedom of expression. Muslim leaders argued that the West was hiding behind the freedom of speech and ignored cultural differences

* offense 冒犯；攻擊

and sensitivities after in the aftermath of anti-Islam slurs.

In many Islamic countries, the online video "the Innocence of Muslims" had evoked protests, or even attacks, against U.S. and other Western embassies. Terrorists and jihadist groups had also launched several bombings attacks since the video was posted on internet. The crisis had been deepened when a French magazine insisted to publish comics that mock the prophet Muhammad.

Leaders and delegates of major Muslim nations had arrived at the United Nations, preparing to demand international curbs on speech or media that defame their religion or the prophet Muhammad.

The demand is coming from major Muslim nations' leaders, including Turkish Prime Minister Recep Tayyip Erdogan, Egyptian President Mohamed Morsi and Iranian President Mahmoud Ahmadinejad. The Organization of Islamic Cooperation and other leading Islamic groups also demanded for limits on anti-Muslim expression.

These Islamic leaders consider anti-Islamic materials as hate speeches that should be banned around the world. Prime Minister Erdogan of Turkey, whom President Obama views as a key ally in the Middle East, has declared that all 57 Islamic nations should speak forcefully with one voice to demand an international legal regulations against attacks on what people deem sacred.

The demand posted an unexpected challenge for President Obama in the United Nations. Although Western leaders claimed they wouldn't give ground on free speech, President Obama needs to be careful in condemning the anti-Muslim video at the same time not to sound an apologetic note, as Obama still has a presidential race to run. The least thing Obama needs now is to draw political fire from his adversary.

Foreign affair experts say even if the demand does not pass, a battle at the United Nation means a serious setback for U.S. policies on several levels.

在原為推廣普世價值而舉辦的聯合國大會中，穆斯林和西方國家卻因對言論自由的看法產生嚴重分歧。穆斯林領袖認為西方國家以言論自由為藉口，罔顧文化差異與敏感性，對伊斯蘭教進行毀謗。

網路影片「穆斯林的無知」引發了許多伊斯蘭國家的民眾到美國及西方國家的大使館進行示威反對，甚至造成衝突。在網路影片公布後，恐怖分子及聖戰組織成員已策劃多起爆炸攻擊。而在法國雜誌刊登諷刺先知穆罕默德的插畫後，此危機愈行惡化。

來自穆斯林國家的領袖及貴賓預備在聯合國大會中提案，要求各國節制反伊斯蘭教及其先知穆罕默德的言論。

包括土耳其總理艾爾段、埃及總統穆希、伊朗總統艾瑪丹加在內，回教國家領袖口徑一致提出上述要求。伊斯蘭合作組織及其他領袖級的伊斯蘭組織也要求各國限制反穆斯林的言論。

伊斯蘭領袖認為，反伊斯蘭的言論應被視為仇恨言論而加以制止。被視為是歐巴馬總統在中東關鍵盟友的土耳其總理艾爾段，公開表示全球 57 個伊斯蘭國家應一致要求國際立法，對攻擊宗教的言論加以管制。

這對歐巴馬總統來說是一個意外的挑戰。雖然西方國家已表態絕不放棄言論自由，但歐巴馬仍需格外小心，因為他在譴責反伊斯蘭影片時，不能顯得是在向回教徒低頭致歉。由於歐巴馬正在進行總統選戰，他必須避免任何讓對手藉題發揮的機會。

外交事務專家則表示，就算穆斯林的要求被否決，在聯合國大會中發生這樣的爭議，仍然是美國政策的一大挫折。

Unit 2

Blasphemy
瀆神

代表意義超理解

　　瀆神指的是對神、對宗教上的人事物、或對某種神聖物品的進行褻瀆、侮辱的行為。某些國家在法律上定有對宗教褻瀆的懲罰，而在部分國家的法律中，則允許被污辱的人或團體對褻瀆者進行報復。

Blasphemy is an act of insulting or showing disrespect to God, religious people or things, or something considered sacred or inviolable. Some countries have laws to punish religious blasphemy, while others have laws that allow those who are offended by blasphemy to punish blasphemers.

背景知識大突破
Background

　　在某些國家中，對國教的褻瀆與不敬被歸為刑事法。雖然許多人認為外國人應尊重這些國家的文化及法律，但這些法令也可能被濫用以掩護恐怖主義，或對非國教的信徒進行虐待及謀殺。

In some countries, state religion blasphemy is outlawed under the criminal code. Although some argue these foreigners should

＊disrespect　不尊重、無禮
＊sacred　神聖的；受尊敬的
＊inviolable　不可侵犯的
＊outlaw　宣布……不合法

respect these laws and the culture, such laws may be used to justify and sanction the terrorism, abuse and murder of non-members of the state religion.

M 使用方法一把罩 Method

世界三大宗教為佛教、基督教及伊斯蘭教。其中佛教有大乘 (Mahayana) 及小乘 (Hinayana) 兩大派別。基督教主要可分為三大派別，分別是天主教 (Catholicism)、東正教 (Eastern Orthodoxy）、新教 (Protestantism)，以及其他眾多規模較小的派別。而在中文語彙當中，「基督教」一詞則常被用來專指前面所提到的「新教」，這是僅有出現在中文的特殊情況，因此有些人會改以「基督宗教」來稱整個基督教。伊斯蘭教也有兩大派別，分別是遜尼派 (Sunni) 和什葉派 (Shiah)。而目前在法律上訂有瀆神法規的國家則大多數為伊斯蘭教（回教）國家。

A 主題文章 Article

The blasphemy laws in Pakistan, which carried death penalty and life imprisonment, was primarily created to govern religious insults against Islam, but not other minority faiths. However, recent events show an intriguing twist, as the blasphemy laws may be used to punish Muslims suspected of attacking a Hindu temple and its monk.

＊sanction 制裁、處罰　　＊abuse 虐待

Police officers in Pakistan reported anti-Hindu attacks took place on 21 September, 2012. The whole Islamic world marched several protests against the anti-Islam film "The Innocence of Muslims" made in the U.S. The government of Pakistan had tried to avoid violent protests, declaring September 21 a national holiday and called for peaceful demonstrations However, the rallies still took violent turns, and more than twenty people were killed during demonstrations.

Groups of Muslims attack a Hindu neighborhood. The mobs marched into a temple, broke religious statues, tore up a copy of a Hindu scripture, and beat up the temple's monk. The attackers robbed the monk's family, stealing away his jewelry, and took away golden ornaments from the temple, which are used for religious decoration.

The monk and other Hindu leaders turned to the police for help, and the police department opened a case against nine Muslims, including a member of clergy. However, none of the suspects had been found yet. Police officials said the case against these mobs was registered under the blasphemy laws, and the section of the law can apply to any religion, carrying a fine, or imprisonment up to 10 years.

Human rights activist group in Pakistan said the blasphemy laws are very vague, often used by people who are trying to bring false charges against rivals or particular minority religions. Although Muslims are also accused of insulting the Koran, the Muslim holy book, or Muhammad, the prophet, minorities in Pakistan are still disproportionately accused of blasphemy.

The blasphemy laws had drawn attentions from the world this year after a young Christian girl was accused desecrating the Quran (Koran). The girl had been released on bail later, and a Muslim cleric is accused of fabricating evidence against her.

巴基斯坦法條中，瀆神罪原先是為管理對回教不敬的行為而設，而非為其他宗教所設，其刑罰最重可處死刑及終身監禁。但最近情況產生有趣的轉變，因為涉嫌攻擊印度教神廟及僧侶的回教徒將可能面對瀆神罪的指控。

據巴基斯坦警方表示，該起反印度教的行為發生在 2012 年 9 月 21 日。當時整個回教世界發動數起示威遊行，抗議在美國拍攝的反伊斯蘭電影「穆斯林的無知」。為避免暴力衝突，巴基斯坦政府將 9 月 21 日設為國定假日，並呼籲和平示威。但遊行中仍然發生暴力行為，造成超過 20 人在示威活動中喪生。

穆斯林群眾襲擊印度教的社區，闖進神廟中砸毀神像、撕扯經文、並毆打神寺中的僧侶。暴徒並搶劫僧侶的親屬，奪取僧侶的首飾及神廟中裝飾用的金器。

事後神廟中的僧侶及其他印度教領袖向警方求助。警方列案將九名穆斯林列為嫌犯，其中包括一名神職人員，但警方目前仍未找到任何嫌犯。警方表示，該案件被歸列在瀆神罪中，瀆神罪對任何宗教都有效；違法者可處罰款，或十年以下的徒刑。

巴基斯坦的人權組織表示，瀆神罪是相當模糊的法律，常被人用來進行誣告或打擊少數宗教。雖然也有穆斯林被控褻瀆回教聖典可蘭經及先知穆罕默德，但弱勢宗教仍不合比例的被控瀆神。

在一名基督教女孩被控褻瀆可蘭經後，瀆神罪即成為世界新聞焦點。該名女孩目前已交保出獄，而一名穆斯林神職人員則被控在案中作偽證。

Unit 3

Bird Flu
禽流感

代表意義超理解

禽流感是各種不同種類的流感病毒感染在禽鳥類動物時的總稱。在大部分的案例中，人類會因為處理死禽或與受感染的液體接觸而遭到感染。

Bird flu refers to an illness caused by any of many different strains of influenza viruses that have adapted to birds. Most human contractions of the avian flu are a result of either handling dead infected birds or from contact with infected fluids.

B 背景知識大突破 Background

在飼育寵物類禽鳥的過程中幾乎不會感染流感病毒，自 2003 年以來也並未出現這樣的案例。但在 2013 年多起感染 H7N9 型禽流感事件後，中國大陸官方已在過年前禁止販售活禽，以避免民眾在過年期間遭到感染。

Companion birds in captivity and parrots are highly unlikely to contract the virus, and there has been no report of a companion

＊influenza　流行性感冒
＊contraction（疾病的）感染；（惡習的）沾染
＊fluid　液體
＊companion　伴侶

bird with avian influenza since 2003. Nevertheless, in 2013, authorities in China had banned live poultry sales before the Chinese New Year, after an increase in number of people infected with the H7N9 strain of bird flu, as the busy travel period may help spreading the infection.

Method 使用方法一把罩

Bird flu 也叫做 avian flu，avian 一樣是禽鳥類的意思。flu 是 influenza 流行性感冒的簡稱，流感病毒則稱為 influenza virus。若在 influenza 前面加上名詞，則代表在某種動物間傳染的流感，例如 bird flu、swine flu、human flu 等。不同的病毒則有不同的代號，禽流感部分，目前較著名的有 H5N1 和 H7N9 等。

2009 年爆發的流行感冒即是一種原為豬流感 (swine influenza) 病毒的 H1N1 病毒的變種。和禽流感不同，這種變異型的豬流感病毒會在人畜間相互傳染。世界衛生組織的資料顯示，當時全世界每 5 人就有 1 人感染 H1N1 新型流感；光是在美國就有 5,900 萬美國人染病，並造成 26.5 萬人住院，1.2 萬人死亡。2010 年 8 月，世界衛生組織宣布 H1N1A 型流感大流行已經結束。

---

* poultry　家禽

A deadly new mutant bird strain called H10N8 has so far infested two people. More importantly, China warns that the bird flu has jumped from birds to humans. In the cases that people are infested by this new strain, one patient is dead, and the other is still critically ill in hospital.

The fact that the virus jumped from birds to human brought great concern to researchers. Although the dead patient has been to a live poultry market, but no virus were found. The source of the infection remains unknown. Chinese researchers also said that the new virus can survive in low temperatures, therefore the government must increase the monitoring of poultry farms.

Chinese researchers warn the people that they should always be worried when viruses cross the species barrier, from animals or birds to human, because they don't know if the immunity will protect us from new virus.

China is not the only place where bird flu infected people. Another new and fetal strain of bird flu, H7N9, has infected at least 250 people in China, Taiwan and Hong Kong, killing around 60 of them. A dangerous new strain of bird flu, identified as H5N8, has also spread nationwide in South Korea. South Korea authorities have culled 2.8 million domestic chickens and ducks since the outbreak began. The good news is, there are no reports of human infections yet.

So far, South Korea authorities believe the new virus are likely to have been introduced to Korea by migratory birds. However, some researchers argue that sick birds are not able to fly thousands of miles. Other researchers support the authorities, claiming that migratory birds may carry a mild version of the virus to Korea, where it quickly spread and developed into a

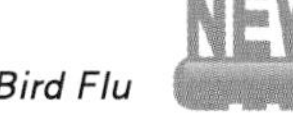

much more dangerous form.

一種新型的致命禽流感病毒 H10N8 目前已造成兩人感染。更重要的是，中國大陸警告各界，禽流感的感染已經從禽鳥類擴及到人類。在目前的兩個病例中，一人已經死亡，另一人病危仍在醫院中接受治療。

禽流感病毒從禽鳥類感染至人類的疫情引發各界關注。研究人員表示，雖然死者生前曾前往家禽市場，但在市場中並沒有發現同樣的病毒，目前仍無法判定感染來源。大陸研究人員並表示，新病毒可以在低溫下生存，因此政府必須提高對養殖場的監測。

中國大陸的研究人員並提出警告：他們表示，當病毒發生跨物種感染時，人們應該更加小心，因為目前仍不知道人體是否對這種病毒具有免疫力。

中國大陸不是唯一感染禽流感的地方。另一種新的禽流感，H7N9，已在中國大陸、臺灣和香港對至少 250 人造成感染，造成約 60 人死亡。另一種新的病毒株，H5N8，則在韓國蔓延，韓國當局已撲殺 280 萬隻國內的雞鴨類家禽。好消息則是，目前仍沒有人感染這一類的禽流感。

到目前為止，韓國當局認為，新病毒可能是經由候鳥進入韓國。但也有學者認為，生病的候鳥無法進行長途飛行。但也有學者支持政府的看法，他們表示，候鳥可能攜帶著較為溫和的病毒進入韓國，透過大量感染，演化為更危險的病毒。

Unit 4

Boston Marathon Bombing
波士頓馬拉松爆炸案

代表意義超理解

波士頓馬拉松爆炸案是一件發生於 2013 年 4 月 15 日的炸彈攻擊事件，這次炸彈攻擊造成 3 人死亡，264 人輕重傷，是 911 事件後美國最嚴重的爆炸案。

Boston Marathon bombing is a bomb attack happened on April 15, 2013, and the attack killed 3 people, injured 264 others. It's the most seriously bombing attack in the United States after the event of 911.

B 背景知識大突破 Background

聯邦調查局在案發後接手調查，並將車臣裔的兩兄弟列為嫌犯。嫌犯在調查過程中槍殺一名警察，並與警方發生槍戰，一名嫌犯在槍戰中被擊斃。另一名嫌犯逃脫現場後，於 4 月 19 日遭到警方逮捕。嫌犯聲稱這次攻擊是要報復美國對伊拉克和阿富汗的襲擊。

FBI took over the investigation, and the suspects were identified as two Chechen brothers. The suspects killed a police officer, and later exchange gunfire with the police. One of the suspects

---

＊attack　攻擊
＊injure　傷害；受傷
＊investigation　調查

was shot and killed by police. The other suspect escaped, and eventually was arrested on April 19. The suspect claimed that they launched the attack to revenge the United States' attacks on Iraq and Afghanistan.

Method 使用方法一把罩

炸彈攻擊一般稱為 bombing 或 bomb attack，和恐怖攻擊 terrorism attack 的分別在於，恐怖攻擊是由恐怖組織所策劃的攻擊行為，其手段不侷限於炸彈攻擊，可能包括毒氣、化學武器、綁票等各種手段；而任何持有炸彈的人都能發動炸彈攻擊，例如上述車臣裔的嫌犯就不屬於任何恐怖組織。

例句：

In June 2014, a massive truck bomb claimed by rebels killed at least 35 people in Syrian.

（2014 年 6 月，敘利亞叛軍發動的卡車炸彈攻擊造成至少 35 人死亡。）

At least one civilian was killed as a car bomb went off in the western part of Afghanistan capital.

（在阿富汗首都周邊則發生汽車炸彈事件，至少造成 1 名平民死亡。）

---

* launch　發動（戰爭等）
* revenge　報仇、報復

A主題文章 Article

Dzhokhar Tsarnaev, the man who launched the Boston Marathon bombing that killed three people and injured more than 260, is being trialed in Massachusetts. Dzhokhar Tsarnaev and his older brother Tamerlan, who was killed in a shootout with police, planned the bombing together. Tsarnaev currently faces thirty federal charges.

In Massachusetts, only one third of the citizens support the death penalty. Observers have claimed that the chance that Tsarnaev will be put to death is very slim. But a recent announcement may turn the tide. The Attorney General has authorized prosecutors to seek the death penalty for Tsarnaev. The prosecutors cited that Tsarnaev intend to kill and maim their victims, and he and his brother planned the attack and were guilty.

On the other hand, death penalty opponents argued that putting Tsarnaev to death will not bring back those who died, nor heal the wounds of those injured. They believe the death sentence is cruel and unusual, and disrespectful for life. They claim that it costs the society more to put Tsarnaev to death than to keep him alive in prison, and justice should not be about revenge.

There are also people who support the death penalty. They argue that punishment is not meant to undo a crime, and the fact that death penalty will not bring back the victims is not the point. To call the death sentences cruel and unusual is also out of the point. Cruel and unusual is what the killers did to the victims. Unlike the victims, the murder will die unconsciously under death penalty, and that is not cruel compared to what he has done to his victims.

Those people who support the death penalty believe the crime is a crime against society, against the state, and against humanity.

It is the state that has the right and responsibility to take action to punish the murderer. The death penalty should be rare. But in this case, it would not be cruel and unusual. It would be just and fair.

造成波士頓馬拉松爆炸案 3 人死亡，260 人輕重傷的兇手 Dzhokhar Tsarnaev 目前正在馬薩諸塞州接受審判。Dzhokhar Tsarnaev 和他遭到警方擊斃的哥哥 Tamerlanu 一起策劃了這場爆炸攻擊，而 Dzhokhar 目前面臨 30 項聯邦起訴。

在馬薩諸塞州，目前只有三分之一的公民支持死刑。觀察者認為，Tsarnaev 被判處死刑的機會微乎其微，但最近的新聞卻有不同的發展。馬薩諸塞州的總檢察長授權給檢察官，讓他們對犯人求處死刑。檢察官認為，Tsarnaev 兄弟意圖殘殺受害者而發動這次攻擊事件。

另一方面，反對死刑者卻認為，判處死刑並不能讓死者復活，也不能治癒受害者的創傷。他們認為，死刑殘忍而不尊重生命，且帶來更高的社會成本。他們強調，報復行為並不代表正義。

但也有人支持死刑。他們認為，懲罰並不能消彌一個人的罪行，死刑會對爆炸事件受害者產生什麼影響，也不是重點。兇殘的是兇手，而不是刑罰；與兇手對受害人所造成的傷害相比之下，死刑並不殘忍。

支持死刑的人強調，罪犯對社會、國家造成傷害，並危害全體人類。政府有權利和責任對兇手做出懲罰，這並不殘忍，反而是公平公正的行為。

Unit 5

Egg Shortage
雞蛋短缺

代表意義超理解

人類吃雞蛋已經有上千年的歷史，今天雞蛋仍是最重要的蛋白質來源之一。雞蛋便宜、方便取得、蛋白質豐富，因此成為許多發展中國家最重要的食物。但若因種種原因發生雞蛋短缺，則會帶來很嚴重的影響。

Chicken Eggs have been eaten by human for thousands of years, and they are still one of the most important protein sources today. Eggs become one of the primary foods in many developing countries, as they are cheap, easy-to-get, and protein rich. However, if eggs run short for various reasons, it will also bring critical impacts to the people.

背景知識大突破 Background

幾年前發生禽流感後，許多國家迅速以撲殺雞隻的方式避免病毒擴散。禽流感爆發後，有上億的雞遭到撲殺。這些行為的結果造成在許多發展中國家，雞蛋的價格迅速上升，使得一般家庭無法維持在日常飲食中供給雞蛋。

* protein　蛋白質
* primary　主要的、首要的
* critical　關鍵的

Since the break out of avian flu years ago, many countries had responded with lethal authority quickly to stop the virus from spreading. Hundreds of millions of chickens were slaughtered after the outbreak of avian flu. As the result, the price of eggs in developing countries had risen in many countries, making it difficult for regular families consumption.

M使用方法一把罩 Method

養雞生蛋是全世界共通的文化之一，雞蛋量產化則是全世界共通的產業。根據 2009 年的資料顯示，全世界大約有 64 億的雞隻在生產雞蛋，每年能產出超過六千萬噸的雞蛋。量產雞蛋用的機器產房英文稱為 battery cage，是能將母雞生蛋的過程全自動化的設備。這種設備日前因違反動物保護原則被歐盟禁用。

A主題文章 Article

Mexico has the highest-per-capita egg consumption rate in the world, about 22.4 kilograms (about 50 pounds) per person in 2011. In another word, everyone in Mexico consumes more than 400 eggs a year, according to Mexico's National Poultry Industry. However, at this moment, the public in Mexico faces an extreme shortage of eggs.

In Mexico City, the country's capital, there have been price

* lethal 致命的、致死的
* slaughter 屠殺
* consumption 消費；消耗

spikes and two-hour lines to buy eggs. Stores in the city are forced to limit how many boxes of eggs per day a customer can buy.

An outbreak of AH7N3 avian flu virus is partly to blame. The deadly bird flu was detected on poultry farms in the Pacific coast states. The Mexican government responded with lethal authority quickly, slaughtered 11 million chickens to prevent the avian flu from spreading. Within weeks of the outbreak, 90 million hens were vaccinated against the flu virus, and a second round of inoculation is now underway.

As the result, the price of eggs has doubled in Mexico, from less than 20 pesos to more than 40 pesos a kilogram. In another word, it has increased from 1.5 dollars to more than 3 dollars a kilogram. There is about 16 or so eggs in a kilogram.

President Felipe Calderon went on television to promise to bring egg prices down, and to punish speculators. The government had already suspended tariffs on egg imports in order to stabilize the market. Thousands of tons of U.S. eggs were imported to Mexico to help Mexico solving the crisis.

President Calderon also announced an emergency financing of 230 million dollars to restore the nation's egg production by replacing the chickens slaughtered months earlier after the bird flu outbreak. The government accounted that 3 million hens were sent out to the farms to replace the slaughtered ones. The government's Office of the Consumer also began a public health campaign called "You Can Choose to Eat Healthy" that offers egg-free breakfast menus.

Mexico's Association of Egg Vendors warns its members not to sell eggs at prices above 40 pesos; otherwise they may face fines by the government. However, many sellers still prefer to keep their eggs instead of selling them at a loss.

墨西哥是世界上每人平均雞蛋食用率最高的國家，根據 2001 年的資料，每人每年約食用 22.4 公斤（約 50 磅）的雞蛋。根據墨西哥國家禽畜業的資料顯示，每人每年吃下逾 400 顆的雞蛋。但此時此刻，墨西哥人正面臨極度的「蛋」荒。

在墨西哥的首都墨西哥市，蛋價屢創新高，而排隊買蛋的時間長達兩小時。商店必須對每人每天可買的雞蛋數量設限。

缺蛋的原因之一是因為當地爆發 AH7N3 禽流感。在太平洋沿岸的農場中被偵測到這致命的疾病。墨西哥政府反應迅速，撲滅一千一百萬雞隻以避免疫情擴大。在疫情爆發一週內，共有九千萬隻雞接種禽流感疫苗，而政府正準備施打第二波的疫苗。

但其結果就是墨西哥蛋價倍增，一公斤蛋的價格從 20 披索一路衝破 40 披索。換句話說，蛋價從每公斤 1.5 美元衝到 3 美元。一公斤約為 16 顆雞蛋。

墨西哥總統卡爾德龍在電視上承諾將降低雞蛋價格，並懲罰投機商人。墨西哥政府已取消雞蛋關稅，試圖藉此穩定雞蛋價格。政府也將進口數千噸的美國雞蛋來化解這次的雞蛋危機。

而卡爾德龍總統亦公布一筆 2 億 3 千萬的緊急預算，用以買進新的雞隻，恢復雞蛋產量。政府向各農場送出 3 百萬隻雞，以取代先前遭撲殺的雞群。政府的消費者辦公室則推廣一項名為「你可以吃得更健康」的活動，向民眾宣傳不含蛋的早餐菜單。

墨西哥的蛋業協會警告所屬成員，政府將對超過 40 披索的蛋價做出罰款。但許多業者寧可維持庫存，也不願低價賣出雞蛋。

Unit 6

China's Smog
霾害

代表意義超理解

霾害是空氣污染的一種，其來源是在城市中大量燃燒煤炭的結果。中國大陸的工業化帶來各種嚴重的環境問題，其中就包括非常嚴重的霾害。

Smog is a type of air pollution caused by the burning of large amounts of coal within a city. China's industrialization has brought in its train a host of collateral problems, one in specific is the smog problem.

B 背景知識大突破 Background

在 2013 年底，北京的空氣汙染超過世界衛生組織認定對人體有害的標準。根據美國駐北京大使館在 2014 年 1 月 12 日的監測紀錄，空氣汙染的指數則高於世界衛生組織標準近 35 倍。大陸呼吸道疾病專家指出，空氣汙染遠比 SARS 還要可怕，因為所有人都受到空氣汙染的影響。

In the end of 2013, Beijing's air pollution soared past levels considered hazardous by the World Health Organization. On

＊pollution　污染
＊collateral　間接的、附屬的
＊hazardous　有害的

January 12, 2014, the air-quality monitor operated by the U.S. embassy in Beijing recorded a number that is nearly 35 times what the World Health Organization considers safe. According to Chinese specialist in respiratory diseases, the pollution is more frightening than SARS, because no one can escape from the air pollution and indoor pollution.

Method 使用方法一把罩

煙霧、塵霾、廢氣等都稱為 smog，汽車的廢氣排放測驗則是 smog check。Smog 這個字本身是一個複合字，是由煙 (smoke) 和霧 (fog) 兩個字組合而來，以說明塵霾這種汙染。造成塵霾的因素很多，包括工廠燒炭排出的廢氣、汽機車排放的廢氣，甚至森林大火、火山活動等自然現象都可能造成塵霾。中國大陸近年來由於經濟快速發展，造成大量的塵霾，甚至影響到周邊區域。

世界衛生組織 (World Health Organization，WHO) 是聯合國屬下的專門機構，致力於提高全世界人民的健康；世界衛生組織的最高權力機構稱為世界衛生大會 (World Health Assembly, WHA)，每年召開一次大會審議世界衛生組織的報告。

＊ embassy　大使館

＊ respiratory　呼吸道的

A 主題文章 Article

China's smog problem has grown to a degree that aircraft pilots are forced to train for blind landing. The nation's airports are dealing with extreme air pollution, which lowers visibility and creates airline troubles.

Beijing Capital airport and Shanghai Pudong airport are two of the world's worst records for on-time flights, and one of the main reasons is the smog problem. Chinese officials are aiming to decrease flight delays in these two airports. Chinese authorities have mandated that pilots at domestic airlines who fly into the ten most congested airports be qualified to land when visibility falls below 400 meters. That means, pilots will need to land airplanes using the auto-landing instruments.

NASA Earth Observatory posted a satellite image in December 2013. China's smog problem has grown to a degree that people can see Chinese smog from space. Another report shows that there is nothing stopping China's smog from drifting back across the Pacific Ocean, and the smog has plagued Los Angeles.

China is well aware of its pollution problem. The smog problem not only affects transportation, but also brings negative impacts to public health. According to Chinese specialist, the pollution is more frightening than SARS. Chinese authorities plan to further limit new license plates in order to curb pollution and traffic.

Beijing's lottery for car license plates was instituted in 2011, and it was designed to control the number of vehicles on the road and to curb both the air pollution and traffic. In 2014, Beijing's municipal government plans to issue only 150,000 new license plates, down from 240,000 in 2013. Additional license plates may be available for electric cars or cars running on natural gas.

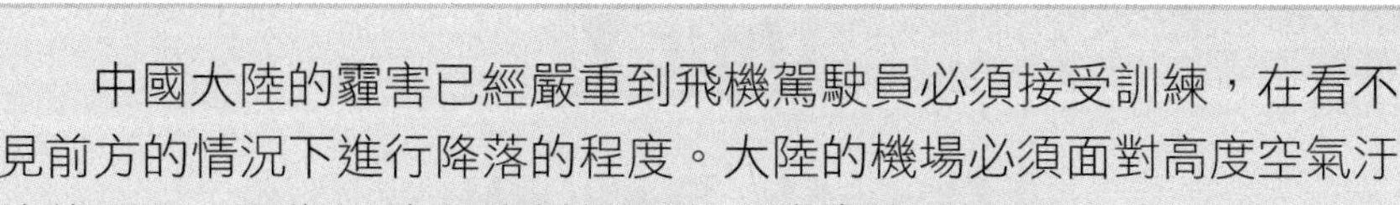

中國大陸的霾害已經嚴重到飛機駕駛員必須接受訓練，在看不見前方的情況下進行降落的程度。大陸的機場必須面對高度空氣汙染的問題，因為汙染已降低能見度，造成航班問題。

北京首都機場和上海浦東機場是世界上班機最常誤點的兩個機場之一，而其主要的原因就是霾害問題。大陸官員的目標是要降低這兩個機場的航班延誤率，日前大陸當局甚至要求飛入前十大擁塞機場的國內航班飛行員要取得能夠在能見度小於 400 公尺時降落的資格。這代表著，飛行員必須使用飛機上的自動降落儀器來進行降落。

美國太空總署在 2013 年 12 月公布太空觀察站照到的照片，大陸的霾害已經嚴重到從外太空可以看到煙霾的程度。另一份報告指出，沒有東西能阻止大陸霾害飛越太平洋，來自大陸的煙霾對洛杉磯造成困擾。

中國大陸也知道汙染的嚴重性，霾害不但影響交通，更對公共健康造成影響。大陸專家指出，空氣汙染遠比 SARS 還要危險。目前大陸當局正計畫限制新車牌的發放，以遏制污染和交通情形持續惡化。

北京自 2011 年開始施行以抽籤的方式限制新車牌的發放，藉以從車輛數量上遏制空氣汙染和交通惡化。在 2014 年，北京市政府僅計畫發行 150,000 個新車牌，比起 2013 年的 240,000 新車牌為少。但電動汽車或天然氣汽車則不在此限。

Unit 7

Death Penalty
死刑

代表意義超理解

在歷史上，大部分的文化都曾以死刑來處罰罪犯，或用以處罰在政治或宗教上持不同意見的反對者。以往被判死刑的人往往也會受到折磨，最後在公眾前處刑，以警告其他人不要犯同樣的罪。

Historical speaking, death penalty has been practiced by most cultures as a punishment for criminals, and political or religious dissidents. In the past, the execution was often accompanied by torture, and execution was performed in public to warn the people not to practice the same crimes.

B 背景知識大突破 Background

目前世界上有 58 個國家仍在執行死刑，105 個國家已廢除死刑，另有 35 個國家已有 10 年未曾執行死刑或已明文停止行刑。歐盟是世界上最努力提倡廢除死刑的政治集團之一。

There are 58 countries in the world actively practice Capital punishment, 105 countries have abolished death penalty, and 35 countries have not used it for at least ten years and/or under

---

* dissident　反對者；持不同意見的人
* execution　死刑、處死
* torture　折磨、拷問
* abolish　廢除、廢止

moratorium. The European Union is one of the largest political groups advocating for the abolition of death penalty.

M 使用方法一把罩 ethod

死刑除了 death penalty 這個詞外，又稱做 capital punishment，會被處以死刑的犯罪則稱為 capital crime，死刑的判決稱為 death sentence。任何形式的處死行為則稱為 execution。廢除死刑的運動則被稱做為 abolition of death penalty 或是 abolition of capital punishment。Abolition 是廢除的意思，例如歷史上的廢除黑奴運動，當時就稱為 abolition of slavery。

A 主題文章 rticle

In April, the European Union had expressed its disappointment over execution of five death row inmates in Taiwan through the European Economic and Trade Office in Taipei. The office spoke the European Union's stance against death penalty and again called for a moratorium on executions in Taiwan.

The European Union had consistently called for a universal abolition of capital punishment. The head of the European Economic and Trade office said that the death penalty "is inappropriate and may make irreversible mistakes due to misjudging." The officers also added that "The European Union

---

* moratorium （行動、活動等）的暫停、暫禁
* advocate 鼓吹、提倡

hopes to cooperate with every other nation to promote a more enlightened path."

Five inmates were put to death on April 29, who were found guilty of eleven murders. The government's stance is to keep the death penalty while reducing its frequency of use, citing the Ministry of Justice's efforts to review the law on the matter. There are still forty-seven death row inmates in Taiwan after the executions.

The last time Taiwan executed convicts was in April 2013, when six inmates were put to death. There are 22 countries around the world still practice capital punishment. Those who promote the abolishment of capital punishment argue that death penalty is no longer a majority phenomenon in the world.

On the other hand, those who support capital punishment argue that people do seek the return of death penalty in countries that no longer practice capital punishment. For example, death penalty is currently present in the Russian Criminal Code, but legislators introduced a moratorium on it in 1997. Russia signed the Convention on Human Rights and Freedoms in order to enter the Council of Europe.

The head of Russia's Investigative Committee has asked the Parliament members to consider the return of capital punishment earlier in May 2014.

"I am not suggesting to restore the actual death penalty, but I think that it must be present in our legislation as the hypothetical possibility of such an outcome can stop a potential criminal," said the Russian officer.

今年四月，歐盟透過臺北歐洲經貿辦事處針對臺灣執行五件死刑表達失望。辦事處重申歐盟反對死刑的立場，並再次呼籲臺灣停止死刑。

廢除死刑是歐盟的一貫立場。歐洲經貿辦事處負責人表示，死刑「不恰當，也可能造成無法挽回的錯誤」。這名官員補充說，「歐盟希望能和所有國家合作，邁向一條更開明的道路」。

這五名犯人在 4 月 29 日因 11 起謀殺案遭到處刑。法務部的立場是保留死刑，但減少行刑。臺灣目前仍有 47 名死刑犯。

臺灣上一次在 2013 年 4 月執行死刑，當時有六名犯人被處刑。目前世界上只有 22 個國家仍在執行死刑，因此部分主張廢除死刑的人認為，死刑已不再是世界的主流。

但支持死刑的人則強調，在世界上有些已停止執行死刑的國家，人們仍希望回復死刑。舉例來說，俄羅斯的刑法中雖然仍有死刑的規範，但國會已在 1997 年停止執行死刑。當時俄國為了進入歐洲委員會而簽署了人權自由公約。

但在 2014 年 5 月，俄國調查委員會的首長要求國會員考慮回復死刑的可能性。

“我並不是說一定要執行死刑，但我認為死刑必須出現在我們的法律中，以阻止潛在的犯罪可能”這名俄國檢察首長做出上述發言。

Unit 8

Detroit Bankruptcy
底特律破產

代表意義超理解

美國城市底特律於 2013 年 7 月 18 日宣布破產。這起破產事件是美國歷史上人口最多、債務最為龐大的都市破產事件。近年來該城市的經濟情況每況愈下。

The city of Detroit went bankruptcy on July 18, 2013, and it is the largest city by population and by debt in the U.S. history. The economics of the city had declined greatly in recent decades.

背景知識大突破 Background

底特律是美國傳統的汽車產業中心，但近數十年來，該市的經濟和人口皆大幅下降；受全球競爭的影響，汽車產業亦不斷外移。在破產前，底特律的犯罪率高居全國第一，大部分的市區處於老化狀態。

Detroit is traditionally known as the nation's automobile industry center, but it has gone through a major economic and demographic decline in recent decades. The automobile industry in Detroit has suffered from global competition and has moved

* debt　債務
* decline　下滑、減少
* demographic　人口、人口統計的

the production out of the city. Before the bankruptcy, the city has one of the highest crime rates in the United States, and large areas of the city are in urban decay.

Method 使用方法一把罩

破產 (bankruptcy) 是指法律上宣告債務人無力償付債務及其後的一連鎖還款予債權人過程的法律程序。企業資產低於負債不代表破產，因為企業可能有足夠的收入來支付所有到期債務。在不同國家對破產也有不同的處理方式，例如在英國大部分使用財產清算 (Liquidation) 或債務重組 (administration) 等詞彙。

2013 年 7 月，底特律市負債超過 180 億美元，正式申請破產保護，成為美國史上最大的破產案件；光是為了申請破產的官司，底特律就要付出約 2300 萬美元的律師費和會計費。昔日有汽車之城美譽的城市，人口也從鼎盛時期的 400 萬，下降到現在的 70 萬。為了支應負債並重新建立財政，勢必將進行加稅、裁減預算、裁減公務員等措施，使底特律未來的發展更為艱困。

＊ decay 腐敗、衰退

主題文章 Article

Rick Snyder, the governor of Michigan, has asked the federal government to set aside fifty thousands of work visas over five years for Detroit, reviving the bankrupt city by attracting talented immigrants who are willing to stay in the city.

The proposal involves visas which are offered to legal immigrants who have advanced degrees or exceptional ability in certain fields. The governor believes that immigrant entrepreneurs will be a powerful potential force for Detroit's economy. Under Snyder's plan, immigrants would be required to live and work in Detroit. The plan is expected to be formally submitted to federal authorities soon.

According to the governor, his plan would require no federal financial bailout. All the federal government needs to do is to ease immigration rules and visa limits to help the city fill jobs in automotive engineering, information technology, and health care.

The fate of Snyder's plan is uncertain, because the visas are not currently allocated by regions or states. In addition, the number of visas he is asking would be a quarter of the total visas offered to immigrants with talents. The federal authorities have yet to receive a formal request so far, and the proposal is said to come as a part of a plan to push Midwestern cities' economy by attracting immigrant entrepreneurs.

Detroit filed for bankruptcy in July 2013, becoming the largest city in the nation's history to do so. The Obama administration pledged support, but has not offered any direct assistance. In Washington, the State Department says they are aware of the governor's comments but had no immediate response.

Mike Duggan, the new mayor of Detroit, and many of Detroit's

city leaders who attended the governor's announcement, support the idea. The mayor has said that he wanted to see an increase in the population within five years.

密西根州長瑞克史耐德日前要求聯邦政府在五年內撥出五萬個工作簽證名額給底特律，以吸引有專業能力的的移民前往底特律，復興這座破產的都市。

這項建議涉及對在特定領域有專業能力或特殊才能的人發送移民簽證。州長認為，移民企業家將成為底特律經濟發展的潛在力量。在這項將提交給聯邦政府的計畫中，新移民必須在底特律工作及生活。

據州長所言，這份復興計畫不需要聯邦政府的援助。聯邦政府需要做的，就是降低移民簽證的限制，以補足底特律在汽車、資訊、醫療等產業所需要的人才。

史耐德的計畫能否成功仍有待觀察，因為簽證從來不受地區分配所影響。此外，他所要求的簽證數目，已超過簽證總額的四分之一。聯邦當局目前尚未收到正式的計畫。該計畫是透過吸引移民人才，推動整個中西部城市經濟成長計畫的一部分。

底特律在 2013 年 7 月申請破產，成為歷史上最大的破產城市。歐巴馬政府曾承諾給與支持，但至今尚未有直接援助。在華盛頓，政府部門表示他們知道州長的計畫，但尚未做出反應。

底特律的新市長麥克杜根及許多市民領袖都支持這項計畫。市長說，他希望在五年內看到底特律的人口出現成長。

Unit 9

International Worker's Day
國際勞工日

代表意義超理解

國際勞工日又稱為勞工節，是社會主義者和共產主義者提倡為工人和勞工階級所設立的紀念日。勞工節在許多國家中都被明定為國定假日。

International Worker's Day is also known as Labor's Day. It is a celebration holiday of labors and the working class that was promoted by the Socialists and Communists. It is announced as a national public holiday in many different countries.

背景知識大突破 Background

5 月 1 日也稱為五月節或五一節，是歐洲傳統上的春季節日。因此勞動節有時候也被稱為五月節或五一節。但這並不是這一天被選為勞工節的原因。在 1886 年 5 月 4 日，勞工在芝加哥的乾草市場示威，要求每天八小時的工作時間。但事件最終演變成一場動亂，造成多人死亡。5 月 1 日是因為這個原因而被訂為勞工節，以紀念這次的事件。

May 1 is also known as May Day, which is a traditional

＊celebration　慶祝

European spring holiday. Therefore Labor's Day sometimes is also known as May Day. However, it is not the reason to be chosen as the holiday for the workers. On May 4, 1886, labor demonstration took place at Haymarket Square in Chicago. The workers demanded an eight-hour working hour, but the event eventually became a riot which led to the death of many. May 1 was then chosen to commemorate the event.

M使用方法一把罩 Method

雖然世界上大部分的國家都將 5 月 1 日設為國際勞工日，但部分國家並不跟隨這個俗成節日，另行訂有自己的勞工日。例如在美國，勞工節 (Labor Day) 是九月的第一個星期一。但美國許多勞工團體和社會主義人士仍會在 5 月 1 號進行各種示威抗議，爭取勞工福利。

＊demand　要求

＊riot　暴亂、暴動

主題文章 Article

The labors of Iran had a harsh International Worker's Day. The government arrested a large amount of workers to prevent labor demonstrations on the holiday. It also summoned numerous workers to warn them to stay away from participating in demonstrations. The government even prevented any kind of ceremonies from being held in the country.

The clerical regime also stationed a suppressive force in front of the Ministry of Labor to thwart possible gatherings. The alleys were blocked by armored vehicles and motorcycle guards.

Nevertheless, about a thousand workers still gathered and marched to the Ministry of Labor. They eventually reached the ministry building; however, they were prevented from assembling. The protestors were outnumbered, and many of the workers there were arrested by the suppressive force. These workers petitioned for raise in their wages.

According to journalist's reports, leaders of the Free Trade Union of Iranian Workers who called for the rally were apprehended in a raid on their homes by the intelligence agents. Other labor activists' houses were also raided by the intelligence agents. Some of these activists avoided the attack, but were still arrested hours later.

Workers of the urban bus system who had assembled in other places in the city were also attacked and arrested by the clerical regime's suppressive force. The shopkeepers in the local markets had also closed their shops to protest against the government.

The government of Iran is known as the clerical regime. The clergy established hegemony over Iran's political system in 1979. They emerged from a crowded field for many reasons. First, Islamic revolutionaries ruthlessly eliminated other rivals. The regime also tapped into the popularity and legitimacy conferred by its call to Islam, a force rooted in Iran's social history. None of other revolutionary political factions benefited from the traditional legitimacy and social network provided by the Shiite clerical establishment.

伊朗勞工渡過一個痛苦的國際勞工節。伊朗政府當局在勞工節逮捕大量工人，以防止勞工在假期間進行示威抗議。政府同時警告工人不得參加示威，並禁止人民進行任何形式的慶祝活動。

由神職人員組成的政府也在勞工部外圍部署鎮暴部隊，以防止人民集會。附近小巷則被裝甲車和警衛機車封鎖。

然而，為數千人的示威群眾仍在集結後往勞工部前進。他們最終抵達勞動部建築，卻無法進行集會。這些抗議者寡不敵眾，許多人被優勢的鎮暴部隊逮捕。當時他們遊行的訴求是希望得到加薪。

根據記者的報導顯示，伊朗工人自由貿易公會的領導人遭到逮捕，其他勞工領袖的住家也遭到襲擊。部分人士雖然避開了政府的襲擊，但仍在幾個小時候遭到逮捕。

在城中其他區域集結的公共運輸工人也遭到神職政府的鎮壓逮捕。當地市場的攤販則以罷市進行抗議。

伊朗政府被稱為神權政府。伊朗的政治體制在 1979 年遭神職人員獨佔，其背後有諸多原因。首先，當時的伊斯蘭革命份子無情的排除了其他的競爭對手；而根植於伊朗社會歷史的宗教力量則給予神職人員無比的合法性及正當性，其他的各種政治革命團體無法從什葉教派的組織中得到這些傳統支援及人脈。

Unit 10

"Let's Move!" Campaign
「動起來運動」

代表意義超理解

「動起來」是美國第一夫人蜜雪兒歐巴馬所發起的綜合性運動，致力於解決當代的兒童肥胖問題，並讓學童長大後能更加的健康，追逐自己的夢想。

"Let's Move!" campaign is a comprehensive initiative, launched by Michelle Obama, dedicated to solving the challenge of childhood obesity within a generation, so that children born today will grow up healthier and able to pursue their dreams.

B 背景知識大突破 Background

根據官方網站的説明，「動起來運動」的目標包括讓學童在年輕時培養健康的未來，提供家長們有關健康的資訊，支持健康的環境，在學校中提供健康餐飲，確保每個家庭都得以取得價格低廉的健康食物，並讓孩子更常運動。

According to its official website, "Let's move!" is about putting children on the path to a healthy future during their earliest

* dedicate　致力於
* obesity　肥胖
* pursue　追求、追逐

months and years. Giving parents helpful information and fostering environments that support healthy choices. Providing healthier foods in our schools. Ensuring that every family has access to healthy, affordable food. And, helping kids become more physically active.

Method 使用方法一把罩

Let's move! 是這項運動的專有名稱，因此在使用時會連著驚嘆號一起使用，也較為容易區別。這項運動日前引發部分學生和家長的反對，因為學校提供的健康午餐並不受歡迎。在網路和媒體上若看到蜜雪兒的午餐（Michelle's Lunch），多半是和「動起來運動」有關的新聞。例如：

First Lady Michelle Obama's anti-obesity campaign is claiming that salad bars have increased student participation in school lunch, despite a report that found one million children fled the lunch line in response to Michelle's lunch standards.

（雖然有報導指出，約有百萬名學童因為蜜雪兒的午餐標準而停止在學校用餐，但第一夫人蜜雪兒歐巴馬的反肥胖運動仍指出，學校裡的沙拉吧讓更多學生在校園餐廳用餐。）

Part 3 民生 People's Livelihood

＊foster 培養；促進　　＊ensure 確保

主題文章 Article

"I blame Michelle Obama." High school students in the United States are now very clear about whom they blame for the "nasty" lunches in their schools.

One of Michelle Obama's tenure as the First Lady of the United States has been to help Americans get fit and eat right. She has launched the "Let's Move!" campaign to end childhood obesity in the country. She encourages healthier food in schools and more physical activity for children. However, students don't seem to appreciate their new meals.

However, many of the students found their lunches sick and nasty, and the portion of these lunches is not enough to feed the kids. "Starving kids at school isn't exactly a way to get kids' obesity down," one student said; "it's great that schools are trying to make lunches better, they are not doing a very good job of it." The new lunch requirements are not welcome among the students, as news reported that some school nutrition directors want the Department of Agriculture to loosen up the new lunch requirements so students will stop throwing away their food.

Other students are more willing to acknowledge others might be at fault. "It's gonna be a combination of Michelle Obama and the servers at the school, although the servers are probably just doing what they are told," said a senior high school student.

Many students have started bringing their own lunch. Some students argue that although the school-prepared food may be beneficial, "if nobody chooses to eat the gross food, then it can't possibly be helping anyone. It's just being thrown out anyway."

According to information from the White House Office of the Press Secretary, nearly 2,000 chefs have volunteered to help schools become healthier. However, the impact of said

volunteerism remains unknown. The students' reaction to the campaign may tell us something about it.

「我責怪蜜雪兒 · 歐巴馬」。面對學校裡「難以下嚥」的午餐，美國高中生很清楚的知道要責怪誰。

蜜雪兒 · 歐巴馬成為美國第一夫人以來，不斷推動健康飲食生活的運動。她推行「動起來」運動，希望能降低肥胖兒童的數量，同時鼓勵學校提供健康食物和提倡運動。但學生們似乎並不欣賞他們的新午餐。

許多學生覺得他們的午餐噁心又難吃。午餐的分量也不足以餵飽這些學生。「挨餓不會減少肥胖學生的數量」，一名學生說，「學校希望把午餐變得更好，這是一件好事，但他們並不成功」。根據媒體報導，新的午餐並不受學生歡迎，一些學校的營養顧問也希望農業部放寬相關規定，以避免學生把他們的食物當成垃圾丟掉。

有些學生則認為這不是蜜雪兒一個人的錯。「學校和蜜雪兒都有份，雖然學校的人可能只是奉命行事」。一名高中生這樣說。

許多學生已經開始自行攜帶午餐。有些學生則認為，雖然學校提供的食物對身體有益，「但如果這些噁心的食物乏人問津，那也不可能對人有益，因為大家只會把食物丟掉」。

根據白宮新聞處的資料顯示，有近 2,000 名的廚師自願協助學校，讓學校的膳食更加健康。但這些志願者的成效並不明顯，至少從學生的反應可見一端。

Unit 11

Looted Art
遭掠奪的美術品

代表意義超理解

遭掠奪的美術品是人類歷史上因戰爭、暴動、或天然災害而造成的掠奪結果的總稱。掠奪美術品、考古物品等文化財產被認為是一種犯罪行為，更可能是衝突中勝利者組織性的行為。

Looted art has been a result of looting during war, riot, or natural disaster in human history. Looting of art, archaeology and other cultural property is a criminal act or may be a more organized case of unlawful pillage by the victor of a conflict.

B背景知識大突破
Background

一般而言，被掠奪的美術品常被用來專指納粹德國在二戰期間所進行的掠奪行為。然而，納粹德國並不是唯一對美術品進行掠奪的國家。蘇聯和美國軍隊也在戰爭中參與掠奪，前者進行較為系統化的掠奪，後者則多維持在個人行為的水準。

Looted art is a term often reduced to refer to artwork plundered by the Germans during World War II. However, the Nazi Germany was not the only one to loot artwork on a large scale.

＊archaeology　考古學
＊unlawful　非法的
＊pillage　搶劫、掠奪
＊plunder　奪取、搶劫
＊systematically　有系統地
＊artifact　手工藝品

The Soviet and American armies also participated in war plundering, the former more systematically, and the latter at the level of individuals stealing.

M 使用方法一把罩 Method

Looted art 常被用來單指為納粹德國在二戰期間所進行的掠奪，2014 年的電影大尋寶家（The Monuments Men）就在敘述研究人員從納粹手中奪回藝術品，再物歸原主。Looted art 的範圍只涉及美術品，再更廣泛層次的國家級掠奪行為，則會以 looted artifact （藝品）做為總稱。

A 主題文章 Article

The government of Turkey launches an aggressive campaign to reclaim antiquities looted by foreign powers. Turkey has successfully reclaimed an ancient sphinx and other golden treasures from its glorious past; however, it has also drawn condemnation from the world's largest museums, which consider the Turkish campaign cultural blackmail.

Last year, Turkish officials from its Cultural Heritage and Museums presented the Metropolitan Museum of Art with a stunning ultimatum: prove the provenance of ancient antiquities, including figurines and gold wares, in the collection, or Turkey would stop lending treasures.

Turkish archaeologists say they are 100 percent sure that these objects at the Met are from ancient ruins of Turkey. "We only want back what is rightfully ours," a Turkish archaeologist claims.

Turkish officials filed a criminal report in their court system this year, seeking to investigate into 18 objects that are now in the Met collection. Archaeologists believe these antiquities are originally found in an illegal excavation.

The campaign to reclaim looted antiquities has spurred an international debate about who owns these antiquities after centuries of power and borders shifting. Museums all over the world, including the Met, the Getty, the Louvre, and the Pergamon, are under the threat of Turkish campaign.

Turkey is not alone in requesting the return of looted antiquities; both Egypt and Greece have made similar demands of museums, and Italy also persuaded the Met to return an ancient bowl years ago.

However, the Turkish tactics are more aggressive than others, as the officials start to refuse lending treasures and delay the licensing of archaeological excavations. These actions have particularly alarmed the museums in the western world.

Turkey's campaign still enjoyed major success. The Pergamon in Germany agreed to return a 3000-year-old sphinx, when the Turkish officials had threatened to block important archaeological projects if the sphinx did not come home. Government officials indicated that the Pergamon still needs to return other disputed items before Turkey would resume the loans.

At the same time, Turkish officials put the same pressure on the Met, as they refuse to lend antiquities to a Met exhibition.

土耳其政府積極的向國外政府取回過去遭強權取走的古物。土耳其成功取回其古代繁盛時期的一座獅身人面像及金製品，但也引起世界各大博物館的譴責，認為土耳其的行為是文化勒索。

去年，土耳其文化遺產及博物館部門的官員向大都會文化藝術博物館開出令人震驚的最後通牒：證明包含雕像及金器在內一部分古物的出處，否則土耳其將停止外借其他文物。

土耳其考古學家表示，他們百分之百確定這些古物出於土耳其的遺跡。「我們只想取回我們合法擁有的東西」，考古學家如此說。

土耳其官員於今年在他們的法院體系中完成一份犯罪報告，希望能對其他 18 件在大都會博物館的文物進行調查。考古學家認為，這些都是非法的出土文物。

土耳其的行為引起國際上對歷史文物歸屬權的爭論。世界各地的博物館，包括美國大都會博物館、蓋提美術博物館、法國羅浮宮、德國佩加蒙博物館等，都是受到該計畫的威脅。

土耳其不是唯一要求取回文物的國家。埃及和希臘也對這些博物館提出類似的要求，而義大利在多年前也曾說服大都會博物館成功要求取回一個古老的器皿。

但土耳其的手段遠比他國來的積極，土耳其官方已經開始拒絕外借文物，並暫緩發放考古挖掘執照。這些行為讓西方的博物館萬分警惕。

土耳其的計畫仍舊取得重大成功。由於土耳其官員揚言阻擾重大考古計畫，德國佩加蒙博物館同意歸還一座有三千年歷史的獅身人面像。政府官員表示，在佩加蒙博物館歸還其他存有爭議的文物前，土耳其將繼續停止文物外借。

土耳其同時也對大都會博物館施壓，並拒絕出借文物給大都會博物館。

Unit 12

MH370
馬來西亞航空 MH370 班機

代表意義超理解

馬來西亞航空 MH370 班機於 2014 年 3 月 8 日從吉隆坡起飛飛往北京，但在起飛後不久即與空中管制中心失去聯絡。該班機隨後被視為失蹤，來自世界各地的搜救隊伍至今仍無法找到任何飛機殘骸或是飛機的失事地點。

Malaysia Airlines Flight 370 was an international passenger flight from Kuala Lumpur to Beijing that lost contact with air traffic control on 8 March 2014. The flight was then reported missing, and search and rescue teams from all over the world had not been able to locate any flight debris or its crash site yet.

B 背景知識大突破 Background

MH370 機上載有 12 名馬來西亞籍的機組人員及 227 名乘客，其中大部分乘客來自中國大陸。事件發生後，從世界各地前來進行的搜救行動規模之大史無前例，但至今仍無法找到失事地點，所有乘客也下落不明。搜索行動至今仍由無人潛水器進行中。

＊rescue　救援、營救
＊debris　殘骸、碎片
＊crash　site　失事地點、墜落地點

MH370 carried 12 Malaysian crew members and 227 passengers, most of them from mainland China. The largest search and rescue operation in history was launched after the crash, but the crash site remains unknown, and all the passengers are still missing. The search is continuing today with robotic submarines.

Method 使用方法一把罩

MH370 的正式名稱是馬航 370 班機（Malaysia Airlines Flight 370），簡稱 MH370 或 MAF370。飛機的機型則是波音 777（Boeing777）。波音 777 是目前全球最大的雙引擎客機；為因應不同的需求，波音 777 也發展出各種不同的機型，例如 777-200ER、777F、7779X 等。

＊robotic 自動的、機器人的

A 主題文章 Article

The tragic MH370 incident had brought a dramatic impact to Malaysia Airlines, as it had reported its largest quarterly net loss in two years. The incident had brought down the traditionally weak first quarter's performance to a new degree, as passengers shunned the company after flight MH370 disappeared earlier this year, with 239 people on board.

The jet vanished from radar screen in March as it was travelling from Kuala Lumpur to Beijing. According to a newly released preliminary report by the government of Malaysia, the air traffic controllers did not realize that Malaysia Airlines Flight 370 was missing until 17 minutes after it disappeared from the radar.

In the same report, detailed actions taken by the Malaysian authorities during the hours of confusion that followed the jet's disappearance are also shown to the public. It also showed that the Malaysian authorities did not launch any official search or rescue operation until four hours after the crash. The jet had disappeared near the border between Malaysian and Vietnamese airspace. Most of the information had previously been disclosed by the Malaysian government.

The report also consisted of information from investigating into the flight. It claimed that the uncertainty about Flight 370's last position before the crash had made it much more difficult to locate the plane afterward. It suggested that the international aviation authorities should examine the safety benefits of introducing tracking standards to commercial aircraft.

The report indicated that Malaysia Airlines thought the plane may have entered Cambodian airspace. The airline said that "MH370 was able to exchange signals with the flight and flying in Cambodian airspace; however, the Cambodian authorities said that they had no information or contact with Flight 370. It is still unclear which flight it was referring to that supposedly exchanged signals with MH370.

MH370 悲劇事故對馬來西亞航空帶來巨大衝擊，並帶來馬航近兩年來最大的季度虧損，並讓傳統上表現一向較弱的第一季業績雪上加霜。馬航班機 MH370 日前在航程中消失墜毀，當時飛機上共有 239 人。這起事件讓乘客對馬航避之唯恐不及。

根據馬來西亞政府最新出爐的初步報告顯示，三月份時，馬來西亞航班編號 370 的客機當時正由吉隆坡前往北京，但當時的管制員並沒有在第一時間發現航班失蹤，而是在該班機從雷達螢幕上消失 17 分鐘後，才意識到該班機已失蹤。

這份報告向大眾透露馬來西亞當局在飛機失蹤後的一段時間陷入混亂的情況。當時馬來西亞當局並未立即展開搜救，直到墜機四小時候才展開行動。飛機是在馬來西亞和越南領空之間消失。這些消息之前由馬來西亞政府陸續披露。

這份報告也包括航班飛行的調查報告。報告指出，由於 MH370 墜毀前的最後座標不定，更加深了後續定位工作的困難。報告建議國際航空管理單位應研究商用機型的追蹤系統標準，以增加安全效益。

報告中也指出，馬航認為飛機曾進入柬埔寨領空。航空公司表示，MH370 曾在柬埔寨領空與其他航空載具交換訊號，但柬埔寨表示他們並未收到相關的訊息。究竟 MH370 是和哪一架載具交換訊號，至今仍舊不明。

Unit 13

Mountain Gorillas
山地大猩猩

代表意義超理解

山地大猩猩大部分居住在剛果的維龍加火山地區，全世界共約有 950 隻。科學家自 1990 年代開始近距離的對山地大猩猩進行觀察研究，而在國際自然保護聯盟的瀕危物種名錄中，山地大猩猩被列為極度瀕危物種，靠著人類的保育工作才得以生存。

The mountain gorillas are found in Virunga volcanic mountains in Congo. The estimated total number of mountain gorillas in the world is around 950, and scientists started to monitor and research mountain gorillas closely in the 1990s. Mountain gorillas are listed as critically endangered on the IUCN Red List and are dependent on conservation efforts to survive.

B 背景知識大突破 Background

世界上倖存的 950 隻山地大猩猩中，約有 750 隻生活在剛果的維龍加國家公園。科學家不斷致力於保育工作，2010 年時，維龍加國家公園的官方網站宣稱在過去幾年中，山地大猩猩的數量約增長了 26.3%。山地大猩猩的數量自 1981 年以來幾乎成長三倍，當時的調查

＊endanger　危急；危害　　＊conservation　保護、保存

顯示只剩下 254 頭大猩猩。

There are about 950 remaining mountain gorillas in the world, of which about 750 of them lived in Virunga National Park, Congo. Scientists worked hard to preserve the mountain gorilla population, and in 2010, the official website of Virunga National Park announced that the number of mountain gorillas had increased by 26.3% over the past few years. The population of mountain gorillas has almost tripled since 1981, when a census estimated that only 254 gorillas remained.

Method 使用方法一把罩

INCU（International Union for Conservation of Nature）是國際自然保護聯盟的簡稱，INCU Red List（瀕危物種名錄）則是由國際自然保護聯盟編製關於全球動植物保護現況最全面的清單。該名錄將瀕危物種分為滅絕（EX）、野外滅絕（EW）、極危（CR）、瀕危（EN）、易危（VU）等不同等級。

Article 主題文章

There are few places left for the last remaining mountain gorillas in the world, and Virunga National Park in Congo is one of them. There is more than 270 rangers risk their lives to do their jobs, as the rebel groups had taken control of the area. The rebel groups had ambushed the rangers several times, and nobody is invincible.

Virunga National Park, located in eastern Congo, was just beginning to enjoy the increase of tourist arrival when the war

broke out months ago. The rebel groups soon took control in the area, and the park was forced to shut down. The rebel groups' involvement had not only endangered the gorillas, but also made it very difficult for the rangers to police the reserve.

There are about 800 mountain gorillas remain in the world, and they live on the borders of Congo, Rwanda, and Uganda. The gorillas' presence is a draw for wealthy tourists. The national Park would draw six thousand tourists, making two million dollars a year, if the war did not break out.

However, monitoring the remaining gorillas had become a difficult task for both the scientists and the rangers in the park. The rebels are accused of war crimes, including murders, rapes, and forced recruitment of soldiers. On some occasions when the rangers tried to locate the gorillas, they were arrested and disarmed by the rebels.

One of the orphan gorillas has already died, after the mother gorilla, rescued from a poacher's net five years ago, became ill. The whole area had become dangerous for the gorillas to live, because of the shelling from battles. The scientists and rangers are forced to withdraw from the area, but they are still trying to locate two groups of gorillas after more than four months.

It is the most violent period in Congo in twenty years. United Nation experts claim that Rwanda has supplied the rebels with weapons and recruits through the gorilla-inhabited section of the park. Rwanda denied the above accuse. Park officials say that they have no evidence of Rwanda's involvement.

剛果的維龍加國家公園是世界上僅存不多的山地大猩猩棲息地之一。但因為叛亂團體目前已控制該區域，使得在此工作的 270 名管理員冒著生命危險執行勤務。叛黨已多次突襲該地的管理員，無人能保證下一次的襲擊不會造成任何傷亡。

維龍加國家公園位於剛果東部，數個月前前往該地的觀光客人數仍不斷上升。但在內戰發生後，叛亂組織迅速控制鄰近地區，而國家公園則被迫停止營運。叛軍的活動不但對棲息在國家公園中的山地大猩猩造成危險，更對管理員造成影響。

在剛果、盧安達、及烏干達的國界處居住著世界上僅存約 800 隻的山地大猩猩，而這些山地大猩猩能吸引大量富豪遊客前來參觀。在內戰爆發前，維龍加國家公園每年能吸引六千名遊客，為剛果帶來兩百萬美元的收益。

但對管理員和科學家來說，保護和研究山地大猩猩的工作卻越來越難，因為叛軍在該地進行謀殺、強暴、及強制徵兵等各種行為。當管理員在國家公園內尋找山地大猩猩時，曾有數次被叛軍逮捕、繳械的經驗。

一隻在數年前被管理員從陷阱中救出的山地大猩猩病情惡化，而牠的小孩隨後死亡。對山地大猩猩來說，該區域已不再適合居住，因為戰區的砲火太過危險。科學家與管理員雖仍努力嘗試尋找過去四個多月來持續追蹤的兩個山地大猩猩家族，但他們亦被迫撤出該區域。

剛果處於近二十年來戰亂最嚴重的時期。聯合國的專家則表示盧安達正透過山地大猩猩的棲息地向叛軍支援武器及人力，但盧安達方面否認上述指控。國家公園的管理員則表示，他們沒有證據證明盧安達介入內戰。

Unit 14

MV Sewol
世越號

代表意義超理解

韓國遊輪世越號沉沒事件發生於 2014 年 4 月 16 日，當時船上共有 476 名遊客，其中大部分是高中學生。事件發生後許多人獲救，但仍有 286 人死亡，18 人失蹤。目前韓國政府和美國海軍仍持續進行搜救行動。

The sinking of South Korean ferry MV Sewol occurred on 16 April 2014 while carrying 476 people, mostly high school students. Many passengers were rescued by other vessels after the tragedy; however, there are still 286 deaths, with 18 missing. There are ongoing recovery efforts by the South Korean government and the United States Navy.

背景知識大突破 Background

世越號沉沒事件在韓國引起廣泛的政治社會反應。大眾指責韓國政府和媒體在後續的救災行動中試圖淡化政府應負的責任。世越號的船長則被以謀殺罪起訴，因為他在遊客離開前即自行棄船逃生。

The sinking of the ship has resulted in widespread social and

---

＊sink　沈沒

＊vessel　船

＊tragedy　悲劇；災難

political reaction within South Korea. The public blames the South Korean government and media for its disaster response and attempts to downplay government culpability. The captain of the ship was also charged with murder, as he left the ship before other passengers.

M 使用方法一把罩 ethod

MV Sewol 前面的 MV 是商船 merchant vessel 的簡稱，用來作為船隻種類的區別，Sewol（世越）則是船名。一般而言，無論是軍船還是民間船隻，都會以類似的代碼進行區別，例如美國航空母艦企業號常見的代號是 USS Enterprise，其中 USS 代表 United States Ship。

在和海事相關的新聞中，也常會看到各種商船代號名稱；例如：

The Somali pirates freed 11 crew of Malaysian-owned cargo vessel MV Albedo in June 2014. The vessel was hijacked in November 2010 while sailing from the United Arab Emirates to Kenya. The freed crews are all healthy, and no ransom has been paid so far.

（最近索馬利亞海盜釋放馬來西亞貨運船亞伯貝多號 (MV Albedo) 上的 11 名船員。該船於 2010 年 11 月在從阿拉伯聯合大公國前往肯亞的途中遭到劫持。被釋放的船員身體健康，他們的家屬也沒有向海盜付出贖金。）

* reaction 反應　　* culpability 苛責；有罪

A 主題文章 Article

The sinking of the MV Sewol left more than 300 people dead or missing, with many of them school children. The Prime Minister of South Korea, Chung Hong-Won, had resigned from the position and admitted he had not been up to the task of overseeing rescue operations after the tragedy.

The tragic incident had amid huge public anger over what is seen as a bungled response. Parents and friends of the dead and the missing had blasted the government's response to the sinking, saying the rescue operation was too slow to swing into action, possibly costing lives. People also claimed that perceived corruption and lax safety standards may have led to the disaster, as the ferry was overloaded and the passenger list was inaccurate and incomplete.

"I offer my apology for having been unable to prevent this accident from happening and unable to properly respond to it afterwards," said Chung Hong-Won. "I believed I, as the prime minister, certainly had to take responsibility and resign."

"I sincerely hope the South Koreans and families of the Sewol victims will forgive and understand me for being unable to fulfill my obligations until the end." Chung said in a national press conference.

The confirmed death from the tragedy stood at 187, with 115 missing, in April 2014. Many of the bodies are still trapped in the sunken vessel. Divers are still battling weather and decompression sickness in hope to search for corpses. However, it becomes more difficult every day, as the ferry sinks slowly into the silt of the seabed. The weather is not friendly to the mission either, as the waves are up to three meters tall.

世越號沉沒造成超過 300 人失蹤或死亡，其中包括多名學生。韓國總理鄭烘原辭去職務，並承認他在悲劇發生後並未妥善監督後續的救援任務。

這場悲劇發生後韓國政府的拙劣回應引發大規模的民怨。死者及失蹤人士的父母和親友抨擊政府反應緩慢延遲了救援行動，並讓他們親屬喪生。也有群眾聲稱貪腐和鬆懈的安全標準導致這場悲劇，因為渡輪不但超載，旅客名單也不準確、不完整。

「我為無法阻止這起事件發生，及無法在事件發生後做出適當的反應道歉」，鄭烘原說。「身為總理，我應當負起責任辭職」。

「我衷心希望韓國民眾和遇難家屬能原諒並理解我在結束職務前無法善盡職責的行為。」鄭烘原在一場記者會上這麼說。

這場悲劇發生在 2014 年 4 月，當時已確認有 187 人死亡，115 人失蹤，許多屍體仍被困在沉船中無法打撈。潛水員仍在水壓和天氣的威脅下持續打撈屍體，但隨著輪船漸漸陷入海底淤泥，搜索的難度也一天天增加。不利的天候條件也加深了打撈的難度，當地的海浪可高達三米。

Unit 15

Oil Export in Sudan
蘇丹石油出口

代表意義超理解

石油是蘇丹的主要出口貨品，而蘇丹也因為外銷石油的利潤，享有一段經濟快速發展的時光。然而，隨著 2011 年南蘇丹從蘇丹分裂出去，蘇丹的經濟成長也逐漸放緩，因為南蘇丹據有原蘇丹 80% 以上的油田。蘇丹未來的經濟走向仍是未知數。

Oil was Sudan's main export, and Sudan experienced rapid development from oil profits. However, since the secession of South Sudan in 2011, Sudan's economic growth slowed down, as South Sudan contained over 80% of Sudan's oilfield. The economic forecast for Sudan is uncertain in the future.

B 背景知識大突破 Background

在 2011 年南蘇丹獨立前，蘇丹原本是非洲面積最大的國家。2011 年舉行的南蘇丹獨立公投中，98.83% 的人投下贊成票，使南蘇丹成為一個獨立國家。

Sudan was the largest country in Africa until 2011, when

＊ secession（從宗教、政黨、聯盟等組織中的）退出、脫離

＊ forecast　預測、預報

South Sudan separated into an independent country. In 2011, a referendum was held to determine whether South Sudan should declare independence from Sudan, and 98.83% of the population voted for independence.

Method 使用方法一把罩

公投的英文是 referendum，有時候也稱為 vote on a ballot question。公投（referendum）和選舉（election）並不相同，選舉是針對特定職務從參選人中選出對象，公投則是對特定議題進行意見表決。而在 2011 年的公投中，多數人的贊成，而使得佔有原蘇丹 80% 以上油田的南蘇丹正式獨立。而兩國之間則因為領土上的糾紛，常會以停止原油生產及原油運輸作為制裁手段，也因此造成蘇丹石油出口的不定因素。

＊declare　宣告、宣布　　＊ballot　無記名投票

Sudan and South Sudan made a major progress on trade and security agreements in 2012, aimed to cease hostilities and set up a buffer zone on their shared border. This also means the oil export is likely to set to resume from these two countries after both of their leaders signed the agreements.

Sudan and South Sudan became hostile toward each other in April 2012, as clashes on the border had resumed in April. The deal would prevent the two from going into an open war. Although the deal is likely to end the clash between the two, it has no territorial deal to resolve the most enduring source of the conflict. Both Sudan and South Sudan claim the region of Abyei, and the disputation is likely to continue.

If Sudan and South Sudan does not reach a peace agreement, they would face United Nation Security Council sanctions.

The African Union had mediated President Omar Hassan Ahmed Bashir of Sudan and President Salva Kiir of South Sudan to reach an agreement. The two had finally signed the deal in Addis Ababa, the capital of Ethiopia.

Sudan and South Sudan has fought each other for more than twenty years. The two sides signed a peace deal in 2005 to end the war, and eventually South Sudan became independence in July 2011. However, both border and oil transit issues remain unsolved. The two had a dispute over oil transit fee this year, and South Sudan shut down oil production when the two became hostile. The suspension of oil exports cost both countries millions of dollars, and hit both economies hard.

President Salva Kiir of South Sudan calls the agreement a "great day in the history of the region," while President Omar Hassan Ahmed Bashir of Sudan says the deal is a "historic moment

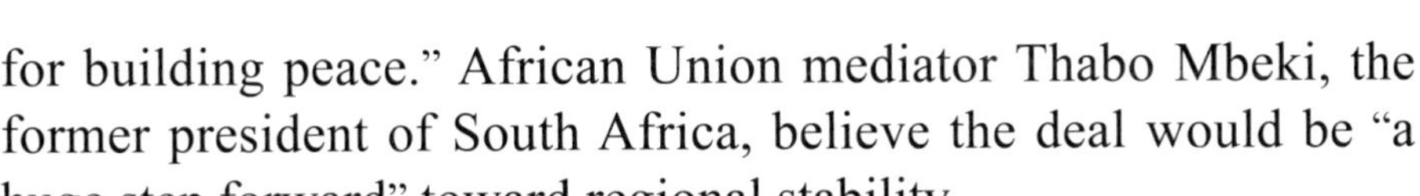

for building peace." African Union mediator Thabo Mbeki, the former president of South Africa, believe the deal would be "a huge step forward" toward regional stability.

蘇丹和南蘇丹在 2012 年的貿易安全協定上取得重大進展，兩國同意停止敵對，並在國境上設立緩衝區避免衝突。這也表示在兩國領導人簽定協定後，兩國將恢復原油出口。

蘇丹和南蘇丹在 2012 年 4 月因領土問題走向敵對，這次的協議將避免兩國開戰。雖然這次的協定將暫緩兩國間的爭議，但協議中並沒有解決兩國間的領土糾紛。蘇丹和南蘇丹都宣稱對阿拜伊地區擁有主權，未來兩國仍可能在此爭議上持續交鋒。

但若蘇丹和南蘇丹無法達成和平協議，兩國都將面臨聯合國安理會的制裁。

在非洲聯盟的調停下，蘇丹的拜希爾總統和南蘇丹的奇爾總統終於在衣索比亞首都阿迪斯阿貝巴達成協議。

蘇丹和南蘇丹在過去有超過二十年的爭戰歷史。兩國在 2005 年簽約停戰，隨後南蘇丹在 2011 年完成獨立。但兩國間的領土爭議及原油運輸問題從未獲得解決。今年雙方因運油費用產生爭議，而南蘇丹在雙方交惡後即停止原油生產。原油停運對雙方都造成數百萬美元的損失，並嚴重影響經濟。

南蘇丹的奇爾總統稱這次協定是「此地區史上美好的一日」，而蘇丹的拜希爾總統則稱之為「締造和平歷史性的一刻」。非洲聯盟的調停人、南非前總統姆貝基則稱該協定邁出區域穩定的「重大一步」。

Unit 16

Pope Francis
教宗方濟各

代表意義超理解

教宗方濟各本名 Jorge Mario Bergoglio，他於 2013 年 3 月 14 日獲選為天主教會第 266 任教宗。其稱號為羅馬教區及梵諦岡城市的主教，也就是一般所稱的教宗。

Pope Francis, born Jorge Mario Bergoglio, is the 266th and current Pope of the Catholic Church, having been elected Bishop of Rome and absolute Sovereign of the Vatican City State in 14th March 2013.

B 背景知識大突破 Background

教宗方濟各以謙遜著稱，他長期關懷窮人，並承諾將對不同背景、不同理念、信念的民眾一視同仁。教宗方濟各在尊崇天主教教義的同時，也曾表示現在的天主教徒過分專心於譴責墮胎，避孕和同性戀等行為，卻忽略對世間應有的憐憫與同情。

Pope Francis has been noted for his humility, his concern for the poor, and his commitment to bring people of all backgrounds, beliefs, and faiths together. While affirming

---

＊humility　謙遜、謙卑　　　＊affirm　聲明

present Catholic doctrine, he has stated that Catholics have concentrated excessively on condemning abortion, contraception, and homosexual acts, while neglecting the greater need for tenderness, mercy, and compassion.

Method 使用方法一把罩

教宗的正式稱號是羅馬主教 (Bishop of Rome)，教宗的統治行為及任期稱為 Papacy，教宗的主教職權則被稱為聖座 (The Holy See)。整個聖座的的行政機構則統稱為教廷或羅馬教廷 (直接使用拉丁文：Curia Romana)，輔助教宗處理事務。由於教廷所在地為梵諦岡，因此一般也以梵諦岡作為教廷的總稱。

＊ doctrine （宗教的）教義
＊ condemn 責備、責難
＊ contraception 避孕

In an interview Pope Francis said that the Catholic Church cannot focus only on contraception, abortion, and gay marriage, and that the moral structure of the church will fall like a house of cards if it does not find a better balance.

In the same interview, the Pope acknowledged that he has been criticized for not speaking more about those three issues, but he said that the Catholic Church must talk about them in a context. Although the Pope acknowledged the teaching of the church on those subjects is clear, he says, it is not necessary to talk about these issues all the time.

The interview is published across the world. "We have to find a new balance," says the Pope. "Otherwise even the moral edifice of the church is likely to fall like a house of cards, losing the freshness and fragrance of the Gospel."

Pope Francis has been noted for his humility, his concern for the poor, and his commitment to bring people of all backgrounds, beliefs, and faiths together. Since his installation in March 2013, he has focused on the poor and those on the margins of societies. He has also personally returned the phone calls of some of the faithful who had written to him.

On homosexuality, the Pope says that when he was still in Argentina, he used to receive letters from those who were socially wounded, and he felt that the church had condemned them. "But the church does not want to do this," said the Pope. "Religion has the right to express its opinion in the service of the people, but God in creation has set us free: It is not possible to interfere spiritually in the life of a person."

When people asked him if he approved of homosexuality, Pope Francis replied with the following question: When God looks at

a gay person, does he endorse the existence of this person with love, or reject and condemn this person?

教宗方濟各在接受採訪時說，天主教教會不能只注重避孕、墮胎和同性婚姻等議題；如果教會不能（在各種議題間）找到平衡，教會的道德觀將會像紙牌做的樓房一樣倒塌。

在這次訪談中，教宗公開表示，很多人批評他對上述三個議題的表態不足。但他也說，教會必須從整體上來討論各種問題。教宗表示，他知道教會在這三個議題上的態度，但不代表教會要整天討論這些問題。

以上的採訪在世界各地播放。「我們必須找到一個新的平衡」，教宗說。「否則的話，教會的道德觀將會像紙牌做的樓房一樣，喪失福音的精華」。

教宗方濟各以謙遜著稱，他長期關懷窮人，並承諾將對不同背景、不同理念、信念的民眾一視同仁。自從他在 2013 年 3 月成為教宗以來，他持續關注窮人和社會邊緣人；他甚至親自致電給來信的信眾。

對同性戀問題，教宗則表示，當他還在阿根廷時，曾有人寫信給他，表示同性戀族群受到社會傷害，教會也不斷譴責他們。「但這不是教會的原意」，教宗說。「宗教有權對它所服務的信眾發表意見，但上帝造人是平等的，我們不可能干涉別人的靈魂和生命」。

當他人質問教宗是否認可同性戀，教宗則回以下列問題：當神面對同性戀的時候，神會以愛來包容這個人，還是會拒絕、甚至譴責這個人？

Unit 17

Spanish Financial Crisis
西班牙金融危機

代表意義超理解

西班牙金融危機是歐債危機的一部分，受影響的國家多為南歐國家，例如西班牙和希臘。在西班牙，危機主要來自於長期貸款和嚴重的失業問題；西班牙的失業率在 2013 年 4 月曾飆升到 29.16%。

The Spanish financial crisis is part of European sovereign debt crisis, which has primarily affected southern European states such as Spain and Greece. In Spain, the crisis was generated by long-term loans and severe increase in unemployment, which rose to 29.16% by April 2013.

背景知識大突破 Background

歐元區會員國的財政部長們在 2012 年時同意提供給西班牙一份救助貸款，歐洲委員會和西班牙也同意設立經濟復甦計畫。同年西班牙也宣布增稅，並削減公務預算，以表現西班牙削減赤字的決心。

The eurozone finance ministers agreed to provide rescue loans in 2012. The European Commission and Spain also agreed to

＊ severe　嚴重的

establish an economic recovery program. Spain announced tax increases and cutbacks in 2012 to convince the financial market that it is resolute in cutting its deficits.

M 使用方法一把罩 ethod

歐債危機較為正式的名稱是 European sovereign debt crisis，中文一般稱為歐洲主權債務危機。2007-2008 年的全球金融風暴一般則稱為 financial tsunami，其導因之一為次貸危機，英文用 subprime mortgage crisis。

在這些危機中，出現債務問題的歐元區國家包括希臘 (Greece)、愛爾蘭 (Ireland)、西班牙 (Spain)、葡萄牙 (Portugal)、義大利 (Italy) 等，因此曾有經濟學者以這些國家的英文字母開頭組成 PIIGS，中文稱為歐豬五國。但這種稱呼非常負面，現在已鮮少有人使用。

A 主題文章 rticle

Spain, Europe's fourth-largest economy, struggles to avoid another bailout by its European partners, announces tax increases and cutbacks this week, aiming to save 50 billion dollars from its budget next year. The announced plan will further reduce government spending and raise taxes in order to convince the lenders and financial market that Spain is resolute in cutting its deficits.

＊recovery　復甦、恢復
＊deficit　赤字；不足額
＊tsunami　海嘯；金融海嘯

According to the cutback announcement, all civil servants' salaries would remain frozen for a third year, all government departments would cut about 9% of its budget, and the government would start levying new lottery winning taxes.

However, thousands of Spaniards launched an "Occupy Congress" movement earlier, surrounding the Spanish parliament, protesting against the government's policy to cut budgets from education, public healthcare, and pensions. The officials of Spain respond that the government would use social security reserve fund to keep paying the pensions, and even increase the pension payment by one percent.

Prime Minister Mariano Rajoy of Spain, elected last year, had promised not to touch pensions, at the same time avoid a second bailout by other European countries. The government also distributed precious tax revenue to jobless benefits, as the unemployment rate continues to rise. Spain's unemployment rate, about 25%, remains the highest in the Eurozone; with unemployment among young people double that.

Prime Minister Mariano Rajoy said Spain is midway through the second deepest recession in its history. He has also warned the public several times that Spain's problems would not come quickly – in other words Spain is in for a long period of economic difficulties as it struggles to find exit recession and save its banks.

In 2012, officials claimed that the unemployment rate is likely to remain the same next year, but Spain would emerge from recession the year after. Spain's austerity plan appears to be well-received in the financial markets, with Spanish bond yields falling again. However, experts are warning that Mariano Rajoy's new austerity package will drive the Spanish economy deeper into recession.

身為歐洲第四大經濟體的西班牙這星期公告增稅計畫並大規模削減開支，希望在明年能省下五百億美元的預算，藉以避免其他歐洲國家對其進行新一輪的緊急救助。這項計畫將進一步的增稅並減少政府支出，並讓其債權國及金融市場相信西班牙減少赤字的決心。

根據這項削減開支計畫，所有公務員的薪水將第三年凍漲，同時所有政府部門都將刪減約 9% 的預算。政府也將開徵新的樂透稅。

但數千名西班牙群眾發起「占領國會」運動包圍西班牙國會，抗議政府刪減教育、公共醫療支出及退休金等預算。西班牙政府官員回應時則表示，政府將透過社會安全基金發放退休金，實質退休金甚至將成長 1%。

去年當選的西班牙首相拉霍伊曾承諾不對退休金做出改變，同時避免其他歐洲國家對其進行新一輪的緊急救助。在失業率持續攀升的情況下，政府也將稅收分配在失業救濟補助。西班牙的失業率高達 25%，是歐元區中最高的，其中青年失業率更高達失業率的兩倍。

拉霍伊首相表示，西班牙正經歷有史以來第二嚴重的經濟衰退期。他也多次向公眾示警，西班牙的問題無法迅速解決。換句話說，西班牙在拯救銀行、走出經濟衰退的困境上，仍有很長一段路要走。

在 2012 年時，政府官員表示，失業率在明年仍將居高不下，但西班牙將在後年擺脫經濟衰退。西班牙緊縮政策在金融市場上受到好評，西班牙公債價值也停止下滑。但也有專家認為，拉霍伊的緊縮政策會進一步的把西班牙推向經濟衰退的深淵。

Unit 18

Tornado
龍捲風

代表意義超理解

龍捲風是快速、強烈且暴力的氣旋，其中一端連接雲層，另一端則與地面接觸。龍捲風的風速太強，通常會摧毀途徑上的房屋與樹木，並對附近的人造成傷害。

A tornado is a fast, powerful and violent rotating column of air that is contact with both the earth and the clouds. The wind speed of tornado is strong that it often brings down trees and buildings and harms anyone who's nearby.

B 背景知識大突破 Background

龍捲風有各種不同的形狀和尺寸，但通常都是肉眼可見的漏斗狀氣旋，較窄的一端與陸地連結。大部分的龍捲風風速都小於每小時 160 公里，但強烈的龍捲風風速可達每小時 500 公里以上。龍捲風通常會在地面上徘徊幾公里後才會消失。

Tornadoes come in different shapes and sizes, but they are all typically in the form of a visible air funnel, with the narrow end touches the ground. Most tornadoes have wind speed lower than

＊ column　圓柱　　＊ funnel　漏斗狀；漏斗

160 kilometer per hour, but powerful tornadoes may have wind speed higher than 500 kilometer per hour. Tornadoes would travel for a several kilometers before dissipating.

M 使用方法一把罩 ethod

Tornado 是最常用來稱呼龍捲風的詞，另外能用來稱呼龍捲風的英文單字還包括 twister 和 cyclones。Twister（旋風）在口語上也常用來指龍捲風，例如 1996 年的電影龍捲風就是以 twister 為名。Cyclone 則較常指氣象上的氣旋，比起其它兩個字較少被用來形容龍捲風。龍捲風著陸則是用 touch down 這個詞來表現旋風著地的一瞬間，這個詞一般是用來形容美式足球的達陣得分。

A 主題文章 rticle

Nine people were hurt when a tornado roared through a small town near Watford City, North Dakota, earlier in March this year. The tornado also destroyed thirteen trailers. The National Weather Service said that the twister packed winds that peaked at 120 miles per hour.

The tornado hits at a small town about five miles south of Watford City. A fifteen-year-old girl was flown away by the twister and received a serious head injury. Luckily she was

＊dissipate　消散

expected to survive. There are also eight other people who were sent to a local hospital for lesser injuries.

A volunteer at an American Red Cross shelter recalled that the tornado touched down so quickly that nobody had time to take shelter. "I saw it coming at me" said another men who suffered a head wound and cuts on his arms.

Not long after the event, another tornado did damage in Riverview, Florida. The tornado touched down and damaged throughout the area. "This car got dents and bangs all over it. This one just got broken windshield and some more damage on the side," said an eyewitness of the tornado. The roofs were also torn off buildings, and there was debris strewn around. Luckily, there is no report of injuries involved this time.

In other cases, tornados also damage forests that would take decades to heal. Experts say that in tornado-damaged areas, it will take between 50 and 100 years for the forests to replenish. Even the shade trees would take about 25 years to grow back to their full size.

According to Meteorology data, the top 10 tornado warning areas in the United States in 2013 are Jackson, Mississippi, Birmingham, Alabama, Memphis, Tennessee, Paducah, Kentucky, Raleigh, North Carolina, Huntsville, Alabama, Denver, Colorado, Mobile, Alabama, Springfield, Missouri, and Richmond, Virginia. Alabama is the top tornado warning state in the United Sates.

美國北達科他州沃特福德市附近在今年三月發生龍捲風，造成九人受傷。龍捲風襲擊時也摧毀周邊 13 輛大型拖車。國家氣象局顯示，當時龍捲風周圍的最高風速達到每小時 120 英里（約每小時 192 公里）。

龍捲風發生在沃特福德市南方約五英哩處的小鎮，一名 15 歲的女孩被龍捲風捲起，頭部受到重傷。幸運的是，她在接受治療後並沒有生命危險。此外還有 8 人受到輕傷，都被送往當地的醫院進行治療。

美國紅十字會的義工在避難所回憶時說，龍捲風發生的太快，沒有人能及時做出反應前往避難。「我看到它（龍捲風）朝著我過來」，一位頭上受傷，手腕也被割傷的受害者說。

這次事件發生後沒多久，另一個龍捲風發生在佛羅里達州的河景，龍捲風著陸後破壞了整個地區。「這輛車遍體鱗傷，到處都有凹痕，擋風玻璃全毀，車體側面也被破壞，」目擊者說。現場建築物的屋頂也被捲起，碎片四散。幸運的是，這起事件並沒有造成任何人員的傷亡。

不僅如此，在其他事件中，龍捲風也破壞當地的森林，造成數十年後才能回復的傷害。專家們說，遭到龍捲風破壞的森林區域，預計要花 50 年到 100 年的時間才能回復。即使是造景、林蔭用的植樹，也要 25 年才能長回原本的尺寸。

根據氣象資料顯示，2013 年美國前十名的龍捲風警示區分別是密西西比州的傑克遜，阿拉巴馬州的伯明翰，田納西州的孟菲斯、肯塔基州的帕度卡，北卡羅來納州的羅利，阿拉巴馬州的亨茨維爾，科羅拉多州的丹佛，阿拉巴馬州的莫比爾，密蘇里州的斯普林菲爾德，以及維吉尼亞州的里士滿。阿拉巴馬州則是美國龍捲風警報最多的州。

Unit 19

Whaling in Japan
日本捕鯨活動

代表意義超理解

千年來，捕鯨活動是日本傳統上非常重要的一個活動，但這項傳統近年來卻遭到反捕鯨國家或組織的強烈反對。一般而言，日本從鯨魚身上獲取鯨肉、鯨油、和其他各種原料。

Whaling has been an important part of Japanese society for over a thousand year; however, this traditional practice is recently under fire from nations and organizations that strongly oppose it. General speaking, Japanese have obtained meat, oil, and other materials from whales.

背景知識大突破 Background

國際捕鯨委員會於 1982 年投票決議禁止任何形式的商業捕鯨行為。該禁令於 1986 年生效，而日本也受迫於壓力，停止捕鯨行為。但近年來日本已著手研究如何在國際捕鯨委員會的管理範圍內重啟商業捕鯨行動。

In 1982, the International Whaling Commission voted on a resolution to ban commercial whaling. The moratorium came to

---

＊resolution　決心

＊moratorium　（行動、活動等）的暫停

active in 1986. Japan was forced to stop its commercial whaling under pressure. However, recently Japan had begun researching ways to restart its commercial whaling under the jurisdiction of the International Whaling Commission.

Method 使用方法一把罩

類似於 fishing 這個字用來表示釣魚或捕魚，whaling 這個字是從 whale（鯨魚）而來，用以表示各種形式的捕鯨行為。例如：

The Japanese whaling fleet has slaughtered 30 whales off its northeast coast, against UN rules.

（日本捕鯨船隊無視聯合國的規章，在日本東北海岸周遭捕殺 30 頭鯨魚。）

若要用英文表達臺灣常見的釣蝦活動，一般則會使用 shrimp fishing，例如：

Shrimp fishing in Taiwan has moved indoors over the years, and it is a popular activity in Taipei and elsewhere.

（在臺灣，釣蝦在多年前已成為一種室內活動，在台北和其他地方，都是一種很受歡迎的活動。）

＊jurisdiction　管轄範圍；管轄權

A 主題文章 Article

The International Court of Justice in The Hague ordered Japan to stop hunting whales in the Antarctic. It says Japan's "research whaling" program contravened a 1986 moratorium on whale hunting. Although the ruling prompted Japan to decided not to send whaling fleets to the Southern Ocean, Japan still started its annual north-west Pacific whaling operations. In order to defuse international criticism, Japan had decreased its planned catch by 23%. Japan also plans to resume whaling in the Antarctic in 2015.

The Japanese Government plans to resume a lethal hunt next year as it tries to revive legal commercial whaling. Four ships will be sent before the lethal hunt, with plans to use biopsy guns instead of harpoons, since the International Court of Justice had outlawed the Antarctic hunt. This none lethal research program will undertake research programs before the hunt, in Japan's usual whaling grounds south of Australia and New Zealand.

Japanese researcher will be aboard these ships, and international researchers have been invited to join the course too. They will use darts guns and crossbows to gain biopsy samples on large whales.

However, anti-whaling groups have condemned the research activity as a cover for commercial whaling. They argue the research boats would sneak around the International Court of Justice ruling. Anti-whaling groups confirmed that they would return to the Antarctic to track the Japanese vessels. "We will be going down, definitely," a spokesman from anti-whaling group said. "We are yet to decide which ships will go."

The Australian Government, which has been particularly vocal in its opposition to Japan's waling activity in the Southern Pacific, also stated in the strongest terms that it will not cooperate with Japan. It claims that it will take whatever actions necessary to prevent Japanese plans to bring back commercial whaling.

海牙國際法庭下令日本須停止在南極的捕鯨行為。國際法庭指出，日本「研究性捕鯨」的計畫已違反 1986 年的暫停捕鯨協議。這個判決雖然使日本暫停前往南冰洋捕鯨，但日本仍照常派遣前往西北太平洋的捕鯨作業。而為了緩和國際社會的批評，日本也將原先的捕鯨額度降低 23%。日本同時計畫在 2015 年恢復在南極的捕鯨作業。

為了能在明年恢復合法的商業捕鯨並重新地展開致命性的獵捕行為，日本政府計畫先派出四艘非致命性的捕鯨研究船，並以用在活體檢驗的切片槍取代魚叉，以符合國際規範。這些船隻將進行捕鯨前的研究項目，其目的地是在日本捕鯨活動最常出沒的澳大利亞和紐西蘭南方。

這些船上載有日本的研究人員，而國際研究人員也受邀加入這支船團。他們會以標槍和十字弩取得活體檢驗標本。

然而，反捕鯨團體紛紛提出譴責，認為日本在為商業捕鯨行為進行掩護。他們認為這些研究船隻是在鑽國際法院判決的漏洞。反捕鯨團體證實，他們會回到南冰洋追蹤日本船隻。「我們還沒決定好哪些船會去」，反捕鯨團體的發言人說，「但我們一定會去監視」。

而一向大力反對日本捕鯨的澳大利亞政府則強烈表態，他們絕不會與日本合作。澳大利亞政府也表示，他們會採取一切必要的措施，防止日本重新進行商業性的捕鯨行為。

Unit 20

Wildfire

野火

代表意義超理解

野火是在荒野中自然發生的火災。由於野火蔓延的非常迅速，而且會延燒至其路徑中的所有東西，因此對生物和各種天然資源都造成非常大的威脅。

A wildfire or wild fire is an uncontrolled fire in an area that occurs in the wilderness. Because wild fire could spread out so quickly and combust anything on its path, it poses a great threat to lives and natural resources when it happens.

B 背景知識大突破 Background

野火通常發生在乾熱、廣闊的自然地形中，例如澳大利亞和美國加州就時常傳出原野火災或森林火災。野火在一年四季都對人命和各種設施建築造成威脅，尤其在夏天時更為危險。美國每年可發生多達八萬場野火火警，燒毀高達一千萬英畝的平野或森林。

Wildfires usually occur in large landscape with hot and dry climate, such as Australia or the state of California. They pose a great risk to life and infrastructure during all time of the year,

---

＊ combust　燃燒；消耗

＊ landscape　景觀、園林

＊ infrastructure　基礎建設、基礎設施

especially in summer time. In the United States, up to 80,000 wildfires may occur each year, burning down up to 10 million acres of lands or forests.

M 使用方法一把罩 ethod

Wildfire 和字面上的意思一樣，就是野火，泛指中文一切類似的稱呼，包括山火、林火、森林大火等。不同植被引發的火災可用不同的詞彙，例如灌木叢引發的火災稱為 bushfire，草原上引發的火災則稱為 grass fire 等。例如：

Grass fire burns close in LA hills, the fire was contained to 3 acres and did not damage any structures.

（洛杉磯附近發生草原火災，火災面積被控制在 3 英畝內，並沒有破壞到任何建築。）

野火不一定發生在森林中，但一般無法控制、造成災情的野火多半發生在森林中，因此 wildfire 常被用來形容森林大火。若在其他情況下要形容野火，尤其是在和森林、原野無關的場合，可以用 uncontrolled outdoor fires 等直白的詞句進行說明。

A 主題文章 Article

According to the California state government, there are nearly a dozen wildfires sparked in May, causing more than twenty millions in damage. The state government readied five thousand firefighters and appropriated six hundred millions to battling blazes. However, with the worst wildfire season ahead, it's far from enough. "We're getting ready for the worst," said the state governor. "Now, we don't want to anticipate before we know, but we need a full complement of firefighting capacity."

According to the governor, California may still need thousands of firefighters in the future. The weather is hotter because of climate change, and the chances of wildfire are much higher than before. "And in the years to come, we're going to have to make very expensive investments and adjust. And the people are going to have to be careful of how they live, how they build their homes and what kind of vegetation is allowed to grow around them." Said the governor.

The California Department of Forestry and Fire Protection has responded to more than 1,500 fires this year already, compared to about 800 in an average year.

A blaze started in San Diego County earlier in May, eventually grew to ten fires spanning 39 square miles in the area, destroying 11 houses, an apartment complex, and two businesses. A burned body was found, and a firefighter suffered heat exhaustion.

Firefighters had to douse remaining hotspots with backpacks filled with water to ensure the ground was moist enough to prevent fires from returning. They also covered the hotspots with soils and large logs to prevent further sparks. All these works required great amounts of labor, and the state firefighting agency went to peak staffing in the first week in April, instead of its usual start in May. "It's almost like a 12-month fire seasons this year," said one Fire Department officer in central California.

根據加州政府提供的資料，今年五月上旬加州發生十餘場森林火災，造成超過兩千萬美元的損失。加州州政府已動員 5000 名消防隊員並撥款六億美元以因應野火，但面對野火最為嚴重的夏季，這些準備可能遠遠不足。「我們已做好最壞的打算」，加州州長說。「我不想在事件發生前預言，但我們需要做好防治的一切準備」。

根據州長的說法，加州在未來仍須追加數千名消防隊員的人力。因為氣候變化的關係，天氣比過去來的熱，這使得野火發生的機率大為提高。「在未來幾年中，我們必須為預防工作投入大量昂貴的預算並進行調整。居民也必須十分注意他們的生活細節，例如他們建造房屋的方式及建材、以及居家附近可以種植的植被」，州長說。

加州的林業及防火部門今年上半年已處理了約 1,500 起森林大火，而在過去，平均一年只有 800 多起森林火警。

稍早在五月時，聖地牙哥發生一場大火，火災最後從十個地方外竄，災區遍及 39 平方英里，摧毀 11 棟房屋，1 棟公寓，以及兩座商業建築。災後現場發現一具被燒毀的屍體，及一名消防員在工作中發生熱衰竭。

消防員必須以裝滿水的背包覆蓋著有起火危險的地點，以保持地面濕潤，預防起火。為防範任何可能的意外起火，他們還要以土石泥磚覆蓋可能的危險起火點，而這些工作都需要大量的勞力。加州消防機構往年在五月才需啟動尖峰工作期，但今年則在四月初就被迫啟動。「這簡直像是一年 12 個月都是火災季」，一名來自中加州的消防員這樣說。

PART 4

anagement, securities investent, information processing,
il engineering, asset manage-
ent, etc. Their monthly salary
ll be set at NT$31,000.

There will also be 209 new
fice clerks to be recruited this
ar, with their starting salary
t at NT$24,000 per month. The
rgest number of new
nployees, at 459, will be mail
rriers, with their starting pay
so set at NT$24,000 per month,
us an extra driving or delivery
lowance of NT$5,732.

Based on the average employ-
ent rate of 2% to 6%, the
xpected number of applicants to
ke the examination is around
8,000, the spokesm

For furth

Inter-party consultations to

The China Post news staff

The Kuomintang-controlled Legislative Yuan completed the first reading of an amendment to its own procedural bylaw yesterday, promising to make all closed-door inter-party consultations public record. Known popularly as "black box" operations, the inter-party consultations held behind closed doors may last as long as four months.

"The horse trading

Moreover, the records will be published in the Legislative Yuan bulletin, together with the conclusions reached, Ting said.

Should there be discrepancies between the published conclusions and the results of action on bills, full explanations will be able to be discovered in the record, the Kuomintang legislator said. "We want the secret horse trading exposed under bright sunshine," Ting stressed.

Lawmakers have to complete the second and third readings before the legislature adjourns for the summer. "There won't be difficulty," another Kuomintang legislator said. The

Kuomintang contr
majority in the 1
Yuan.

In addition, Art
cedural bylaw w
The inter-party c
can go on for four
to that article, sho
in one month.

Democratic Pro
islators c
Kuomintang-prop
as "going a little to

"All of us are
party consultatio
improved, but act
be seriously dela
ment were mad

NSC dismisses Ma death in war scenario

The China Post news staff

Taiwan's top security body yesterday dismissed a report that the military's upcoming war chess would drill a scenario where President-elect Ma Ying-jeou was assassinated. The National Security Council (NSC) described the Next Magazine report as unfounded, irresponsible and with a political agenda.

Next claimed that the war chess, to be conducted later this month, would assume that Ma's assassination would plunge the nation into chaos and trigger a surprise invasion by China. The drill was meant to see how different government and security bodies could cope with such a situation, and how Taiwan would interact with the United States, the tabloid magazine cited unnamed presidential sources as saying.

It would be a test to see whether U.S. intervention should be sought or whether other solutions would be possible, and whether a state of emergency should be declared, the report said.

Ma's spokesman Lo Chih-chiang declined to comment on the report, saying the Presidential Office owed the public an explanation. President Chen Shui-bian had invited Ma to the war chess, which is part of the NSC's annual drill, but the president-elect declined the invitation.

The opposition camp called for the drill to be postponed until Ma is inaugurated, but the NSC insisted on conducting it as scheduled. The NSC said yesterday that the drill, to be conducted in three stages between April 21 and 27, is a test of government bodies' responses to military crises and of the nation's defense facilities.

But Kuomintang legislators have repeated the opposition camp's call for the drill be postponed, so as to let Ma oversee it. KMT Legislator Lin Yu-fang said it is "very ridiculous and impolite" for an outgoing president to conduct a drill on the mock assassination of his successor. "The Chen administration has designed such a drill apparently to vent its anger over its loss in the presidential election," claimed Lin.

KMT Legislator Chang Hsien-yao said such a drill has already raised concern in the United States and Taiwan's neighbors.

Fugitive ex-Hsinchu Council speaker returns

TAIPEI, CNA

Former Hsinchu County Council speaker Huang Huan-chi returned to Taiwan and was taken into custody Tuesday after fleeing to China two years ago, following his sentencing to eight years in prison on corruption charges, judicial sources said yesterday.

Following unsuccessful kidney transplant surgery in China, Huang recently informed Hsinchu County police that he would be returning to the Taiwan. Shortly after Huang's plane landed in Taiwan, he was escorted away by police, who later turned him over to the Hsinchu District Prosecutors Office.

Huang served two terms as Hsinchu County Council speaker before running in the legislative elections in December 2001 as a candidate of the Taiwan Solidarity Union. He ended up losing the election. In that race, Huang was accused of vote-buying violations for allegedly using the county council's budget to purchase tea and moon cakes for voters. He was later released on bail.

Two years ago, after being convicted on corruption charges related to an incinerator scandal in the county, Huang decided to flee to China to avoid serving his prison sentence. He was then placed on the Hsinchu District Prosecutors Office's wanted list.

More g
Parkin

TAIPEI, CNA

An internation
ject has
Parkinson's-relat
that only develop
Those who carry
twice more li
Parkinson's disea

The mutation,
is found in ge
codes for pro
repeat kinase 2
paper produced
partially funded b
National Science
lished in the scie
of Neurology.

Parkinson's di
as Parkinson syn
erative disorder
nervous system
the patient's sp
ment.

A group of exp
Singapore, Japa
States have alrea
Parkinson's-relat
linked to LRRK2,
relations betwee
groups and ind
For example, the
LRRK2-G2019S is
of Parkinson's an
and Ashkenazi Je

In 2004, the g
a mutation, G238
linked to Parki
especially Han Ch

綜合篇

Miscellaneous

Unit 1

2014 Olympic Winter Games
2014 年冬季奧運

代表意義超理解

2014 年冬季奧運於 2014 年 2 月在俄羅斯的索契舉行，是一場重要的國際綜合性體育盛會。2014 年的冬季奧運和帕拉林匹克運動會都由索契組織委員會舉辦。這是俄羅斯自 1991 年蘇聯解體以來首次主辦奧運會，共有來自 88 個國家，近 3000 名運動員共襄盛舉。

The 2014 Winter Olympics was a major international multi-sport event held in Sochi, Russia, in February 2014. Both the 2014 Winter Olympics and 2014 Winter Paralympics were organized by the Sochi Organizing Committee. It was the first Olympics in Russia since the breakup of the Soviet Union in 1991. Nearly 3 thousands athletes from 88 nations participated in the event.

B背景知識大突破 Background

冬季奧運會每四年舉辦一次，是國際重大賽事之一，運動項目多為冰上或雪上運動。2018 年的冬奧會將由韓國舉辦，而歷史上第一次的冬季奧運會則在 1924 年由法國主辦。

---

* breakup　（關係、聯盟）的終止

The Winter Olympic Games is one of the major international sporting events that occurs once every four years. It features sports practiced on snow or ice. South Korea is to host the 2018 Winter Olympics. The first Winter Olympics was held in 1924 in France.

Method 使用方法一把罩

除了一般的奧林匹克比賽和冬季奧運外，國際奧林匹克委員會 (International Olympics Committee, IOC) 也舉辦青年奧林匹克運動會 (Youth Olympic Games，青年奧運) 和帕拉林匹克運動會 (Paralympics Games，帕運會，身心障礙人士奧運) 等各種賽事。此外還有國際聽障運動總會 (International Committee of Sports for the Deaf, CISS) 舉辦的聽障奧林匹克 (Deaflympics)，都是國際間的重大賽事。

A 主題文章 Article

Pyeongchang had missed its opportunity to host the Winter Olympics four years ago, only by a handful of votes. Again, it has lost the opportunity to host the Winter Olympics this year. But this time, Pyeongchang is ready to welcome the 2018 Winter Olympics, as it won the 2018 bid in a landslide over Munich.

Pyeongchang is a county in Gangwon Province in South Korea. It is home to several Buddhist temples. It is located approximately 180 kilometers east of Seoul, the capital of South Korea.

According to South Korean organizing committee official, "It was a very difficult moment to come back after the second loss and ask people to go for another bid." The Korean people are disappointed and skeptical. "But the International Olympic Committee encouraged us to bid again."

It had been decades since last time the Winter Olympics was hosted in Asia. The continent had held it only twice, both times in Japan. It also means that South Korea is the second Asian country to host the important event. "Asia is a bit underdeveloped for winter sports when compared to other continents," said the South Korean official.

The evidence is also true when it comes to the medal table. Asian countries had only won seven gold medals in the 2014 Winter Olympics. South Korea won three gold medals, and eight medals overall. The total gold medals won by Asian countries are fewer than the Dutch speed skaters alone.

South Korea plans to spend 9 billion for the coming Winter Olympics, which includes infrastructure improvements. The government also has plans to build high-speed railway to Pyeongchang. However, it is still relative pittance, compared to the Russians who spent 50 billion in the 2014 Winter Olympics.

Pyeongchang had hosted the 2013 Special Olympics World Winter Games before. It will also host the Paralympics in 2018.

平昌過去曾以少數幾票的差距痛失主辦四年前冬季奧運的機會。之後，它又再次失去舉辦 2014 冬季奧運的機會。但在日前一場在慕尼黑舉辦的會議中，平昌贏得 2018 冬季奧運的主辦權，準備迎接下一屆的冬季奧運。

平昌是韓國江原道轄下的一個縣。它位於首爾東方約 180 公里的位置，以傳統佛寺聞名。

韓國爭取主辦的委員會官員說，「對我們而言，在連續兩次競爭失利後要繼續進行申請是一個相當艱困的處境。韓國人民對此頗為失望，但國際奧運委員會鼓勵我們繼續進行申請」。

上一次由亞洲國家主辦冬季奧運已經是幾十年前的事了。位於亞洲大陸的國家中只主辦過兩次冬季奧運，兩次都是在日本。這也意味著，韓國是亞洲中第二個主辦冬季奧運的國家。「和其它大洲相比，亞洲在冬季運動方面較為落後」，這名韓國官員說。

在實際證據上也確實如此。在 2014 年的冬季奧運中，亞洲國家總共只奪得七面金牌。韓國隊則奪得八面獎牌，其中包括三面金牌。亞洲國家取得的金牌總數，比荷蘭滑冰隊拿到的獎牌還少。

韓國計劃斥資 90 億美元為即將到來的冬季奧運會作準備，其中包括改善基礎設施，並興建通往平昌的高速鐵路。但和在 2014 冬季奧運中花費 500 億美元的俄羅斯相比，這個數字仍顯得微薄。

平昌之前曾主辦過 2013 的特殊奧林匹克運動會。它還將主辦 2018 年的帕奧會。

Unit 2

3D Printing
3D 列印

代表意義超理解

3D 列印機可以被解釋成一種有限制性功能的工業用機器人，它能在電腦的控制下進行「積層」的程序。3D 列印的技術從 1980 年代就已經出現，但直到 2010 年以來才得到廣泛的商業應用。

3D printer can be explained as a limited industrial robot which is capable of carrying out an additive process under computer control. The technology has been around since the 1980s, but it didn't become widely available commercially until the 2010s.

B 背景知識大突破
Background

3D 列印又被稱為「積層製造」，是一種透過數位導引製造實物的程序。這種技術透過「積層」的程序，逐層將原料堆疊累積成不同形狀的物件。這和傳統上依賴以切割或鑽孔模式改變外形的加工技術有根本上的不同。

3D printing, also known as additive manufacturing, is a process of making solid object from a digital model. It uses an additive

＊ additive　　＊ solid

process where successive layers of material are laid down in different shapes. It is distinct from traditional machining techniques, which rely on the removal of material by methods such as cutting or drilling.

Method 使用方法一把罩

3D 列印技術的核心技術「基層造形法」的概念在各領域都有其實用性，包括工業設計、建築工程、航太、牙科、土木工程、國防、以至於珠寶、休閒用品等產業都對 3D 列印有廣泛的應用。3D 列印已運用在矯正中，假牙就是 3D 列印產品之一。例如：

Dentists around the world are now embracing next generation 3D printing to produce durable, accurate dental models. It's known as rapid manufacturing. 3D printer is delivering much higher capacity, at lower costs, and with excellent quality with increased customer satisfaction.

（世界各地的牙醫師開始使用新的 3D 列印技術來提供更耐用、更合適的齒模，進行大量生產。3D 列印機的效率更高，價格更低，品質優良，滿意度也較高。）

＊ distinct 明顯的

Large 3D printers have been in existence for several years, and they have been used to produce plane parts. Recently in Shanghai, a Chinese construction firm has succeeded in building ten houses each measuring 200 square meters by 3D printer, in less than 24 hours.

Each of these houses costs around five-thousand U.S. dollars, and all of these houses are environmental friendly. These houses are all constructed from 3D-printed building blocks, which are made from cement mixture and layers of recycled construction waste and glass fiber.

The said firm spent 20 million Chinese Yuan and 12 years to develop the 3D printer. It holds 77 national patents for its construction materials. The printer is 6.6 meters tall, 10 meters wide, and 150 meters long. Even the firm's office building was constructed with 3D-printed walls. The Office building covers an area of 101,000 square meters, and took a month to build from an assembly line of four 3D printers.

The recipe for the quick drying cement used in the construction is top secret, but is made entirely from recycled materials as well. Quality checks are currently conducted by examining each piece of the structure as it is printed out, but there might have to be more stringent checks if people are to live in the building in the future.

The said firm purchased parts for the printer overseas, and assembled the 3D printer in Suzhou. This new type of building constructed by 3D printer is not only environmental friendly, but also cost-effective. "Industrial waste from demolished buildings is damaging our environment, but with 3D printing technology, we are able to recycle construction waste and turn it into new building materials," said the inventor of the 3D printer. "This would create a much safer environment for construction workers and greatly reduce construction costs."

大型的 3D 列印機器已問世多年，甚至被應用在生產飛機零件。最近在上海，一家中國建築公司已經成立利用 3D 列印，在不到 24 小時的時間內，建造出 10 棟約 200 平方公尺的房屋。

這些房屋的造價大約是五千美元，而且還是綠能建築。3D 列印製造出來的建材原料，包括水泥和從廢棄建材中回收的素材以及玻璃纖維。

這家建設公司花了兩千萬人民幣和 12 年的時間開發 3D 列印技術。它的建材擁有 77 項國家專利。這些 3D 列印機高 6.6 公尺，寬 10 公尺，長 150 公尺。甚至連這家公司的辦公大樓都是用 3D 列印建造出來的。這間辦公大樓佔地超過十萬平方公尺，由四架 3D 列印機經過一個月的時間興建而成。

這間公司施工時的水泥配方雖然仍是機密，但也是由再生材料所製成。當 3D 列印機製造出建材時，每一件成品都受到品質檢查。但若將來有人要進住這些房屋，則會進行更嚴格的檢查。

這家公司在海外訂購 3D 列印機的零件，並在蘇州進行組裝。3D 列印製成的建築不但環保，而且更符合成本效益。這些 3D 列印機的發明人說，「原先，建築廢棄後的廢棄物會汙染我們的環境，但透過 3D 列印機，我們能回收這些廢棄建材，並讓它們成為新建材」。「這將大幅降低建築成本，並為工人打造更安全的工作環境」。

Unit 3

Agribot (Farm Robotic)

農業用機器人

代表意義超理解

農業用機器人 (agricultural robot) 簡稱為 agribot，是專為農業用途所設計的機器人。這種機器人又被稱為農場機器人，因為它們多半被安裝在農場中進行農作。大多農業用機器人被用來協助農作物的收成，但也有其他各種不同的機器人以滿足不同需求。

An agricultural robot is also known as agribot. It is a robot designed for agricultural purposes. Agribots are also known as farm robotics, as many of these robots are installed in various of farms. Agribots are mostly applied to agricultural harvesting, but different Agribots had been invented to satisfy different needs.

B 背景知識大突破 Background

除了常見的收成用機器人外，世界各地也有採收水果、剪羊毛、擠牛奶等各種用途的農場機器人。自動拖拉機和噴水器也算是機器人的一種，被用來減少農場所需的勞動力。另外也有專門為牲畜設計的機器人，能為牲口進行清潔或閹割等工作。

Other than the common harvesting robots, fruit-picking robots, sheep shearing robots, and robotic milkers are also installed in farms around the world. Driverless tractor and sprayers are also types of Agribots created to reduce the labor required for farm works. There are also specially designed robots to take care of other livestock works, such as washing and castrating of livestock.

Method 使用方法一把罩

Agribot 是農業用機器人 (Agricultural Robot) 的縮寫，分別由 Agricultural 和 Robot 兩個字的字首和字尾結合而成。機器人 (robot) 這個字字尾的 bot 也常被用來作為各種機器人的表稱，在網路上也常被用來稱呼各種無人操作的程式或產生器。

農業用機器人的研究早在 20 多年前就已經開始，但大部分的研究都因為預算不足或成果有限而陸續停止。但最近許多研究人員陸續展開新的研究，並提出各種不同的機械農業運用方式。大幅的降低所需的人工成本為機械化農業提供了良好的發展背景。

* shear 剪羊毛
* livestock 家畜、牲畜
* castrate 閹割

A 主題文章 Article

A new type of agricultural robot (agribot) had been invented in upstate New York: robotic milkers. It feeds and milks cows without the help of farmhand. Desperate for reliable labor and buoyed by soaring prices, dairy operations started to install robotic milkers. The cows are milking themselves in the farm now.

These farm robotics had been installed across New York's dairy belt, changing patterns of daily farm life which has been followed for centuries. It also reinvigorated the allure of agriculture for a younger, tech-savvy generation.

Senior agricultural managers believe the switch to robotic milking would play a major part in expansion plans for an increasing number of dairy farmers. The machines are able to take care of both the cows and the routines in the farms, though the farm owners occasionally received distress call from their robotic milkers.

Here are the good things about agricultural robots: they allow the cows to set their own hours, lining up for automated milking several times a day. These machines can also scan and map cows' underbellies to calculate their "milking speed." They also monitor the amount and quality of milk produced, how much each cow has eaten, and even the number of steps each cow has taken per day. Best of all, these robots never have problems getting up early or working late.

A 30 years old, seventh generation dairyman who upgraded his farm to robots told the reporter: "we are used to computers and other stuffs, and it's more in line with that." "It's tough to find people to do it well and show up on time," said another milker who installed four robotic milkers last year. "And you don't have

to worry about that with a robot."

The installation of farm robotics is not just happening in U.S. Robots now account for about half of all milking installations in the United Kingdom, and the number is expected to increase in the future.

紐約北部近期來發展出一種被稱為擠奶機器人的新型農業機器人。這種新型的機器人是缺乏人力時餵食和擠奶的好幫手。由於缺乏可靠的勞動力和勞工薪資不斷上升，越來越多酪農業者都開始安裝擠奶機器人，讓乳牛進入全自動擠奶作業。

紐約的農場普遍安裝了這些農業機器人，這也改變數百年來的農場生態。農業機器人不但振興農業，並吸引年輕技工投身這個產業。

高階農產管理人認為，隨著越來越多酪農開始使用擠奶機器人，這些機器會在農莊的擴張中扮演越來越重要的角色。這些機器能自動管理乳牛和擠奶的程序，但農場主人偶而還是會接到機器人的求救通知。

這種農業機器人的好處包括：它能讓乳牛依設定好的時間，多次進行擠奶作業。這些機器也可以掃描乳牛的腹部，計算乳牛的擠奶速度。它們還可以監督牛奶的產量和質量，並計算乳牛吃掉多少飼料，甚至每天行走的步數。更重要的是，這些機器人完全可以應付長時間的工作。

一名年約 30 歲，家中七代從事畜牧，並已安裝機器人設備的農莊老闆告訴記者：「我們已經習慣這些電腦設備，這樣作更符合潮流」。「現在很難找到技術夠好、又不會遲到的員工」，另一位安裝機器人的農莊老板強調，「機器人不會有這些問題」。

美國不是唯一採用這種農業機器人的國家。在英國，大約有一半的農莊採用這種機器設備，未來這個比例還會增加。

Unit 4

Canonization
封聖

代表意義超理解

封聖指的是天主教或東正教中將已去世的人封為聖人的行為。被宣佈為聖人的人將會出現在教會所認可的聖人名單中。

Canonization is the act by which the Catholic Church or the Eastern Orthodox Church declares a deceased person to be a saint. The declared person is then included in a list of recognized saints.

B 背景知識大突破 ackground

最早的聖人們是以前的殉道者，他們虔誠殉教的舉動被認為是對基督最堅定的信仰。原先封聖的行為並沒有任何正式程序，但天主教和東正教漸漸發展出不同的程序將信徒封為聖人。

The first group of people honored as saints were the martyrs. Pious legends of their deaths were considered to affirm the truth of their faith in Christ. Originally, individuals were recognized as saints without any formal process. Later, different processes were developed by the Roman Catholic Church and the Eastern

---

＊decease 死亡
＊martyr 殉道者；烈士
＊pious 虔誠的

Orthodox Church.

M 使用方法一把罩 ethod

天主教 (Roman Catholic) 和東正教 (Eastern Orthodox) 對封聖的名稱也有所不同。天主教一般使用上述的 canonization，而東正教則使用 glorification 這個字。天主教聖徒必須經過幾個不同的審查過程，包括在申請後，到調查及蒐集證據期間，該名候選人被稱為「天主之僕」(Servant of God)、而在教宗宣布該名候選者的「傑出德行」(Heroic in Virtue) 後則稱「可敬者」(The Venerable)、以及「宣福禮」(Beatification) 之後便享有僅次於聖人位階的「真福者」(Blessed) 稱號。例如：

Originally, individuals were recognized as saints without any formal process. Both the Roman Catholic Church and the Eastern Orthodox Church developed different processes to recognize devoted followers into saints.
（在早期，被認可為聖人的基督徒並不需經過任何官方的程序。但隨著教會發展，無論是天主教還是東正教，都發展出不同的將虔誠教徒封為聖人的程序。）

In the Catholic Church, canonization is reserved to the Holy See. The Church requires a long process and extensive proof that the person is worthy to be recognized as a saint.
（在天主教會中，冊封的行為是羅馬教廷的權責，教會經過長期的程序，並需要大量的證據，才能認定被冊封的人值得被稱為聖人。）

A 主題文章 Article

Pope Francis declared his two predecessors John XXIII and John Paul II saints, with Emeritus Pope Benedict XVI also attended the historic ceremony. Never before has a reigning and retired pope celebrated together in public, much less at an event honoring two of their most famous predecessors.

The canonization of John XXIII and John Paul II is a symbol of unity of the Catholic Church, as it honors popes beloved by conservative and progressive followers. The celebrations would begin with the solemn chant of the litany of the saints, while about 150 cardinals, 1,000 bishops, and 6,000 priests process through St. Peter's Square towards the steps at the base of the Vatican basilica.

Pope John XXIII called the historic Second Vatican Council in 1962, which addressed relations between the Roman Catholic Church and the modern world. The first Vatican Council was called about 100 years ago, in 1864. However, the pope did not live to see it to completion. Pope John XXIII said he wanted to "throw open the doors of the Church and let the fresh air of the Spirit blow through."

Pope John Paul II, the first non-Italian pope since the Renaissance, logged over 750,000 travel miles in 104 foreign trips, more than all previous popes combined. He significantly improved the Catholic Church's relations with Judaism, Islam, the Eastern Orthodox Church, and the Anglican Communion. He supported the Church's Second Vatican Council and its reform.

By canonizing two of the most popular modern saints, Pope Francis is adding a newer element to the expectations of a saintly life: engagement with the world. This is also the heart of Francis's own identity.

Pope Francis made the point clear to praise both popes for their work associated with the Second Vatican Council, which brought the 2,000-year-old institution into modern times. John XXIII convened the council while John Paul II helped ensure its more conservative implementation and interpretation.

教宗方濟各為兩名已故教宗若望二十三世和若望保祿二世主持了封聖儀式，名譽教宗本篤十六世也親自出席這個歷史性的儀式。以前從未有現任教宗和退休教宗同在公共場合中慶祝，更不用說是為了紀念兩個最有名的前任教宗。

若望二十三世和若望保祿二世的封聖儀式象徵了天主教會的團結，因為兩人分別受到保守派和進步派信徒的愛戴。慶祝活動將從對聖徒的莊嚴詩歌開始，將會有約 150 名的樞機主教，1,000 名的主教，以及約 6,000 名的神父，經過聖彼得廣場向梵蒂岡大教堂前進。

教宗若望二十三世於 1962 年召開了歷史性的第二次梵蒂岡會議，這次會議定義了天主教會和現代社會之間的關係。這次會議距離 1864 年的第一次梵蒂岡會議約有 100 年的間隔。但這位教宗並無法在有生之年目睹會議結束。他曾說，他想「敞開教會的門，讓聖靈的新鮮空氣吹過」。

教宗若望保祿二世則是自文藝復興以來的第一個非義大利裔教宗，他出訪超過 104 次，旅途高達 75 萬英里，超過以前所有教宗的總合。他顯著的改善了天主教與猶太教、伊斯蘭教、東正教和英國聖公會的關係。他也支持第二次梵蒂岡會議的結論和改革。

藉由這兩位教宗的封聖儀式，教宗方濟各將與世界接觸新增為聖人的生活要素。這也是方濟各自我認知的核心。

教宗方濟各清楚的讚美兩位教宗和第二次梵蒂岡會議，這次會議將有 2,000 年歷史的天主教帶入近代化的工作。若望二十三世召開這個會議，而若望保祿二世則確保其保守的執行和解釋。

Unit 5

FIFA World Cup
國際足球總會世界盃足球賽

代表意義超理解

國際足球總會世界盃足球賽一般簡稱為世界盃足球賽，是由國際足球總會會員國代表隊間的足球競賽。自 1930 年開始，世界盃足球賽每四年舉辦一次，現任的冠軍是德國隊，他們在 2014 年贏得巴西世界盃的冠軍。

The FIFA World Cup, often simply the World Cup, is an international football competition contested by the national teams of the members of the International Federation of Association. It is held once every four year since 1930, and the current champion is Germany, who won the 2014 tournament in Brazil.

B 背景知識大突破 Background

世界盃足球賽由 32 支隊伍爭奪冠軍。四年一度的世界盃賽事被稱為世界盃決賽，足球總會用三年戰績衡量哪些國家隊有資格晉級決賽。世界盃足球賽是世界上最多人觀看的體育賽事之一，有超過 7 億人觀看 2010 年的世界盃決賽。

＊contest　爭奪、競爭　　＊tournament　聯賽、錦標賽

The tournament involves 32 national teams competing for the title. These games are called the World Cup Finals. A qualification phase of three years is used to determine which teams qualify the World Cup Finals. The World Cup is also one of the world's most widely viewed sports events. Over 700 millions of people watched the final match of the 2010 FIFA World Cup game.

Method 使用方法一把罩

美國一般用 soccer 這個字稱呼足球，用 football 稱呼美式足球（橄欖球）。但在美國以外的國家，則大部分使用 football 來表示一般所說的足球。國際足球總會的正式名稱是 Fédération Internationale de Football Association，這也是 FIFA 這個縮寫的由來，International Federation of Association Football 則是其英文名稱。

相關例句如下：

According to FIFA, the competitive game cuju is the earliest form of football for which there is scientific evidence. It is an exercise in a military manual from the third and second centuries before common era.

（根據國際足球協會的說法，中國的蹴鞠則是最早有科學證明的足球活動。這是西元前 2-3 世界就存在的一種軍事訓練活動。）

* phase　階段；期

The International Federation of Association Football had come up with a new strategy to detect drug cheats for the coming World Cup scheduled to kick off in June in Brazil.

According to FIFA officers, the fight against doping has intensified over the last 10 to 15 years. The increase of simple sampling procedures both in and out of competition controls does not stop some athletes to continue with doping strategies.

Starting in 2014, FIFA will freeze and keep the samples as long as they want, so they can always revisit the samples. They will examine all participating players in the preparation period between now and the World Cup at least once, and then they will perform routine procedures during the World Cup and examine blood and urine. FIFA will compare the data with already existing sample analysis from Champions League, from the Confederations Cup 2013, and from the Club World Cup from 2011 to 2013. That means for the top football players around the world, FIFA will run multiple sampling procedures.

"We can compare different samples from the same athletes being taken over periods of the athlete's career in and out of competition, during different times of the year, pre-competition, during high profile competition. We compare the different parameters in urine for the different steroids and hormones and also in blood which could indicate artificial manipulation of the body by doping substances or methods," said the FIFA official. If the data is suspicious, FIFA can perform much more targeted testing.

Players at the tournament in Brazil are to have their blood and urine compared with previous samples. According to a news article, England's World Cup squad will be among the first to

undergo these new doping test regimes that the scientists hope will cut out the use of performance-enhancing drugs.

為了 2014 年 6 月將在巴西開幕的世界盃足球賽，國際足球總會已擬定新的方法對禁藥進行檢測。

國際足球總會的官員指出，在過去 10 到 15 年中，總會和禁藥間的纏鬥越演越烈。雖然總會不斷增加賽前賽後抽樣的次數，但仍無法阻止運動員服用禁藥。

從 2014 年開始，國際足球總會就會持續凍存檢驗樣品，有需要的時候就可以重複對樣本進行檢驗。他們將會在世界盃開打的準備期間，對所有參賽的選手進行血液和尿液的檢驗。國際足球聯盟將把這些樣本和從歐洲冠軍聯賽、2013 年的洲際國家盃還有 2011 到 2013 年的世冠盃所取得的樣本進行比對分析，對世界上頂尖的足球選手進行檢驗。

「我們可以在重要比賽前比較這些運動員在過去不同場合、不同時期中的樣本，分析樣本中的類固醇和激素指數，以分辨這些人是否服用禁藥或其它配方」，這名官員說。「如果得到的數據是可疑的，總會將對個人作出針對性的測試」。

選手們將在巴西進行賽前的血液、尿液抽樣比較。根據新聞報導，英格蘭的代表隊將成為首批受到檢驗的選手。科學家希望透過這種方式達到打擊禁藥的目的。

Unit 6

Oil Shale
油頁岩

代表意義超理解

油頁岩是一種富含有機物質的沉積岩，主要成分包括油母質，可以用來提煉頁岩油。頁岩油和原油的功用一樣，因此被視為可以取代傳統的原油；但提煉頁岩油需要較高的技術，才不會對環境造成衝擊。

Oil shale is an organic-rich sedimentary rock containing kerogen from which shale oil can be produced. The refined products from oil shale, the shale oil, can be used for the same purposes as crude oil. Shale oil is a substitute for conventional crude oil; however, higher technology is required to extract shale oil without bringing environmental impacts.

B 背景知識大突破 Background

包括擁有大型油頁岩沉積的美國在內，世界各地都有油頁岩。世界各地的油頁岩據估計約能提供約 3 兆桶的頁岩油。

Deposits of oil shale occur around the world, including major

* sedimentary　沉積的
* kerogen　油母岩質
* conventional　傳統的

deposits in the United States. Oil shale deposits around the world are estimated to be able to supply 3 trillion barrels of shale oil.

Method 使用方法一把罩

油頁岩 (oil shale) 和頁岩油 (shale oil) 並不一樣。油頁岩指的是富含油母質的頁岩；透過開採、提煉油頁岩所得到的合成原油則稱為頁岩油。頁岩油的功能雖然和傳統原油一樣，但和傳統原油 (crude oil) 並不相同。油頁岩也被用來當作化學原料和建築原料等不同用途。

目前開採頁岩原油的技術稱為水力壓裂法，是利用高壓將水打入油井內，利用水壓沖裂頁岩層，再使油、氣透過裂縫沖向地表。這種技術英文一般稱為 Hydraulic fracturing，簡稱 Fracking。美國政府的資料則指出，美國油頁岩的儲量，以跨越猶他州、科羅拉多州及懷俄明州的綠河層 (Green River Formation) 最多，估計約有近三兆桶的蘊藏量，在經濟和技術條件許可下，約有半數可獲開採。自頁岩油開採技術成熟後，根據國際能源總署的資料顯示，美國將在 2015 年取代俄羅斯，成為全球最大的天然氣產國，並在 2017 年取代沙烏地阿拉伯，成為世界上最大的產油國；美國的石油進口量和原油對外依存率，也陸續創下歷史新低。

主題文章 Article

US oil output is booming thanks to fast-growing production from oil shale formations in places like Texas and North Dakota. The US government expects oil production to grow from 7.3 million barrels a day to 8.4 million.

At the same time, oil imports have remained resilient in the face of surging domestic supply, helping push stocks to record highs. Information released from the Energy Information Administration showed commercial crude stockpiles had climbed from 394.2 million barrels to 397.7 millions in April - the highest level since the agency started the records in about 30 years ago.

Analysts said that the surging shale production overwhelmed an increase in refinery output. The data showed the US is struggling to accommodate surging domestic output, which hits 8.36 million barrels per day. "With parts of the refinery system continuing to require heavy and sour foreign crudes, insufficient volumes of imports are being displaced by indigenous supplies to prevent stock building," said the analysts.

The fastest increase was again in the US Gulf Coast, the world's largest refining hub. Crude has been piling up since new pipelines connecting the region to the giant tank terminal complex in Oklahoma had come on stream. Just a couple years ago, there was no pipeline connecting Oklahoma to the Gulf Coast. There are two main pipelines, with more capacity on the way.

As for the Gulf Coast, with more refineries planning maintenance work, crude stocks in the region is likely to reach a new high before declining as refineries come back from maintenance. On the other hand, as the result of increasing pipelines, oil stocks at Oklahoma, the delivery point for future contracts, have halved in

these years. Report showed the stocks had declined to a degree that the tanks can barely operate.

由於德州和北卡達他州等地的油頁岩層大幅開發，美國的石油產量增長迅速。根據美國政府估計，美國的石油產量將從每天 730 萬桶成長為 840 萬桶。

與此同時，雖然國內需求增加，但石油進口數量仍維持一定的基礎。根據能源部門的資料顯示，四月的商業原油庫存從 3 億 9,420 萬桶成長為 3 億 9,770 萬桶，創下該部門約三十年來的最高記錄。

分析師表示，雖然煉油廠的產量增加，但油頁岩生產的更快。數據顯示，美國正試著調節國內原油的產量，目前已達到每天 836 萬桶的程度。分析師說，「煉油業仍然需要進口的原油，但不足的部分將被國內生產的石油取代，這樣可以避免原油的庫存問題」。

目前美國煉油業成長最快的是墨西哥灣的沿岸地區。這裡也是世界上最大的煉油中心。自從連接奧克拉荷馬州油庫的巨型油管完工後，這邊的原油便堆積如山。不過在幾年前，當地並沒有這樣的油管，但現在不但已經有兩條主油管，未來還將興建更多的油管。

由於墨西哥灣沿岸許多的煉油廠正在進行維修，因此在煉油廠復工前，該地區的原油庫存可能會持續創下新高。另一方面，由於輸油管的發展，原先作為石油轉運點的奧克拉荷馬州石油儲量則減少了將近一半。報告顯示，目前當地的庫存量，僅能勉強讓油槽維持運轉。

Unit 7

New Horizons
新視界號

代表意義超理解

「新視界號」太空偵測船預計將在 2015 年七月抵達冥王星。它將會採集這個矮行星的大氣、衛星、磁場等資訊，再向海王星前進。

The space probe New Horizons is planned to reach the Pluto system in July 2015. It will collect data about the dwarf planet's atmosphere, moons, and magnetosphere and continue the journey to Neptune.

B 背景知識大突破 Background

「新視界號」是美國太空總署派往矮行星冥王星和海王星古柏帶探索的太空探測器。「新視界號」於 2006 年 1 月出發，並在 2007 年到達木星；如果一切按計畫進行，「新視界號」將在 2015 年 7 月抵達冥王星系。

New Horizons is a NASA space probe launched to explore the dwarf planet Pluto and the Kuiper Belt of Neptune. New Horizons was launched in January 2006, and it reached Jupiter in

* probe　探測器

* magnetosphere　磁場；磁層

2007. If everything goes as planned, New Horizons will perform a flyby of the Pluto system in July 2015.

Method 使用方法一把罩

較為普遍的說法是，太陽系的九個行星分別是金星 (Mercury)、水星 (Venus)、地球 (Earth)、火星 (Mars)、木星 (Jupiter)、土星 (Saturn)、天王星 (Uranus)、海王星 (Neptune) 和冥王星 (Pluto)。但其中冥王星已被定位為矮行星 (Dwarf Planet)，並不符合行星的標準。

國際天文聯會 (The International Astronomical Union, IAU) 在 2006 年正式把冥王星的地位降級為矮行星，因為它不符合國際天文聯會用來定義行星的三個標準。因此嚴格來說，目前太陽系只有八個行星。

2006 年「新視界號」出發時，冥王星還被界定為是行星。雖然稍後冥王星被降級為矮行星，但冥王星系仍然有至少五個衛星。其中一個衛星的體積非常巨大，被部分學者視為和冥王星是雙行星。雙行星是一種非正式的天文學用語，用來描述有巨大衛星的行星。因為這些原因，「新視界號」仍持續向冥王星前進。

A 主題文章 rticle

The National Aeronautics and Space Administration (NASA) is the agency of the United States government that is responsible for the nation's civilian space program and for aeronautics and aerospace research. Its New Horizons is one of the fastest spacecraft ever built. New Horizons was launched in 2006 and traveling at million miles per day, its destination is the ex-planet Pluto, the most distant bodies in the solar system.

According to NASA, New Horizons reached Jupiter in 2007, and by July 2015 it will be only 6,200 miles away from Pluto. Its mission will start in January 2015, with photographs using Long Range Reconnaissance Imager (LORRI). The exact location of Pluto is uncertain to us, so these photos will help mission control pinpoint exactly where Pluto is. "We will use the images to refine Pluto's location, and then fire the engines to make necessary corrections," said NASA official.

Pluto has five moons, but experts believed there is a possibility the New Horizons will discover new moons or rings. "We are flying into the unknown and there is no telling what we might find." After New Horizons passes Pluto, it will continue the journey into the Kuiper Belt. It will study the region up to a billion miles from Neptune's orbit where as many as a billion mini-planets may exist.

Humankind doesn't have the chance to encounter with a new planet after Mars was revealed in 1965, revealing the surface of Mars as a desolate wasteland. Pluto's surface is unexplored, and the mission will give astronomers a new look of what's on the dwarf planet. Progress of the mission can be soon on New Horizons Mission website.

美國太空總署是美國政府負責全國太空計劃及研究的機構。「新視界」太空船是有史以來最快的飛行器之一。「新視界」在 2006 年出發，每天能航行超過百萬英哩，它的目的地則是太陽系中最遙遠的矮行星－冥王星。

根據美國太空總署的資料，「新視界」在 2007 年抵達木星，而在 2015 年 7 月的時候，將抵達距冥王星 6,200 英哩距離的目的地。它的任務將從 2015 年 1 月開始，使用遠距離勘測成像儀（LORRI）拍攝照片。冥王星的確切位置目前仍無法確定，這些照片將會協助任務中心定位冥王星的位置。「我們將使用圖像細化冥王星的位置，然後作出必要的修正」，太空總署的官員這樣表示。

冥王星共有五個衛星，但專家認為仍有可能發現新的衛星或星環。「我們正飛向一個未知的領域，目前仍不知道會有怎麼樣的新發現」。「新視界」將飛越冥王星，並繼續向海王星的古柏帶前進。它會在海王星外圍十億英哩的範圍內蒐集資料，那邊可能有多達數十億的微行星。

人類自從 1965 年看到火星的影像後就不曾再有機會探索新的星球。當時揭示了火星表面只有一片荒地。冥王星的表面尚未有人探索，我們將能知道這個矮行星上到底有什麼新東西。太空總署網站上可以查的到「新視界」的任務進度。

Unit 8

Selfie
自拍

代表意義超理解

自拍是一種以智慧型電話或數位相機自行拍照的行為，它通常透過臉書、Instagram、Snapchat 等社群網路分享。自拍照通常是較為隨性的照片。

A selfie is a self-portrait photo usually taken with a hand-held smart phone or digital camera. It is often shared on social networking services such as Facebook, Instagram, or Snapchat. They are usually casual photos.

B 背景知識大突破 Background

自拍這個字出現於 2005 年，但在此之前，自拍形式的照片就已經在網路上風行。在臉書成為最大的社群網路前，自拍照已普遍出現在部落格或其他網站上。研究顯示，智慧型電話的前置攝影鏡頭的改良，是現在自拍越來越流行的原因之一。

The term "selfie" was introduced in 2005, although this type of photos predates the widespread use of the term. Before Facebook became the dominant networking service, self-taken photos

＊ portrait　肖像
＊ casual　隨性的；偶然的
＊ predate　居先；在日期上早於
＊ dominant　占優勢的

were common on blogs and other online media. According to a research, improvements in front-facing cameras on mobile phones help selfies become popular in modern era.

Method 使用方法一把罩

自拍通常被視為一種休閒性的拍攝行為，一般常與社群網路連結，人們可以隨心所欲的拍照，並將照片放在社群網路上親友分享。但就如同這個字的英文來源一樣，自拍也被視為是比較非正式的拍照模式，在較為正式、嚴肅的場合，應該避免自拍行為。一些政治人物也因自拍引發爭議。

自拍 (selfie) 這個單字日前已被收入牛津英文字典 (Oxford English Dictionary)，並被評選為牛津字典 2013 年度國際詞彙。這個詞在不同地方也被寫成 selfy，但 selfie 仍較常見，也較受歡迎。牛津字典對 selfie 的官方定義是用智慧型手機或視訊拍攝的自身照片，並經由社群網路 (social media) 進行分享。這個字源自於澳洲，最早在 2002 年時澳洲的一個網路論壇上使用。

牛津字典將 selfie 選為 2013 年度國際詞彙時表示，selfie 在 2013 年被人們廣為傳播和使用，牛津字典編輯部進行的語言研究顯示，selfie 這個字的使用頻率比去年同期增加了 170 倍。

＊era　年代、時代

President Barack Obama refused to take a selfie with a 13-year-old girl during his visit to Seoul, South Korea.

A group of teenagers from the U.S. Army Garrison in Seoul were waiting for President's Obama's arrival with a sign that read, "Mr. President May I Have a Selfie with You?" However they were in for a major disappointment.

As the President made his way the lines of spectators, he bypassed the girl, telling her that if he agreed to take a selfie with her, he would have to do it for everyone else. "Just take a picture of me as I'm going by," said the commander-in-chief, according to the news reporter.

It's kind of awkward, right? However, what makes it even more awkward is the fact just less than 24 hours later, Obama took a selfie with Malaysian Prime Minister Najib Razak. Prime Minister Razak shared the selfie on Twitter and wrote "My selfie with President Obama!"

When it comes to selfies, President Obama has been burned before. The President was caught snapping a selfie with Danish Prime Minister Helle Thorning-Schmidt and British Prime Minister David Cameron during former South Africa President Nelson Mandela's memorial service. The three smiled while taking the selfie, but the first lady Michelle Obama didn't seem to approve it. The picture went viral on the internet, with a large number of comments on the lack of propriety shown by the three national leaders.

Mr. Obama also took a selfie with Vice President Joe Biden few days earlier, as the photo was posted on the Vice President's new Instagram account.

Again, just a few weeks ago in April, the President was captured on camera with Boston Red Sox slugger David Ortiz. It was found later that Ortiz has a relationship with Samsung, and the selfie was used to promote their products. This selfie incident led a White House senior adviser to suggest "Maybe this will be the end of all selfies." Clearly, he was wrong.

美國總統歐巴馬在訪問韓國首爾途中，拒絕與一名 13 歲的女童自拍。

當時，一群來自美國駐軍基地的青少年拿著「總統先生，是否可以和你一起自拍」的標語等候歐巴馬到來。但隨後這些人大失所望。

歐巴馬繞過那名女孩向看台走去。他告訴那名女孩說，如果他同意一起自拍，那他必須和其他人也一起自拍。「我走過去的時候，照張相就好了」，他是這樣說的。

這還挺尷尬的對吧？事實上，更尷尬的是，不到 24 小時後，歐巴馬就和馬來西亞總理拉札克自拍。拉札克把兩人的自拍照上傳到網上，並註明「我和歐巴馬總統的自拍！」

歐巴馬之前已經為了自拍的事情惹過麻煩。當他出席南非故前總統曼德拉的追悼會時，他和丹麥首相施密特、英國首相卡麥隆三人一起微笑自拍，但第一夫人蜜雪兒則在一旁冷眼旁觀。圖片被放上互聯網後，許多人都認為三名領袖的行為並不恰當。

歐巴馬幾天前也和副總統拜登一起自拍，照片被放上拜登新設的 Instagram 上。

四月時，歐巴馬也和波士頓紅襪隊的球星奧爾蒂斯一起自拍，結果是後來發現奧爾蒂斯和三星有合作關係，兩人的自拍照被用來推廣三星的產品。這件自拍事件使得一名白宮高級顧問認為，「這或許會結束一切自拍的行為」。但很明顯的，他是錯的。

Unit 9

Super Bowl
超級盃

代表意義超理解

超級盃是美國國家美式足球聯盟 (NFL) 每年一度的冠軍決賽。最近一次的超級盃比賽是 2014 年 2 月 2 日的第 48 屆超級盃球賽，它是 2013 年 NFL 球季的冠軍賽。

The Super Bowl is the annual championship game of the National Football League (NFL) in the United States. The most recent game, Super Bowl XLVIII, was played on February 2, 2014, as the championship game for the 2013 NFL season.

B 背景知識大突破 Background

超級盃是每年全美國和全世界最多人觀看的運動賽事之一。世界上只有歐洲足球協會聯盟 (UEFA) 決賽的觀眾人數能超過超級盃的。根據美國國家美式足球聯盟的數字，全世界大約有來自兩百個國家，約十億人的潛在觀眾。

The Super Bowl is one of the most watched annual sports events in the United States and in the world. The only sports event that

* annual　年度的

gathers more audiences is the UEFA Champions League final. The NFL claims that the Super Bowl has worldwide potential audience of around one billion people from 200 different countries.

Method 使用方法一把罩

過去美國有兩個美式足球聯盟：國家足球聯盟 (National Football League)（文中所提的美國足球聯盟），和美國足球聯盟 (American Football League)。在 70 年代雙方合併成一個聯盟前，雙方協議讓各自的冠軍進行 AFL-NFL 世界冠軍賽，這就是超級盃比賽的前身。原本的兩個聯盟結合成現在的國家足球聯盟 (NFL) 後，則分別成為國家足球聯會 (National Football Conference) 和美國足球聯會 (American Football Conference)。

美式足球在美國只稱為足球，在美國以外的國家特別稱為美式足球，以和國際認知的足球作為區別。在美國以外的地方，美式足球又被稱作橄欖球 (gridiron football)。美式足球是在美國發展出的運動，最早的美式足球比賽開始在 1869 年舉行，由兩個大學校隊進行比賽。

＊audience　觀眾　　＊gridiron　橄欖球場

A 主題文章 rticle

The National Broadcasting Company (NBC) is seeking to represent a new record next year by selling a 30-second spot in Super Bowl XLIX (the 49th edition of the Super Bowl) for 4.5 million dollars. It's not only a new record for pricing in the gridiron classic, but also a 12.5% uptick over prices sought for the Fox Broadcasting Company's 2014 broadcast of the event. NBC is slated to broadcast the 49th edition of the Super Bowl in Glendale, Arizona.

According to journalists' reports, NBC is currently in conversations regarding the sale of more than forty 30-second spots in the game. The source of the information said the sales process is described as "brisk." Others claim that NBC had already sold a large number of ad slots in the next Super Bowl, because there are advertisers who are multiyear buyers of the game. These long term buyers typically pay rates that are below the market. NBC does not deliver an official comment regarding related questions.

Super Bowl ad prices had hiked considerably in the recent years. For all the years, the championship game has always been a place to launch new ad campaigns and get consumers' attentions with better-than-usual creative work. It is the one place where big advertisers known they can reach millions of people in one fell swoop even as new devices have siphoned away TV audiences from traditional TV-watching behavior.

In 2014, Fox sought 4 million dollars for a 30-second ad in the 48th edition of the Super Bowl. The company sold out its ad slot inventory 3 months before the game. The broadcast of Super Bowl XLVIII reached 111.5 million viewers, making it the most-watched television event in U.S. history. The previous record had been set by NBC's 2012 Super Bowl telecast, which had 111.3

million viewers to watch the game. Before the 2013 Super Bowl event, each of the five previous Super Bowl games had set the record as the most-watched event in the United States.

美國廣播公司 (NBC) 將以每 30 秒 450 萬美元的價格出售第四十九屆超級盃比賽的電視廣告，創下美國廣告價格的新紀錄。這不但是這場經典賽事廣告的最高記錄，也比 2014 年福斯公司 (Fox) 提出的超級盃廣告價格提升了 12.5%。NBC 預定將在亞利桑那州的格倫戴爾進行第 49 屆超級盃的轉播。

根據報導，美國廣播公司目前已進行四十多筆 30 秒廣告的商談，知情人士透露，「過程十分順利」。有些人更認為美國廣播公司已經售出大量的超級盃廣告時段，因為許多廣告商早已是超級盃比賽的多年廣告買主。這些長期買主通常能以比市價更為便宜的價格購買廣告。美國廣播公司則拒絕對相關問題進行回應。

超級盃的廣告時段價格近年來大幅上升。這些年來，冠軍賽一直是廠商推出新廣告的場合，希望藉由廣告的創意來引起消費者的注意。這些大型廣告買主認為，在各種新型設備不斷搶走傳統電視收視率的今天，超級盃仍是一個能吸引數百萬人注意的電視節目。

在 2014 年，福斯以 400 萬美元的價格出售第 48 屆超級盃的 30 秒廣告時段，並在賽前三個月就賣完所有的廣告時段。共有超過一億一千一百五十萬的人在電視前收看第 48 屆超級盃的轉播，成為美國電視轉播史上收視人數最高的節目。2012 年的超級盃轉播則有一億一千一百三十萬的收視人數。在這之前五年，每年的超級盃都創下紀錄成為收視史上最高的節目。

Unit 10

World Baseball Classic
世界棒球經典賽

代表意義超理解

世界棒球經典賽 (WBC) 是美國職棒大聯盟 (MLB) 和世界各地其他職業棒球聯盟所創立的國際棒球比賽。經典賽由世界棒球壘球聯合會 (WBSC) 的認可，以聯合會的名義給予勝利隊伍「世界冠軍」的頭銜。

The World Baseball Classic (WBC) is an international baseball tournament created by Major League Baseball (MLB) and other professional baseball leagues around the world. It is the main baseball tournament sanctioned by the World Baseball Softball Confederation (WBSC), which names the final winner "World Champion."

B 背景知識大突破 ackground

世界棒球經典賽原先和奧運棒球比賽和世界盃棒球賽並列為國際棒球聯盟認可的國際賽事。但奧運會在 2008 年後取消棒球項目，世界盃棒球賽也在 2011 年後停辦。現在經典賽是世界上第一個也是唯一一個讓世界各國棒球聯盟中的職業選手以國家隊的名義共聚一堂爭奪冠軍的賽事。

＊ sanction 認可；批准　　＊ confederation 聯盟、結盟

World Baseball Classic coexisted with Olympic Baseball and the Baseball World Cup as International Baseball Federation (IBAF) sanctioned tournaments. However, Olympic Baseball games ended in 2008, and the Baseball World Cup discontinued in 2011. It is now the only and the first to have national baseball teams feature professional players from baseball leagues around the world competing for the championship all together.

Method 使用方法一把罩

除了棒球 (baseball) 外，壘球的英文名稱是 softball，而在中小學較常見的壘球，英文則叫做 kickball。和其他運動不同的是，棒球隊的總教練英文稱為 manager 或是 field manager，而不是用 coach。總教練領導的其他教練則是用 coach，例如 Pitching Coach 是投手教練，Batting Coach 則是打擊教練。先發投手、中繼投手、救援投手則分別稱為 Starting Pitcher，Relief Pitcher，Closer Pitcher。例如：
The American team had decided to fire the general manger, and the press release was announced last Saturday. The pitching Coach will become the new general manager.
（美國隊決定解雇球隊的總教練，這份新聞稿已在上星期六發佈。球隊的投手教練將成為新的總教練。）

---

* coexist 同時共存；和平共處

主題文章 Article

The last World Baseball Classic (WBC) was held from March 2, to March 19, 2013. It was the third iteration of the WBC, following the two previous tournaments held in 2006 and 2009. Those participated in the 2013 WBC included Australia, Brazil, Canada, China, Chinese Taipei, Cuba, Dominican Republic, Italy, Japan, Mexico, the Netherlands, Puerto Rico, South Korea, Spain, the United States, and Venezuela.

In WBC 2013, the Dominican Republic defeated Puerto Rico to become the first WBC champion from the Western Hemisphere, as Japan was the champion for both 2006 and 2009 games. The four teams that made to the semifinal were Dominican Republic, Japan, the Netherlands, and Puerto Rico.

The 2006 and 2009 tournaments had the same 16 teams participating, chosen by invitation. Starting with the 2013 tournament, the top 12 teams from the previous tournament qualified automatically, and a qualifying round will be held to determine the remaining four teams.

The next WBC series, WBC 2017, may expand to a total of 28 teams participating in the game, as the Major League Baseball plans to invite more countries to join the tournament. “This is a tournament that’s actually been going on since November. We’ve offered 28 countries the opportunity of competing with each other, and when you put the best athletes in uniforms that have their country’s names on it, you get a level of passion and competition that generates this kind of excitement,” said a manger of the Major League Baseball. However, how the MLB will determine the qualification of participating teams remained unknown. It is believed those who participated in previous WBCs will be qualified automatically.

"There are a thousand possibilities," said the manager of MLB. "There are going to be competitions in the intervening years because it's going to grow larger. The intention is to play the championship every four years, but we might see more qualifiers two years from now. This tournament is just going to continue to grow."

上一屆世界棒球經典賽 (WBC) 於 2013 年 3 月 2 日至 3 月 19 日間進行，這是繼 2006 年和 2009 年後第三次舉辦的世界棒球經典賽。參加 2013 經典賽的隊伍包括澳洲、巴西、加拿大、中國大陸、中華臺北、古巴、多明尼加、義大利、日本、墨西哥、荷蘭、波多黎各、南韓、西班牙、美國、委內瑞拉。

在 2013 年的經典賽中，多明尼擊敗波多黎各，成為經典賽史上第一個贏得冠軍的西半球國家。日本則包辦 2006 年和 2009 年的冠軍。進入四強決賽的隊伍則分別是多明尼加、日本、荷蘭、波多黎各。

2006 年和 2009 年參加經典賽的是同樣受到邀請的 16 支隊伍。從 2013 年開始，上一屆比賽中排名前 12 名的隊伍將自動晉級下一次的經典賽，其餘四個名額則另行舉辦資格賽決定。

在下一次的 2017 經典賽中，美國職棒大聯盟計畫邀請更多的國家加入比賽，將經典賽程擴張到 28 支球隊相互競爭的賽事。「比賽將從前一年的十一月開始，我們將提供 28 個國家互相比賽的機會，當你看到這些優秀運動員的制服上有自己國家的名稱時，將會令你熱血沸騰，以及振奮人心的比賽」，大聯盟的經理人員說。但未來如何決定參賽資格的方法未定，一般認為，先前參加過經典賽程的國家將被自動列入邀請國家。

該經理說，「這將有上千種可能性」。「這幾年將會有相關的比賽，因為經典賽程將會變得更大。我們希望每四年能產生一次冠軍，而這之間將有更多的預賽。這一系列的賽程將持續不斷的擴張」。

Learn Smart! 037

掌握 News 關鍵字 透析英文報導的要訣

Keywords Catcher - Catch me if you can!

作　　者　James Chiao
封面構成　高鍾琪
內頁構成　華漢電腦排版有限公司

發 行 人　周瑞德
企劃編輯　丁筠馨
執行編輯　陳欣慧
校　　對　徐瑞璞、劉俞青
印　　製　大亞彩色印刷製版股份有限公司
初　　版　2014 年 8 月
定　　價　新台幣 329 元
出　　版　倍斯特出版事業有限公司
電　　話　(02) 2351-2007
傳　　真　(02) 2351-0887
地　　址　100 台北市中正區福州街 1 號 10 樓之 2
E-mail　best.books.service@gmail.com

港澳地區總經銷　泛華發行代理有限公司
地　　　　　址　香港筲箕灣東旺道 3 號星島新聞集團大廈 3 樓
電　　　　　話　(852) 2798-2323
傳　　　　　真　(852) 2796-5471

國家圖書館出版品預行編目(CIP)資料

掌握 News 關鍵字 ： 透析英文報導的要訣 / James Chiao 著.
-- 初版. -- 臺北市 ： 倍斯特, 2014.08
　面 ；　公分. -- (Learn smart ; 37)
ISBN 978-986-90883-0-5(平裝)
1.新聞英文 2.讀本
805.18　　103013622